S0-AGY-434

The Goddess Hangup

Books By Joyce Elbert

A Martini on the Other Table

The Crazy Ladies

The Goddess Hangup

Joyce Elbert

The Goddess Hangup

THE WORLD PUBLISHING COMPANY
New York and Cleveland

Published by The World Publishing Company
Published simultaneously in Canada
by Nelson, Foster & Scott Ltd.

First printing—1970

Library of Congress catalog card number: 70-128484
Printed in the United States of America

WORLD PUBLISHING
TIMES MIRROR

To Sterling

Saturday Evening

IT was nine thirty on a hot, July, New York night when I pushed open the streaked lobby door of my hotel, relieved that at last my weekend was beginning. Sixty beautiful, free hours stretched ahead of me. I wouldn't have to return to my office at the network until nine thirty Tuesday morning, when I'd once more start booking talent for the popular television talk show, unsurprisingly called Talk.

Free. From bartering with agents over things like I'd agree to book a boring journalist if he'd agree to let me have Truman Capote the next time he was available. Free. From writing genial introductory notes for the star of our show who's even more of a pain in the ass off camera than he is on ("People are *Talk*-ing about us . . ."). Free. From taking nervous movie stars to lunch at 21 in order to find out what inanities they wanted to discuss on the show that evening. Free. From the inane world of non-communications.

Psychedelic lights in the lobby blinked on and off, and a large sculpture of pink plastic hairbrushes, the Woolworth variety, was still in its prized place, the center of the room. And of course all the wonderful paintings done by either past or present (future?) occupants of Hotel Splendide, a joke name given it by the man in the penthouse apartment who walked around carrying lizards in his pocket, for reasons he's never bothered to explain, and nobody has bothered to question.

I moved into the hotel last January, on a cold, snowy afternoon, right after my fourth marriage hit the rocks. I've been married to a Jew, a Protestant, a Catholic, and a Negro, and I'm only thirty-two years old. How's that for fast ethnic work? As a result of these assorted (and sordid) marital catastrophes, my full name is nothing short of spectacular: Loretta Irene Silverman Kramer Bjorkman O'Connell Ray.

It's always amused me that I was named after Loretta Young and Irene Dunne, two movie stars who have never been divorced. My mother's sense of the inappropriate is matched only by that of my second husband, a silent Swede, who owns and operates The Green Hornet, a broken-down Village moving company that specializes in moving the furniture of broken-down homosexuals.

The lobby of the hotel was populated by its usual conglomeration of bearded filmmakers, beautiful girls in mini dresses and maxi bangs, a gentleman sweating in an English bush jacket, a lady in a flowered half-size dress carrying a Rheingold six-pack, a handsome well-known painter talking to an ugly well-known writer, a girl in a sailor suit studying the pink hairbrushes, and at the desk was a rock and roll group, either checking in or checking out, it was hard to figure, and my friend, Josephine Jasmin, looking tearful for a change.

"I tried to call you before." Her voice had not dissipated to the whine that made people cringe. "Are you just getting in?"

"Yes, I had to hang around for the taping. I booked that English playwright and he was a nervous wreck. So I stayed and held his hand until he was ready to go on. What a business."

"Do you want to have dinner?"

Another one of those evenings was about to unfold, I could feel it. "I'll meet you at the bar in about an hour. Okay?"

Josephine looked at me with perfectly justified distrust, knowing damn well that if I ran into anyone more interesting I'd either ask them to join us, or I'd dump her. Actually, I liked Josephine, but she had a Southern accent and became maudlin after two drinks. After more than two, she cried into a lightly perfumed handkerchief and wondered aloud why men no longer found her attractive. The funny part was that men did find her attractive—at first. But between the whine and the tears, they soon became turned off, which of course didn't stop them from fucking her. In fact, the only woman who's been screwed by more men in the hotel than Josephine is me. And sometimes they weren't even *in* the hotel, only passing through, my dear.

Josephine and I had discussed this once, and her explanation for our great arithmetic sex score was that I had Dylan Thomas' old room and she had Thomas Wolfe's, which made us immensely desirable because of those two famous ghosts floating around the beds. That was the quality of Josephine I liked, a feyness and whimsicality that thirty-nine years of rough going had not succeeded in stifling. And she really believed her theory as to why we were so ready to peel off our clothes with almost any man who asked. I had my own version: we were desperate. But I knew it would hurt Josephine's feelings if I said that, so I never did.

"Can't you make it sooner than an hour?" she asked.

"I have a little laundry to do first. And I want to shower and change."

"You must be mad to iron shirts in this weather. Particularly if your air-conditioner is still on the blink."

"It's not only on the blink, it's driving me out of my mind. The heat, that is."

"Won't Leonard fix it for you?"

"I told you. He's angry about the washing machine and dryer because they use up so much current."

"Why don't you be sensible, Loretta, and get rid of the washing machine? Then I'm sure he'll fix the air-conditioner."

"I refuse to get rid of it. It's a Whirlpool with permanent press cycles. I won it on You Said It! And besides, I like to wash and iron men's shirts. It gives me a sense of domesticity. I used to wash and iron all my husband's shirts."

"But you're not married any more."

"Yes, I am. Billy and I are still married."

"What I mean is that you're not living with him any more. You're not living with any man, so why turn yourself into a free laundry service?"

"It appeals to my sense of Americana. I pretend that I'm living in a small town in Kansas, and there's a tuna, noodle, and mushroom soup casserole in the oven (I got the recipe from the noodle package), and my husband will be home any minute from his job at the GE plant, and he's going to need a clean shirt tomorrow."

"But you're not in a small town in Kansas, you're on West 77th Street at Hotel Splendide, home of international artists."

"The kids have eaten supper and are playing in the living room, which isn't finished yet because we're up to our necks in hock."

Josephine's eyes became still more misty. "I just received a call from my daughter. She's had a fight with her boyfriend and is coming to visit me tomorrow. He drank all the orange juice."

"Is this Daffodil?"

"That's the only daughter I have."

For some reason I never could remember whether Josephine had two daughters and one son, or one daughter and two sons.

"She's the one at Berkeley, isn't she?"

Josephine nodded. "It might not sound like such a big deal about the orange juice," she earnestly explained, "but you see, it was laced with the last of their LSD. Even though I'm against drugs, I still think it was a pretty rotten thing for him to do."

It turned out that the rock and roll group was checking in. The Naked Seven. Five men and two blank-eyed girls, all wearing paisley Indian headbands. The bellman who specialized in grass was putting their bags into one of the two creaking elevators.

"I'll see you in about an hour," I said to Josephine. "Hold a barstool for me."

Then I turned to the clerk behind the desk, the one who was in his fourth week at Berlitz. "Do you have anything for 701?"

He handed me my copy of *Women's Wear Daily*, my weekly copy of *Variety*, a bill from Bonwit's, a note from Josephine saying that she'd tried to call me and would be in the bar, a note from I. C. Ring asking me to call him, and a letter postmarked Sweden. It was from my fourth and current husband, Billy Ray, whose rock group, Malcolm X, Y, and Z, was playing in Stockholm.

I hadn't heard a word from Billy since our breakup six months ago, and I couldn't wait to get upstairs and open the letter and find out what the black motherfucker had in mind.

I had never gone to bed with a Negro before Billy, mainly because I never wanted to. I was hung up on blond types, like my blond, blue-eyed uncle. Being a German Jew is no laughing matter. They weren't all seen throwing themselves out of windows in Berlin in 1937 for nothing. Call it anomie.

I met Billy when I was still married to John O'Connell, my third husband. The marriage was very much on the rocks, and if it hadn't been for my job I definitely think I would have cracked, but I was too busy booking talent on Talk to have time to crack up. Although there are four of us on the show who do the booking, I'm considered the classy booker which means that I book top movie stars like Burt Lancaster, government figures, novelists, architects, David Susskind, you know. One of the other talent coordinators specializes in comedians, another in musicians and singers, and the fourth is the hooker booker: starlets, people like Ultra Violet. The reason I deal with the higher echelons is because I once was a language major at an insignificant Midwestern college. I'm not kidding. That's how television minds operate.

Anyhow, the booker who specializes in musicians had gotten Billy Ray's group on the show and they were in the studio that afternoon rehearsing their current hit, "Yummy Yummy Yummy." I was in the studio out of sheer lethargy. I didn't have anyone on the show that evening and I wasn't in the mood to talk to agents who were trying to push creepy clients on me. The guy who booked Billy wasn't even around, which is not unusual. Groups are treated like shit.

After the rehearsal, Billy walked over to me and asked where the men's room was. Since he could have asked the stage manager, I knew it was a come-on, but there was something about him, a boyishness, a sweetness. I liked him. He asked if I was going to hang around for the taping.

"That's three hours from now," I said. "And I don't have a reason to be here."

"You do now."

I've never liked cheating, and yet somehow I always seem to be guilty of it. I met every one of my husbands when I was married to another man, except, of course, for my first, but then he took the place of my father, so it's really the same thing, isn't it? After the show, Billy and I went to a jazz club on the Upper West Side, not far, as a matter of fact, from where I'm now living. The one thing I always knew about musicians, sexually, is that they go down on you right off the bat. And I don't just mean the ones with the reed instruments. Even the piano players. But what I was wondering that evening, was whether Billy would do anything different because he was black. It embarrasses me to have to confess to such boring, middle-class thoughts, but I had them.

And he did do something I consider different. We went to his place and he *insisted* that the glaring overhead lights be left on. This was before the Black-Is-Beautiful days, and I realized afterward that it was important to him to know for sure that he was fucking a white woman. I didn't come, but I pretended I did because I didn't want to hurt his feelings (actually, I never do that unless I'm pretty damn sure that I will come with that person eventually, and I was pretty sure in this instance).

Billy lived in a loft in the East Village and I stayed over. I called my husband and said I was spending the night with Peggy, a good friend of mine who likes to make lasagne. I don't know whether John believed my story, but he pretended he did. An odd thing happened the next morning. Billy and I had had a lot to drink and smoke the evening before, and when I woke up I didn't open my eyes right away, because I knew something ominous had happened, and I just lay there with my eyes closed, trying to remember what had taken place before I went to sleep. It didn't even occur to me then that I wasn't home in my own bed. But I couldn't remember a thing, and finally I opened my eyes and there was this coal black body lying next to me. I screamed at the top of my lungs before I realized it was Billy.

"Is that how you usually wake up?" he asked, lighting a cigarette.

"I had a bad dream."

"About what?"

"My husband. He was dead in the dream and the funeral service was at Frank Campbell's. But when everybody was there, listening to the minister, suddenly the casket opened, and John jumped right out, and said, 'I fooled you all, didn't I?' "

"What does your husband do?"

"He's a literary agent."

"Successful?"

"Going downhill. He lost two of his best writers recently."

"Frank Campbell's?"

"No, they went to another agent. Do you have any juice? I'm absolutely dehydrated."

"I think so."

I wanted to see him walk across the long room. Billy was about five nine and wiry. His hair was like steel wool. I vaguely remembered having kissed it last night.

"Wow."

That had been his last word to me before all that wool disappeared between my legs. Now he was returning with a carton of Tropicana orange juice and no glass. The loft would have been a mess if there'd been enough things in it to make it messy, but there weren't. It was one of the barest places I've ever seen. The bed was on the floor, just a mattress. Maybe Billy Ray didn't *own* a glass. And yet there was nothing about the way he behaved that would make you think he didn't have any money. Maybe, as with the glass, he didn't give a damn. He shook the carton of juice and handed it to me.

"All the glasses are dirty."

"I have to call Peggy. I guess she'd better know that I stayed with her last night. She uses Italian sausage meat in her lasagne."

"What's the significance of that?"

"Just that Peggy had a very strange upbringing. You see, her mother was a health nut. She used to give Peggy four raw string beans and two Brazil nuts for breakfast. Then she'd make her sit in the sun in the middle of the winter, wearing nothing but a homemade bikini."

"Where is Peggy from?"

"Herald Harbor, Maryland. And it's cold there in the winter. Peggy used to sit in front of this garage wearing the homemade bikini, for maximum exposure."

"Her mother sounds pretty crazy."

"You don't know the half of it. Peggy's father wouldn't give her mother any money, so one day she stole four hundred dollars out of his pocket while he was asleep, and she stuck it in the Kotex she was wearing. Peggy's father looked everywhere for that money, but naturally it never occurred to him that it was in his wife's Kotex."

"Didn't she bleed on it?"

"Probably. But you can wash paper money, you know."

"That's one of the strangest stories I've ever heard."

"You can say that again. Her mother kept a pet spider and used to wear white ankle socks and Girl Scout shoes. Peggy loves her now, but if you had to eat four raw string beans and two Brazil nuts for breakfast, you'd be making lasagne with Italian sausage meat in it every chance you got."

"I guess you're right," Billy said, looking thoughtful. "By the way, where do you live?"

"Seventy-ninth Street."

"East?"

"Yes. Why? Between Park and Lex."

"Do you feel like you're slumming?"

"No." It was a partial lie. "I've lived in all kinds of places. It doesn't matter to me anymore."

"Actually, this isn't my place. I'm just staying here. It belongs to a guy I know, he plays drums, but he's out on the Coast now."

"Where do you live when you don't live here?"

"I move around, baby."

There was no denying it: I wanted to make love to him again. In fact, I was so excited my legs were starting to tremble. Maybe he didn't want to, although like most men he probably was at his best in the A.M.

"If I see one more morning erection, I'll scream," were my last words to John on the subject. And now, I couldn't wait. I pulled him down to the bed and started to kiss him. I still had the carton of Tropicana orange juice in my hand.

"Why don't you put that on the floor?"

"No, I'm going to drink it."

"How can you drink it if you're kissing me?"

"I'm going to drink it while you go down on me."

"Yes, Captain."

It was very light in the loft, very light, so there was no

need for the glaring overhead light, and I knew that it certainly was light enough for Billy to see anything he wanted to (nothing beats a good vaginal glimpse). I wondered how I looked to him at that angle. The only thing that bothered me was that I was half sitting up, and in that position I looked like I had a stomach, which made me self-conscious. I've always had a phobia about stomachs. My first husband, the racetrack hound, said it was because of my unconscious fear of pregnancy, and maybe he was right, although I never took his word for anything except the daily double at Belmont. Someone crossed the room in the loft above us, and Billy was making it very clear that he knew what to do with his lips besides playing the tenor sax.

"Don't stop."

His muffled response was lost forever on my clitoris, and all I can say is that there's nothing like coming and drinking orange juice at the same time, even if it doesn't have LSD in it.

I read Billy's letter in a state of utter shock, in fact, at first I couldn't believe I was reading what I was reading: the son of a bitch wanted a divorce so he could marry a Swedish girl named Inger. But he loved *me*! All of my husbands loved me, the proof being that none of them had remarried. I knew I could have any one of them back any time I wanted, all I had to do was whistle ("You know how to whistle, don't you, Steve?"), and they'd come running. Who was Billy Ray to screw around with my perfect batting average?

I put the letter on top of the bureau that Leonard Stein claimed was real walnut, the only real walnuts at the hotel being in his head. The room was suffocating. Maybe I was insanely stubborn not to hire my own electrician and get the air-conditioner fixed, but I felt so bitter toward Leonard because of his inferior service and superior rates that I had decided to make him spring for the repair job. So what if I had a washing machine and dryer and did a few shirts now and then? Leonard Stein was raking in a small fortune with his crummy over-publicized hotel, he could afford to absorb a little extra electric current cost. Something like twenty people were turned away every day because there were no rooms available; they were frequently seen pleading with the Berlitz desk clerk who had only recently mastered the French subjunctive.

"Anything," they would plead, "I'll take anything you have. I've read so much about this place. Are you sure you don't have a room somewhere that you've forgotten about?"

English, French, German, Italian, Spanish, Greek, Arabic, Chinese, Japanese, Indonesian, Serbo-Croatian—they babbled in all languages, some even cried. Berlitz loved his job, the power he held over all those poor unfortunates who were being denied the privilege of living at the famous Hotel Splendide, which had long ago become a city landmark.

The hotel was a gigantic dump. Five hundred rooms, some of them lavish apartments, others more like broom closets. Mine wasn't bad. It had a workable fireplace, an electric bed left over from the previous tenant, and a neat kitchenette. The only thing wrong with the bathroom was the toilet paper that the hotel supplied. My lawyer friend, Parker Mason, who lived two floors below me, said that Leonard Stein could be sued because of the miserable quality of the toilet paper. Parker wanted one of the occupants to swear that he'd gotten hemorrhoids as a direct result of the sandpaper that Leonard Stein was passing off on us.

I told Parker that he obviously knew nothing about hemorrhoids, but I did, thanks to my third husband, John O'Connell, who had cornered the Preparation H market, singlehanded. Once, when we were living in Paris, I had to go find the French equivalent of the American product, and it was no picnic marching in and out of Montparnasse drugstores, trying to make my husband's poignant need understood. He was home, bleeding and eating croissants.

The house phone rang. It was my next-door neighbor, the mysterious Chinese, I. C. Ring.

"Are my shirts ready? I have a dinner date in half an hour."

"I just got in. I'll iron one right away. Which do you want?"

"It suddenly occurs to me," he said, "that you have my Bentley Permanent Press, so there's nothing to iron. Providing you've washed it."

"What color is it?"

"Tannish. You know, the window-pane check."

"I'll have to go look. I don't remember. I'll call you back."

"No tickee, no washee."

"No funnee."

The reason for the mystery surrounding I. C. was because of his avowed occupation. Parker Mason was convinced that I. C. was lying when he said he was conducting a survey for a prominent gynecologist. It seemed that this gynecologist, if he existed, planned to write a book dealing with the sexual and birth control practices of unmarried women who led unconventional lives. That was why I. C. had been assigned to the hotel—it was a veritable mecca for unconventional women. I. C. was forever asking me very personal questions, despite the fact that I kept reminding him I was hardly an unmarried woman. That was okay, he said, he didn't mean *unmarried* in the literal sense of the word, he meant women who were living alone. But I still wouldn't tell him anything, and my obstinacy was killing him. He knew I was screwing my brains out, and I wouldn't even tell him whether or not I was on the pill. I could just imagine what his reaction would be if he suspected that I was pregnant; he'd probably carry on like it was the Chinese New Year, absolute bliss.

Aside from suspecting I. C. of something phony, Parker had no clue as to what his real occupation might be. I just figured that I. C. was some kind of nut who got his kicks by listening to women's descriptions of their favorite positions in bed, and whether they used an I.U.D. My friend, Peggy, who lived in one of the broom closets, had told I. C. everything about herself. She liked him. They ate Portuguese sardines together and talked about tubal pregnancies.

"Your Bentley shirt is ready," I told I. C. a few minutes later.

"I'll be there in a sec."

I. C. came in wearing a pair of wide-ribbed corduroy pants and nothing else. He practically had no chest hair at all. Since I had never gone to bed with an Oriental, I was naturally curious what one of them would be like in the sack. Maybe they did it sideways.

"The shirt looks pretty good," I. C. said. "That's a dandy little machine you have."

He sat down on the edge of my electric bed. Now that he had his shirt, he didn't seem to be in any great rush to go to dinner.

"Who are you having dinner with?" I asked.

"The gynecologist. He's really worked up over the prospect of doing this book. He says it will make Kinsey and Masters and Johnson look like nurse's aides. Tell me something, Loretta."

I was putting Fab in my wonderful Whirlpool so I could wash a few of Parker's shirts.

"Tell you what?"

"Have you ever taken it in the ass?"

He really was incorrigible. "Well, I *was* married to a Catholic once."

"No funnee."

I started to sing my favorite detergent commercial.

"There's a new kind of clean I want to get close to, oh, Fab, I'm glad they've put enzyme action, lemon-scented Borax in you."

"You're more than a little *meshuga*, aren't you, Loretta?"

I. C. grew up in Los Angeles and loved to sprinkle his conversation with Jewish words.

"Screw off," I told him. "This is the last time I'll ever use Defend germ-proof fabric softener on your cheap shirts. You're a fine one to be calling *me* crazy, with the questions you go around asking all the women here. It's amazing that nobody has punched you in the nose yet, absolutely amazing."

I. C. picked up his shirt and walked to the door.

"Number two son leaves to go to dinner. Fuckee suckee fifty cents."

While Parker's shirts were tumbling around in the dryer, I took an icy shower to cool off and then I changed into my daisy patterned bra with matching daisy hip huggers, and a green silk sash. Green and blue are my favorite colors because of my auburn hair. When I wear green, my eyes look green, and when I wear blue, they look blue. That old song, "You Must Have Been a Beautiful Baby," really applied to me. My mother said that people were constantly stopping her on the street to get a better view of me in my carriage, and when I was about six or seven, grown men used to give me a nickel and suggest that I call them up in ten years. I picked up a lot of fast change that way.

But lately I've been worried. I'm starting to lose my

looks, there's no doubt about it. I see the insidious beginnings of age, such as those two Fu Manchu lines that have recently emerged, like parentheses, extending from my nose around and down to my mouth. A little crow mark next to each eye, faint, but unmistakably there. When I was in my twenties, I used to laugh at all the hormone cream ads in women's magazines; now I buy the creams myself, and they don't strike me as the least bit funny. Even the prospect of a thigh lift in a few years doesn't amuse me. I'm starting to get slightly crinkly in that area, despite the fifty thigh exercises I do religiously each morning. I've always wondered how unattractive women feel about the whole process of aging. Maybe they're not as threatened by it as I am, maybe they even welcome it. I certainly don't. I want to stay young and beautiful forever, but it's like wishing for the moon.

When I got downstairs to the bar at La Chiripa, it was plain that Josephine was well on her way to being crocked. The whine had worsened. The perfumed handkerchief was already clutched in her hand, waiting to be put into use. I looked desperately around the restaurant, hoping to spot someone I could ask to join us for dinner, but for once the place seemed to be filled with strangers.

"Here you are," Josephine said. "I was afraid you'd changed your mind."

Josephine was drinking a Papa Doble, the specialty of the house. The double daiquiri, which was named in Hemingway's honor, was his favorite drink at his favorite bar, the Floridita, in Havana, and the owners of La Chiripa had reverently hung a blownup photo of the old lush over the bar, directly above all the crucifixes and cheap saint statues. Leonard Stein had nothing to do with La Chiripa. The restaurant, which adjoined the hotel, was owned and managed by three nervous Cubans who had left Havana shortly after Batista. I didn't doubt that, in its origin, a Papa Doble was a hell of a good drinks, but thanks to La Chiripa's typical chintziness, it was a minor catastrophe, much as the food served there. Paella with empty lobster shells.

"I'll have the Papa Doble," I said to Carlos Santiago, one of the owners, who was tending bar. "Try to put a little rum in it."

Carlos gave me a dirty look. He had never reconciled himself to his bohemian clientele, nor to women who sat unescorted at bars and drank hard liquor. To the masculine Spanish mentality, women fell into two categories: saints and whores. There was little doubt in which category he'd lumped Josephine and me, even though he tried to be polite about it most of the time.

"How come you're drinking?" Josephine asked.

"I'm depressed."

As everyone knew, I usually stuck to Coke or ginger ale, but Billy's letter had hit me pretty hard, and then there was the pregnancy business still pending.

"My husband wants a divorce. He wants to marry a Swedish girl named Inger. I just got a letter from him."

"What are you going to do?"

"I don't know. I don't want a divorce."

"You're not in love with him, are you?"

"What's that got to do with it? My pride is hurt. I don't take things like this lying down."

"You can't hold a man against his will, Loretta."

"Really? Why not?"

Josephine was wearing a striped orange and pink mini shift, and she looked very attractive despite her masochistic projection. Like me, she had good legs.

"There's no point in trying to hold a man when he's lost interest in you," she said, looking as though she'd had a lot of experience in that department, and I was pretty sure she did.

Where the hell was my drink? I could feel panic beginning to mount. If Billy divorced me, it would be the first time in my adult life that I'd be without a husband, an admirer, a supportive male figure, a man who loved me. The prospect was terrifying. I was not yet ready for Women's Lib. What had gotten into Billy anyway? It was ridiculous, his request for a divorce, absurd. Inger was just a passing whim, he'd get over her. Or would he? He probably was mesmerized by her blond hair and nordic features. I wondered whether Swedish girls were as exciting as they were reputed to be, or whether Stockholm had a superior chamber of commerce. The Papa Doble finally arrived and I drank it down in two gulps and asked Carlos for another.

"I think I'm pregnant," I confessed to Josephine.

"Who's the father?"

"I don't know."

"How can you not know?"

"Three guesses."

"I mean, who have you gone to bed with lately?"

"You win on the first guess. Everybody."

"Oh, dear."

"I'm not absolutely certain that I am, but I haven't had my period in quite a while."

"Take the rabbit test and find out."

"That's the whole point. I can't take it, not with any degree of accuracy."

"I don't understand."

"Well, it seems that if you've been on the pill, as I was, your system becomes so screwed up that the rabbit test is unreliable. At least that's what Dr. Oiseaux tells me."

"I never heard that."

"And I can't remember when I had my last period, so I

don't even know how far gone I am, assuming that I *am* far gone."

"You might be too far gone to have an abortion. Most doctors won't touch you after nine weeks."

"I suppose I could go to Spanish Harlem and find some butcher who'd do the job."

"I've never had an abortion. I don't believe in it."

"What about the starving masses in India?"

Josephine looked into her Papa Doble. "Do you know that I became pregnant with Daffodil while I was wearing a diaphragm and her father was wearing a condom? When a spirit decides to enter the world, there's just no stopping it."

"You know I don't believe in that reincarnation crap. I had an abortion with John."

"*My* John?"

"Listen, Josephine, he was *my* John before he became *your* John."

She dabbed at her eyes with the perfumed handkerchief. Je Reviens. "Must you always remind me?"

I guess there's something here that I've failed to mention, namely that my third husband, failing literary agent, John O'Connell, was Josephine's current lover. He also was a resident of Hotel Splendide. He'd moved in before I had, right after I left him to go live with Billy in the bare loft with the bed on the floor. That's one of the few consistencies about this hotel: all the permanent residents have moved into Hotel Splendide right after their lives ceased being very splendid: me, after the breakup with Billy; John, after his breakup with me; Parker Mason, after his wife ran off with the family dentist; and Josephine, after her latest novel, *Oh, Trusting Fool*, was turned down by every publisher in New York.

Yes, indeedy, following disaster it was natural to move into Hotel Splendide, and move out of it as little as humanly possible. Go to work, go to the deli on the corner, go to the cleaner. Otherwise, you might as well have needed a pass. Resident-inmates, that's what we all were, afraid of the hostile outer world, afraid of being alone in an apartment of our own, and Leonard Stein knew it, the sneaky Hungarian, that's why he was able to get away with charging one hundred and seventy-five dollars a month to live in a broom closet like Peggy's. Peggy herself said that it reminded her more of a solitary cell.

"All that's missing are the bars," was her interpretation of home sweet home.

The only thing that every room in the hotel had in common, from the cheapest dungeon to the most expensive suite, was the same poison-green wall-to-wall carpeting, which is manufactured by Leonard's carpet company, Stein Broadlooms, Ltd. Naturally. Would he buy from Leeds'?

"You can be as bitchy as you like," Josephine said, "but he's *my* John now."

"Lots of luck."

"I don't understand why he's been unable to sell *Oh, Trusting Fool*. I think it's a very saleable book, don't you, Loretta?"

"How would I know? I haven't read it."

"That's right. I keep forgetting." Self-pity turned outward to anger. "Why haven't you read it? I asked you to read it. And you're supposed to be a friend of mine."

I remembered Dick Cavett interviewing Jackie Susann on ABC. When she asked him whether he'd read her book, he said something like, "No, but then I haven't yet read *Anthony Adverse* and *The Decameron*. After I do, I'll get around to yours."

"I don't read novels," I said. "Nobody in television reads

novels. We're in the age of Aquarius. The printed word is obsolete."

"K. doesn't think it's obsolete. I went to bed with him last night. He's wiggy. The only position he likes is man on top, woman on bottom."

"So?"

"There'd be nothing wrong if he didn't scream at the top of his lungs while he was doing it."

"What does he scream about?"

"Nothing. I mean, there aren't any words, just a terrible, piercing scream. Like near the end of the old Joan Crawford movies, when all her schemes have fallen apart and the law is closing in."

K. was a pretty successful Dutch poet who kept cheating Leonard Stein out of rent money by disappearing from the hotel for months on end and then returning in a new motorcycle jacket with a book of his love poems recently published by Gallimard. Leonard was such a snob about anything French that he immediately forgave K. all his indebtedness. The Jewish middle class is like that, I've discovered: make it in Paris or London and you can rape their arthritic mothers, they're so turned on.

Thank God my father was a kosher butcher in The Bronx and beyond that particular brand of bullshit. He had his own, of course, but I preferred it, it was less vulgar than the pseudo-intellectualism of people like Leonard Stein who thought that modern art started with DeKooning. Once I asked Leonard what he thought about the paintings on the walls of Altamira, in that case, and he raised my rent ten dollars a month to assuage his own aggressive ignorance.

"How come you went to bed with K.?" I asked Josephine. "I thought you were so hung up on John."

"John wasn't around. He went downtown. I think he's got a girl on Fourteenth Street."

"East or West?"

"How should I know?"

"How do you know it's Fourteenth Street?"

"Because she wrote him a letter and I saw the envelope. She uses lavender stationery. That's a bad sign. I distrust anyone who writes letters on colored paper."

Colored made me think of Billy's letter. My father always referred to Billy as being *colored*. Either that or, "The *shvartze* you married." I decided to talk to Parker about the legal technicalities involving Billy's request for a divorce. Maybe it wasn't possible for Billy to divorce me without my consent. Maybe he just couldn't do it, thanks to some weirdo law that went back to the Middle Ages.

"Mind if I join you ladies for a drink?"

It was John himself, wearing a striped sport shirt that I had washed and ironed the day before. John was about six one, and had black hair and very dark brown eyes. His face was flushed with alcohol, and I wondered whether he'd been drinking in his room or whether he was hungover from last night. Even though we'd been divorced for three years, I still felt a strong sense of ownership toward him. I felt the same toward all my husbands. You can't divorce your memories, no matter how hard you may try. Little things a person will say or do, insignificant things to an outsider, bring back a torrent of nostalgia. Are we all victims of our pasts? What a dismal prospect.

There was an empty barstool next to Josephine, and John took it. "Martini on the rocks with a twist," he told Carlos.

Yes, he definitely had been drinking earlier. During the course of our marriage, John had tried AA, and although it worked for him for a while, he eventually went off the wagon in a spectacular way. He was a bad drinker, really bad, with the change of personality pattern that characterizes so many bad drinkers. He would go on periodic binges, and when he returned to our apartment on 79th Street he looked as though he'd been rolling around in the gutter for days. There was one suit of his in particular that the French cleaners on Park Avenue finally gave up on. It was last returned to us with a nasty note pinned to it, saying that all modern and scientific methods of dry cleaning had failed to remove the stains from this garment. After that, I switched to the cleaner on Lex, and John never wore the suit again.

Josephine gave him one of the terrible smiles she saved for occasions like this. "I hope you had a good time last night."

"What are you talking about?"

"There's no point in lying. You can't fool Mother. I know where you were."

Josephine liked to make scenes, she always managed to put herself in a position where the man she cared for had little choice but to insult her. John did not like to go around insulting women, so Josephine had to work particularly hard to get what she wanted from him. Basically, my third husband was a very polite and chivalrous person. The worst kind.

"You were with that girl on Fourteenth Street," Josephine persisted. "You can't fool Mother."

"You're not my mother." Then he seemed to notice that I was drinking a Papa Doble, and it surprised him because of my aversion to alcohol. "Is anything wrong?"

"Billy wants a divorce."

"You can't fool Mother," Josephine said again.

"When did all this happen?" John asked me.

"I just received a letter from him. He's in Stockholm. He wants to marry a Swedish girl named Inger."

"No kidding."

"Also, I think I'm pregnant."

"YOU CAN'T FOOL MOTHER!" Josephine shouted.

I knew that John had never forgiven me for having left him for Billy, and I could see a sly look of satisfaction on his face now that *I* was the one being left behind.

"Are you going to have the baby?"

"I don't know. I haven't decided."

Perhaps he was recalling the abortion I had had while we were married. John had witnessed the entire thing, he was the one who held me down on the table while the doctor poked around inside me with a cold, metal instrument, and I tried my best to muffle my screams. John didn't want me to have the abortion, but I'd insisted on the grounds that our marriage was on the rocks. Actually, it was because I was afraid the baby was Billy's. Since then I've wondered whether I did the right thing. Maybe I should have had the baby, another human being to think about besides myself. After thirty-two years, my own egocentricity and narcissism were beginning to drive me crazy, yet I didn't know what to do about it. The only thought that consoled me was that I would have been an impossible mother, just as my own mother had been, a little girl right to the very end of her life, petulant and unsure.

"I suggest that we take a booth," Josephine said, her hysteria momentarily subdued. "I'm starving."

I was, too. All I'd had for lunch was half a liverwurst sandwich at my desk and a container of over-percolated coffee.

"I'm game," John said.

Like most alcoholics, he was only minimally concerned about food, despite the fact that he went through the motions of eating. He had had a bad bout with hepatitis some years back, before I'd known him, and even though he appeared robust and healthy, he actually had a fragile constitution which alcohol was making more fragile every day. Although he was only in his late thirties, around Josephine's age, there was something middle-aged about him. Maybe he was getting ready for death.

The restaurant section of La Chiripa was separated from the bar section by a fence of iron grillwork. There were several booths available, and we took one near the front, where the air conditioning was more effective. I was starting to feel slightly better, perhaps because of the two Papa Dobles, but I still couldn't get Billy's letter out of my mind. We'd been very happy together until last summer in Provincetown. Then the marriage just seemed to collapse. Billy had wanted me to quit my job, he'd wanted that from the start, but I refused to and he never reconciled himself to my decision. What would I do if I quit, I asked him? Be another musician's wife, following him around to club dates? I'd worked hard to get my job, it wasn't easy for a woman to make much headway in television, and I didn't see any reason to give it all up. It was as much a part of my life as music was of his, but he couldn't accept that and when he finally realized I had no intention of quitting, well, he sort of quit on me. I guess.

"Why don't we split two paellas among us?" Josephine suggested.

"Okay," John and I said.

Parker Mason came into La Chiripa just as we started on the paella with the empty lobster shells. I had a slight crush on Parker, but even though we'd gone to bed a few times I didn't have the feeling that he cared very much about me, which, naturally, was deflating. I knew he was physically attracted to me, but at some point he must have decided not to get in over his head.

"Can I join you folks for a drink?" Parker said.

Josephine looked at him reproachfully. She'd never forgiven Parker for not having made a pass at her. Josephine didn't have to be attracted to a man to want him to want her; it was just one of those essentials she demanded from every man who crossed her path.

"Sit down, Parker," John said. "Sit down."

Parker sat next to me and ordered a cognac from the waiter. John, Josephine, and I were all drinking a white Spanish wine, with an unpronounceable name.

"How can you drink cognac in this bloody hot weather?" Josephine asked him.

"It's easy. I've been doing it for forty-one years."

"No wonder your wife ran off with the dentist."

"He was a dental surgeon," Parker said, with a malicious smile.

I almost began to wish I were back at the network booking talent for Talk. On Tuesday I had to try to get Norman Mailer for the show. Our producer wanted to have Mailer and Tiny Tim on the same show, he thought it would be amusing. Television was a simple world when you got down to it. So long as you followed the ground rules, not too much could go wrong.

"There's something I want to talk to you about," I said to Parker. "Not now. Maybe tomorrow on the roof. It's a legal thing."

"She's getting divorced for a change," Josephine said.

Parker looked at me in surprise.

"She's the Lana Turner of the Hotel Splendide," Josephine said. "In the divorce department, that is."

"Let her alone," John said.

"You're still in love with her."

"No, I'm not."

"What do you mean, you're *not*?" I asked.

"Look, Loretta, I'm very fond of you—"

"You're in love with her," Josephine insisted, putting down her fork.

"I tell you, I'm not."

Parker Mason ordered another cognac.

"You can't fool Mother," Josephine said to John.

"Oh, Christ, are we going to start that again?"

Josephine Jasmin started to cry. "Just because I'm not as young as she is—"

Parker looked at his watch. "You're a little late tonight. It's a quarter past eleven. The waterworks usually start by ten, ten-thirty, the latest."

"I don't see why you cry so much," John said to her. "It's really very tedious."

"*Tedious*?" Josephine sobbed, indignantly.

"Yes, dear, I wish you'd try to knock it off."

"I'll knock it off, you miserable bastard."

Josephine opened her purse and took out a five-dollar bill which she flung across the table. It landed on my saffron rice.

"That's for my part of the check," she said. "And do me a favor, John. Don't come crawling up to my room in the middle of the night."

Tears were streaming down her face and her eyeliner was blurred.

"Josephine, don't act this way. Please, sweetheart."

"Miserable bastard. I don't want you to be my agent any longer. I want you to give me back *Oh, Trusting Fool.* Tomorrow."

"Tomorrow is Sunday. The manuscript's at my office."

"What the hell is it doing at your office? Why isn't it at a publisher's? No wonder you can't sell it. You don't send it anywhere. Maybe you've never sent it anywhere. Maybe it's been sitting in your office all this time."

She ran out the door that led to the hotel, dabbing at her eyes.

"Crazy broad," John said affectionately.

"What do you mean, you don't love me?"

Parker finished his second cognac. "I can't stand domestic squabbles. I'm going upstairs to Eric Ambler and the simplicity of a triple murder story."

I was sorry to see Parker leave. I had hoped he would ask me to spend the night with him, but if there's one thing I've noticed about men, it's that they become very docile and unaggressive when confronted with an ex-husband. *Any* ex-husband. You could tell them that you hate the son of a bitch, that he used to beat you when you were married, that he cheated you out of your joint checking funds—it still doesn't make any difference. Men are reverent about ex-husbands.

"Who's the father?" John asked, as soon as Parker had left.

For a second I didn't understand.

"You said earlier that you thought you were pregnant."

"Parker Mason."

I don't know why I said it, although it seemed vaguely possible that it might be Parker. I've never been very good when it comes to remembering dates, monthly cycles, etc.

"I didn't know you were having an affair with him."

"It's not exactly an affair."

John's Irish Catholic upbringing saw fit to rear its head at that point. Instant disapproval. John really had fantasies about my sex life. It's true that I do sleep around a bit, but to John my activities in that area assumed the numerical proportions of a DeMille epic. Cast of thousands.

"I must admit, I've never understood you, Loretta."

"That's news."

"Why you do the things you do. What you want. *Who* you want. What kind of man. What are you looking for?"

"A good ten-cent cigar."

"You see?"

He pushed aside the paella plate and looked around for the waiter, who pretended not to see us. All the waiters at La Chiripa were anti-waiters at heart. On their day off, they turned up at the restaurant in their best gangster suits and became imperious customers.

"If anyone asks a serious question, you retaliate with a wisecrack," John said. "Why is that? Why are you unable to communicate?"

Because I was in the communications business. No. The reason I was in the communications business was because I didn't know how to communicate. For that matter, neither did anyone else in television, they merely went through the grotesque motions. The talk shows were worst of all, since the people involved pretended to be talking about things close to their hearts. I've never ceased to marvel at the way a well-known guest will come dashing out from behind those ubiquitous curtains, shake hands with the star, sit down, and start yakking a mile a minute while the cameras grind away. The star, of course, is even more facile than his guests, mainly because he's been at it longer.

The star of Talk is a genius in the facility department, just about nothing throws him. He knows a little bit about everything and has no hesitation in displaying his flimsy knowledge before millions of viewers. Also, he has a fat contract with the network, which reinforces his ego five days a week at 8 P.M. when we tape the show. I must admit, though, that in many ways I admire him. He never heard of the word *introspection*. You can't afford to on television. *Spontaneity* is the thing. Keep the waves filled with sound. Any sound is better than no sound. Dead air is a dead show. And besides, as the analyst said, "Who listens?"

"I'm sorry, John. I didn't mean to be flippant. It's just that I'm so damned depressed."

John gave me one of those I-told-you-so looks. He probably was thinking that I was getting what I deserved for having left him for Billy. And maybe I was. My marriage to Billy had lasted even less time than my marriage to John (slightly less than two years, as opposed to slightly more than three). Most people were appalled when they learned that I'd been married four times, but not as appalled as I was. My mother had died while I was still married to Chip Kramer, my first husband, so she'd been spared the painful odyssey of my divorces. As for my poor father, he'd gone into deep shock when I married Paul Bjorkman, my second husband. What bothered him most about Paul wasn't that he was crazy, but that he wasn't Jewish. A goy in the family! *Gevalt*!

"Does Parker know you're pregnant?" John asked.

"No, I haven't told him yet."

Maybe Parker would be my fifth husband. The dubious father of my dubious unborn child. I had to call Dr. Oiseaux tomorrow and tell him that the pills he'd given me hadn't worked. Hopefully, they were supposed to bring on my period, which had not been seen or heard from in some time. Dr. Oiseaux was very concerned about my condition and said that that's what I got for having ever taken the pill. "It makes your system crazy," he told me. "*Completement fou, tu entends*?" Like John, Dr. Oiseaux had a tough, vindictive streak, and wouldn't let you forget a past mistake.

"Oh, oh."

At John's warning, I looked up and saw Josephine's Dutch poet of last night, the elusive K., soft-shoeing it from the hotel into the restaurant and through the kitchen door leading to the parking lot. He had a small suitcase in his hand, and was obviously making another successful escape from Leonard Stein and back rent.

"The Berlitz desk clerk will really get it from Leonard this time," John said. "Leonard's going to want to know how K. managed to slip past him."

"The hell with the desk clerk. Leonard will never fix my air-conditioner when he hears about this latest getaway. I wonder how much money K. owed him."

"We'll find out soon enough when Leonard raises our rents ten dollars a month on some phony excuse."

"Like the maids' salaries have suddenly gone up."

"You'd think that by now Leonard would have figured out how these escapes are made," John said.

"He's too busy figuring out how to chop up more rooms into broom closets."

"The window washer hasn't been to my room in months. Has he been to yours?"

"Now that you mention it, no. Leonard probably got rid of him to save money for a change."

John nodded in mute agreement, and we ordered another round of Papa Dobles. The man who usually carried lizards in his pocket entered La Chiripa, but tonight he had a boa constrictor slung over his shoulder. He waved at us and we motioned him to come over for a drink. A few minutes later, Peggy and I. C. Ring came in together from the street entrance. They were both laughing and went to the bar, which was jammed. Every booth was taken and the conversational noise was overwhelming. Nobody either at the bar or in the restaurant seemed to be alone, people were in twos, threes, fours, fives, and at the back of the room, two tables had been pushed together to accommodate a party of ten, the nucleus being made up of the rock group who'd checked in earlier. The Naked Seven. At moments like this, La Chiripa reminded me of a gigantic ocean liner sailing through perilous waters, while snug inside its passengers ate and drank and smoked and talked themselves into frantic oblivion.

"I think I'll have a Papa, too," the man with the boa constrictor said, having sat down next to John.

Then I noticed a peculiar bulge in the snake's middle.

"What's that?"

"Oh, nothing, dear." The man looked slightly pained. "He just ate one of my lovebirds by mistake. That's all."

Sunday Morning

THE first thing I heard when I woke up was the grinding sound of a garbage truck down below on Broadway, so I knew immediately that I was not in my own room. My room faces the parking lot at the rear of the hotel and is relatively quiet. I also knew it couldn't be my room because of the pleasantly faint whir of an air-conditioner.

Then I opened my eyes and saw my third husband, John O'Connell, stretched out on the floor, on Leonard Stein's poison-green wall-to-wall carpeting. John was lying on his back, naked, and appeared to be asleep.

I was in his bed, naked, too, the top sheet pulled over me, last night's bra and hip huggers on a chair across the room. My head really hurt and my stomach didn't feel so hot either, thanks to the wine and all those Papa Dobles that I'm not accustomed to. I've had perhaps three hangovers in my entire life, and as far as I'm concerned that's three too many. I don't know how John stood them. When we were married, he was hungover practically every day, but he didn't seem to mind. He told me that after a while you got used to feeling rotten in the morning, it was a way of life. Not true for Loretta Silverman. I will never get used to hangovers, any more than I'll get used to losing my looks. But that's the way John has been for as long as I've known him: cheerfully resigned to his miserable fate.

"Hey. What's this? What am I doing on the floor?" He raised himself up on one elbow. "What did you do? Push me out of bed, like you used to when we were married?"

"I never pushed you out of bed."

"You used to push me out all the time. Don't you remember?"

"No."

"Sure. You used to say that I snored too loud. Then you'd roll me over until I landed on the floor. Bang. It's amazing I wasn't brain damaged."

All of my husbands were crazy, no doubt about it. "I'm not in the habit of pushing people out of bed. You must be thinking of your first wife."

"Sue didn't do things like that. She was a very docile girl. I'm thinking of *you*, dear."

"Docile? She was a cow."

"It wasn't her fault. She had a low metabolism. You probably have the metabolism of a go-go dancer."

Carping insults. What did I care? The room was pleasantly dark, unlike mine which had a southern exposure and was baking in the July heat this very minute. John had a nice place: bedroom, living room, and Pullman kitchenette. He once told me how much he was paying, but I'd forgotten. It was a considerable amount, though, and I wondered how he managed to afford it since he kept complaining about the agency business being so lousy. Actually, I wondered how most people in the hotel managed to pay their rent which Leonard Stein raised whenever the whim struck him. The whim struck him pretty often, because Hotel Splendide was not rent controlled.

"My head is killing me," I announced. "Do you have any Alka Seltzer?"

That was like asking Jackie Onassis if she had any money; John lived on Alka Seltzer. Which reminded me that the producer of Talk wanted me to try to book Rose Kennedy for the show. The plan was to get her on by herself, the first guest of the show, and have the star conduct a very dignified interview with the stoic ex-mother-in-law of Jackie O. I doubted that Rose Kennedy would be interested in appearing on Talk, but it certainly was worth a try. Monti Rock you can get any time. Or, as Al, the producer, kept telling me: "Class. We've got to out-class Johnny and Merv. Joey don't count. Give him one of the Gabor broads and he's happy as a clam." It was a well-known fact in television that Joey Bishop's guests tended to be singers, dancers, actors, and comedians, primarily because Joey was afraid of anyone too literate. He was afraid they might make him look dumb.

"What's the matter?" John asked, slowly getting to his feet. "Do you have a hangover?"

"A bad one."

He disappeared into the bathroom, which was off the bedroom, and I could hear him filling a glass with water. Then he peed and it reminded me of when we were living in Paris, and we used to pee in the bidet because there was no toilet in our hotel room, only a tub and a bidet.

John handed me the glass which was fizzing like crazy. "I put two tablets in. You look like you need them."

I drank the vile stuff down as fast as I could, and belched

discreetly. "Thanks. My stomach is upet, too. I never should have had that last round of Papa Dobles. That's what did me in."

"You didn't eat much either."

"I'm on a diet."

He got into bed next to me. "Again?"

When we were married I was always on a diet.

"I gained a few pounds before the summer, and I'm trying to lose them," I said.

He lifted the sheet and looked at my body. "Beautiful. Slim and beautiful as ever. Frankly, I'm beginning to prefer more rounded types, like Josephine."

"Since when?"

"Since Josephine."

His affair with Josephine had been going on for more than two years. "Josephine sags."

"Well, she's not a young kid. What do you expect? It'll happen to you, too, in time."

I didn't want to think about that any more than I had to. Also, what was he doing in bed with me, lifting sheets? On the other hand, it *was* his bed.

"Don't sound so gleeful about my eventual demise, John. I'm only thirty-two, and besides I exercise every day and take very good care of myself. Except for last night."

"I suppose you still smoke two cigarettes a day. Period."

"That's right."

John reached over to the end table and lit a Winston. "Dreadful habit, smoking first thing in the morning, but I can't help it. I'm hooked. I'm not disciplined, like you, Loretta. Maybe that's why we got divorced—because you never approved of my various self-indulgences."

It was a question, not a statement, and a question that I preferred not to answer. People didn't get divorced for any one reason, it was always a combination of things gone bad. Besides, it had happened so long ago, and I hadn't thought about it for so long that I wasn't sure exactly why we did decide to get a divorce. Except for the fact that I had fallen in love with Billy. I wondered what time it was in Stockholm, and whether Billy was in bed with his Inger, and if so, what they were doing. My pounding head and aching stomach only made Billy's unexpected request for a divorce seem that much more appalling. Yes, I definitely had to talk to Parker today and find out what my legal rights were. There was no point in getting all worked up until I found out precisely where I stood in the eyes of the law.

John lifted the sheet again. "You don't look pregnant."

"Stop doing that. Anyhow, you know that it doesn't show for the first couple of months."

John inhaled slowly, meditatively. "Maybe you never should have had that abortion when we were married. Do you ever think of that, Loretta?"

"I don't like to mull over the past. It's a waste of time. What's done is done. Why look backward? What good does it do?"

"You know what the poet said—he who has no knowledge of history is doomed to repeat it. Don't you think it goes for individuals as well as countries?"

He was like a dog with a bone, unwilling to let go until the last bit of marrow had been sucked dry. How did I end up here, anyway? Ever since I opened my eyes I had been trying to remember whether we made love last night, or just passed out from too much alcohol. I no longer found John attractive, but I knew that that wouldn't have stopped me from going to bed with him. Always ready for another sexual disaster, that was me.

John crushed out the butt and lit another cigarette. The

ashes started to pile up in the hotel's cheap glass ashtray. When we were married, the first thing I remember seeing upon opening my eyes was an ashtray filled with last night's cigarette butts. When I was married to Billy, the first thing I saw in the morning was the small paring knife he used for shaving hash, and next to it the intricately carved pipe we used for smoking it. I wasn't much more of a smoker than I was a drinker, but I did try it from time to time, mainly because it put me right to sleep and didn't contain any calories.

The telephone on the end table rang, and John picked it up. "Yes? Hello. Oh hi, dear. How are you this morning? Are you feeling better?"

From my side of the bed, I could faintly hear Josephine's Southern-accented voice.

"No, I just woke up," John said. "I'm not doing anything. I should say, I've been lying here *trying* to wake up. What are you doing, dear?"

Josephine said something about breakfast, and John looked at me regretfully. "No, I'm not up to ham and eggs at Stark's, not in my present condition. Why don't I ring you after I've recovered? Do you want to have dinner this evening?"

John seemed to feel guilty about finding himself in bed with me. I merely felt idiotic.

"I forgot about Daffodil," he said. "But I'd love to take both you girls to dinner. Sure, love it. We could go to that Middle Eastern place down the street. I'm sated with paella and saffron rice. I'll call you around seven. And I'm glad you feel better, dear. You were foolish to run out that way last night."

Josephine said something else, and John quickly added, "You know I love you. Yes. Good-bye, dear. I'll talk to you later."

"Why do you keep telling Josephine you love her?" I asked, after he had hung up.

"Because I love her."

"Don't be ridiculous. You're still in love with me."

He smiled. "You'll never change, will you, Loretta?"

"I don't know what you mean. I also don't know what the hell I'm doing in bed with you."

"As I recall, you wanted to come up here."

"Really? What for?"

"You still curl your lip the same way when you get mad. It's quite charming."

"I'm not mad. I'd just like to know what happened here last night."

"Don't you remember?"

"If I did, I wouldn't be asking you. That's all right. You needn't tell me, if you don't want to. It will come back, eventually."

"We made love," my third husband said. "And you passed out in the middle."

"Why would you make love to me, if you're so wild about Josephine?"

"I must admit I'm a little ashamed of my behavior, but you were so eager. . . ." He stopped, embarrassed for both of us. "You couldn't wait to get up here and rip off your clothes. I never saw a woman undress so quickly. You ought to drink more often, it does interesting things to your libido."

"There's nothing wrong with my libido, and if anyone should be aware of that, it's you, John. The next thing I know you'll be telling me that Josephine is more exciting in bed than I am."

John lit another cigarette. "She is."

"*What?!*"

"There's no need to shout, Loretta. I have a pretty bad

headache myself. Besides, it's strictly a subjective judgment. I'm sure there are many men around who would find you more exciting than Josephine. We can't all have the same tastes, you know. Anyhow, what difference does it make what I think? You're not married to me any more. You're not in love with me. Why should you care about my opinion?"

"I have never been so insulted in my life."

"The trouble with you, Loretta, is that you've spent thirty-two years deluding yourself you're a sexpot."

"What do you mean, *deluding*?"

"Just what it sounds like. Now don't get me wrong. You're a very pretty—"

"—beautiful."

He nodded. "Okay, I'll go along with that. Yes, you are a very beautiful girl, it'd be foolish of me to try to deny it, but beauty doesn't have as much to do with sensuality as Hollywood would like us to believe. The best lay I ever had was a one-legged woman who'd never see forty again. God, she was something, I'll never forget her."

I was beginning to wonder whether I had ever known him at all. Three years of married intimacy apparently had failed to reveal certain unpleasant aspects of John O'Connell to me. I felt as though I were in bed with a stranger, and not a very nice stranger at that.

"You see, Loretta, you have the notion that men want to make love to you because you're so sexually irresistible, whereas the real reason is because you're so childishly charming. You're like a naughty little girl."

My world was starting to disintegrate. First, there'd been the letter from my fourth husband, asking for a divorce, and now my third husband was not so politely trying to tell me that I was a lousy lay. An L.L.! But why should I listen to him? A lot of people thought I was terrific in bed, or wherever it was that we happened to do it. Like the floor of my office at the network, where the star of Talk had once screwed me. That was a strange interlude, but then he was a strange man. I had heard all the stories about him before I came to the network, how he used to go on periodic fuck binges and make it with every girl he could lay his hands on, chambermaids, movie stars, secretaries, talent coordinators. I didn't know whether to believe the stories due to the fact that, as on all networks, rumors ran rampant, particularly rumors about people in high places. When it comes to gossip, backbiting, and intrigue, networks make Louis XV's court at Versailles look like a PTA meeting in Des Moines.

The star of Talk came into my office one day, shortly after our routine five o'clock meeting. I had booked a very well-known Western movie actor on the show that evening, and I'd told the star not to ask him about his forthcoming divorce.

"He won't talk about it," I said, at the meeting.

"Are you sure?"

I said that I was positive. "Don't bring it up. I had lunch with him today and he's really touchy on the subject. It would be a mistake even to mention the divorce."

The star reluctantly agreed not to say anything, but when he came into my office a few minutes later he was still conflicted.

"It's not as though this divorce is a big secret," the star said. "It's been publicized in all the papers, and our viewers will be curious. For years this was considered the perfect Hollywood marriage. It's only natural for people to expect Wade to comment on it."

"Don't bring it up. It's dynamite. Wade's wife is going to marry the guy who directed his last movie. Remember?

The one that laid such a big egg you could smell it half way around the world?"

"I didn't know about the wife and the director."

"That's the dynamite part. Not only does our Western hero go from number two to number six at the box office as a result of that movie, but he loses his beautiful wife to the guy he considers responsible for his drop in popularity. How would *you* feel?"

It was hardly a well-kept secret that the star wouldn't care if his wife of many years screwed Soupy Sales on top of the Pan Am building—that's about how concerned he was with her.

"Okay, you've convinced me," he said.

"Stick to his new movie and the problems they had on location. With that and the film clip, you've got plenty."

"Okay."

But although he stood up, he made no attempt to leave my office. The star of Talk is a relatively attractive man in his early forties, his most outstanding feature being his eyes, which look like transparent blue glass. Their full effect does not come across on television because of the thick horn-rimmed glasses that encase them. The incident I'm about to describe took place over four years ago, during my marriage to John, yet I can still remember what I was wearing: a poor-boy sweater and suede skirt. I had kicked off my shoes under the desk, and when the star leaned over and put a hand on the bare section of my arm, something told me I wouldn't be needing those shoes for a while, and I was right.

"Take off your panties," he said.

"Not *here*." I was stunned by his casual aggressiveness. "The door doesn't lock."

He promptly fixed that by sliding a chair under the door knob, then he removed his glasses and put them on my desk.

"What are you waiting for?" he wanted to know, looking at his watch that had a slot in it for the date and day of the week. "I've got some things to do before the taping."

I knew what they were, too. Put them all together and they spelled S-C-O-T-C-H. Well, anyhow, I decided to go through with it because it struck me funny, and because I was curious what the great man would be like once his pants were down. They never got down. He just took *it* out and stuck it in me so fast that I hiccuped, and once having started hiccuping I couldn't stop, which didn't stop him in the least from going about the business at hand. Thump thump thump. Hiccup hiccup hiccup. He seemed blithely oblivious to my affliction, in fact he seemed pretty oblivious to me in general, except for the one area he had so swiftly penetrated. I felt like a fucking machine that hiccuped, not a very flattering self-image no matter how you looked at it.

"Yeah!" the star kept saying in a sort of dazed stupor, those blue glass eyes rolling around in his head. "Yeah! Yeah!"

We were lying on the network's carpet, which was vastly superior to the Leonard Stein variety, when I suddenly noticed that the chair he had put under the door knob was moving back and forth in a very ominous fashion. I tried to warn the star of what was happening, but my hiccups got in the way of coherent speech, and then it was too late. The chair fell over and in walked our prize guest for that evening's show, Rugged Wade, Western Movie Star, and he was dressed for the role, too, right down to his tight Levis and hand-crafted boots. The star still had no idea that anyone had entered the room. Thump thump thump. But no hiccup hiccup hiccup. I was so startled by this sudden intrusion that I had stopped hiccuping and started laughing, which is the way I typically react to disaster.

"What the fuck are you laughing about?" the star asked.

I pointed to Wade across the room. "Him."

Panic flooded the star's face until he turned around and saw who it was. Then relief replaced the panic.

"Oh shit, it's only you, Wade. Thank God. I was afraid the V.P. in charge of programming had busted in."

"Fascinating, simply fascinating," Wade said, that famous Cinemascope smile on his lips. "At least in Hollywood we take the precaution of locking the door."

"The door doesn't lock," I said, feeling very informative, as I lay there with my legs wrapped around the star's head. Then I noticed that Wade had a tremendous erection—it was a pretty hard thing not to notice considering the skin tightness of his Levis. He walked closer to us with a curious expression, much like an archaeologist about to examine a rare Cro-Magnon fossil. The star had stopped thumping, but it was still in me and getting softer by the minute.

"Mind if I get into the act?" Wade asked.

"You're the guest," the star said, laughing at his own witticism.

I reached up and touched Wade's erection, boy was it hard, but as soon as I did that the star extricated himself from me, pulled my hand away, and put his own hand on Wade. At that point Wade unzipped his levis and took the gigantic thing out. I thought the star would die of ecstasy shock, that's how big it was, and he promptly put it in his mouth, leaving me stranded. But not for long. Wade was far more considerate than the star, a true gentleman of the old West who didn't believe in letting ladies down. And down he went on me while the star was still going down on him. After Wade and I had come, we realized that the poor star was the only one who hadn't so we decided that he should fuck me to orgasm this time. He did. I was really getting it coming and going, because after that Wade fucked me for quite a while and it was very nice, or would have been if the damn star hadn't had his glassy blue eyes fastened on us the whole time.

"Go guard the door," Wade told him. "That chair idea of yours is for the birds. Don't you remember the scene in my last picture when I bust into the whore's room with a flick of my elbow, and knock the chair on its ass? That was no stunt, amigo."

The star guarded the door while Wade and I had a good session. He was really a sweet guy in his own way, very direct, very straight, I could see why he'd endeared himself to millions of movie goers over the years. He said what he meant, and he meant what he said, so that I could have killed the star a few minutes later when he pulled his double cross. Wade and I were all finished and the three of us were putting ourselves together again, zipping and straightening and all that, then the star lit a cigarette, inhaled, and said, "No shit, Wade, why are you getting divorced?"

I never told John about that three-way circus, although I did tell Billy, who thought it was amusing. Billy had a very sane and healthy attitude toward sex, and was not one of those puritanical fanatics like John, who rigidly insisted upon monogamy at all cost. But then John's Irish Catholic upbringing and Midwestern background had victimized him in a most unfortunate way. He didn't have much fun with sex, even when it was of the monogamous variety. The fires of hell burned brighter in his soul than the fires of passion ever would, the poor inhibited fuckup. And he called *me* an L.L.!

"Are you hungry?" John asked. "Would you like some breakfast?"

"I don't think I could eat in my present condition. How about a cup of coffee?"

"Coming right up."

He got out of bed and put on a blue terry-cloth robe, the same one he used to wear when we were married.

"That robe brings back memories."

He looked at it as though he'd never seen it before. "I didn't realize it was that old."

"You had it when I met you."

"I did?"

"Yes, I remember the first time we made love you wore it the next morning. You asked me then whether I wanted breakfast, and I said no, only coffee."

"You have quite a memory, Loretta."

He seemed impressed, flattered, that after all these years I should still remember the details of our beginning, but I'm like that. Little things stick in my mind, the color of a lover's tie, but ask me something weighty like why we finally broke up and I draw a blank. To this day I remember how each of my husbands liked their eggs done, yet I've forgotten what it was that made me stop loving them. Parsley. John liked his scrambled eggs sprinkled with parsley, and when we were married I used to keep a manicure scissors in the kitchen for the express purpose of snipping parsley leaves. Billy liked fried eggs with thick slices of Virginia ham. Paul liked eggs Benedict. Chip liked cheese omelets, made with Gruyère. I didn't like eggs.

"Here we go."

John had returned with freshly perked coffee and glasses of orange juice with pieces of lime on the side.

"Do you have a robe I could wear?"

"Are you cold?"

"Yes, slightly."

"Would you rather I turn off the air-conditioner?"

"No, please leave it on. It feels wonderful after living in

Torrid Zone. Sometimes I. C. lets me come into his room and stand next to the air-conditioner until I cool off."

"That's big of him."

"I. C. is okay in a Chinese kind of way. The only complaint I have is that the wall between our two rooms is so thin that we each can hear everything the other one says. No privacy whatsoever. And Leonard Stein has the nerve to advertise *soundproof rooms*. There's simply no end to his vicious lies."

"Yet we all go on living here."

"This hotel is like an addiction."

"I'm thinking of moving," John said. "I look at the classified ads for apartments every day."

"I know. But you never find anything."

"Rents are hopeless in New York."

"How much do you pay here?"

"Four fifty."

"For four fifty you could get a two-bedroom apartment on the Upper East Side where they pick up the garbage regularly."

"I don't like the Upper East Side, it's sterile. And besides, what would I do with two bedrooms?"

"You could use one as an office, and save money."

"I've thought of that, but it seems like a very lonely existence, living that way. Isolated. If I lived in an apartment building, I'd have to make formal appointments to see people. Here, I can wander into La Chiripa whenever I feel like it, have a drink, and maybe run into someone I know, or someone I don't know, but it's casual, it's not such a big deal. And I like all the impromptu parties. There's fluidity here."

"Companionship."

"What's wrong with that? Most people are lonely."

"The people here are lonelier than most."

"Their emotional needs are greater. You criticize my living here, but what about you? You don't seem to have any great plans to check out despite all your bitching."

John was right. Like him, I needed the companionship, the aura of warmth that made Hotel Splendide a sanctuary for dislocated people with uncertain pasts.

"Hey, how about that robe?" I said.

"Sure."

He went to the closet and took out something that looked suspiciously feminine.

"What's this?"

He seemed a bit embarrassed. "Josephine wears it when she stays over."

"That's what I thought. I can still smell the Je Reviens."

"You shouldn't be so hard on her. She likes you, and you always give her a hard time."

"She asks for it. She's not satisfied until someone tells her off. You know that."

He nodded reluctantly and sipped his coffee. To me, it tasted like poison, or was that the taste in my mouth? Awful. I put my cup on the end table and got into Josephine's robe, which was one of those Oriental things with floppy sleeves and no buttons. I. C. Ring should see me now.

"I wonder whether I. C.'s survey is on the level," I said.

"Probably. It sounds dumb enough to be for real."

"Dumb isn't the word. It's a typically masculine approach: statistics. What have statistics ever proven about anything? I don't know why men are so hung up on statistics; women aren't. That's the trouble with the pill. It was invented by man for the convenience of man. I'll never take it again. Never. Do you know why I got pregnant?"

"Why?"

"Don't look so interested."

"But I am interested."

"Well, I forgot to put it on my toothbrush for two days in a row, and the result was instant fertility. How do you like that?"

"You forgot to put *what* on your toothbrush?"

"The pill, idiot. I used to put it on my toothbrush before I went to sleep so I'd remember to take it in the morning."

"You never did that when we were married."

"I didn't take the pill then. I used a diaphragm. Christ, don't you remember anything?"

"I remember that you stole all our ashtrays when you left me for that black saxophone player. You even took the one we swiped from the Palace Hotel in Madrid."

"Don't remind me of Madrid. That's where you refused to buy me a lousy pair of shoes."

"I was getting back at you for being constantly drunk in Rome. Remember how you'd get up in the morning and drink seven cheap Italian brandies as openers?"

"The only reason I drank cheap brandy was because you were so damn cheap."

"Broke. Not cheap."

"Cheap and petty. That's why you got along so well in Paris. The French are as cheap as you, it was a real meeting of the souls, you and the French. And you know that I had to be pretty upset to be drinking at all when we were in Rome."

"Why *were* you drinking? I never did find out."

"Because I was miserable. I thought that maybe if I drank, I'd feel closer to you. That's why."

"You never loved me," John O'Connell said.

At that, I burst into tears because it wasn't true (or was it?). "Yes, I did. You know I did."

"For how long? Three minutes? You've never loved anyone in your life, Loretta. That's why you're so fucked up."

I stopped crying. "The fuckup of the century calls me a fuckup. Intriguing. Remember that scene in *Gilda* where Rita Hayworth looks straight at the camera and says, 'you wouldn't think one woman could marry *two* crazy men in a lifetime, would you?' And I married four."

"Three. I'm the only reasonably sane one you chose."

He believed it, too, conveniently forgetting his crackup some years ago in New York. It was the first time I saw the whole alcoholic d.t. business in action, and hopefully the last. John's drinking had gotten so bad that he believed there was a fifty-piece symphony orchestra in our bathroom. They started to play every time he opened the door. When he left the bathroom and closed the door, they stopped playing. I said how come I didn't hear any music when I went into the bathroom?

"Ah," was John's reply, "that's because you open the door too fast."

I really became scared then. The next time I had to go to the bathroom, I opened the door very slowly and said, "Yes, you're right. Now I hear the music."

I tried to get him to knock off the drinking, but none of my efforts were successful. After he stopped hearing the symphony orchestra in our bathroom, he began to see a bicycle in front of our apartment door. He could not open the door without first removing the bicycle. For some reason, the bicycle obstacle really annoyed me and I said, "Oh for Christ's sake, there's no bicycle there, you're just imagining it."

"You mean you don't see it? You must need glasses, Loretta. And you always told me you had twenty-twenty vision."

I decided it was no use, no use at all, and in utter desperation I removed the bicycle so we could get into our apartment. But I knew that things had hit an all-time low the day he started to cry, and said, "If you ever get out of this alive, go back to Cleveland." He thought I was his first wife, Sue, whom he'd met and married in his home town of Cleveland. I've never been to Cleveland in my life, I'm happy to report. Rita Hayworth wasn't the only one with troubles.

"Please don't cry," John said to me now. "Please, dear. What are you crying about?"

"I don't know why I do it," I said, in between sobs.

"Do what, dear?"

"*Stop calling me dear*. I'm not Josephine. I don't know why I left Chip for Paul, Paul for you, and you for Billy. What sense does it all make?"

"Maybe Parker will marry you when you tell him about your condition. He seems like a decent sort."

"I don't want to marry Parker, I'm not in love with him. Besides, I have no intention of getting married again. Four times is enough for me, more than enough."

John finished his coffee. "Twice was enough for me. I guess the idea of another divorce scares me more than I thought, otherwise I would have proposed to Josephine a long time ago."

I lay back against the hotel's soggy pillows. They felt like they were stuffed with damp handkerchiefs, and probably were, but I was so happy to be in an air-conditioned room for a change that I didn't care about much else. Except, of course, John's infantile reluctance to admit that he was still in love with me. Pride. Pride and penises. That's what men were made of, and if anyone should know it's Loretta Irene Silverman Kramer Bjorkman O'Connell Ray.

"John, do you remember the first time we met?" I asked, feeling a familiar stirring in my lower regions.

"Sure do."

I had booked a client of John's on Talk, a clinical psychologist named Robert Fingerhood who'd written a psychosexual suspense novel about how he killed his unfaithful girl-friend. I thought that the idea of a psychologist writing a murder novel might be interesting, different. The average writer stinks on television, he's too inhibited. Also, as on most big talk shows, we save writers for last (when our viewers are fast asleep and snoring), so that as a result of all that waiting around backstage in the windowless green room, most writers are half deranged by the time they finally face the red eye of the camera.

John had come to the studio with Robert Fingerhood, trying to give him moral support. I stayed for the taping of the show because I found myself violently attracted to John. At that time I was married to Paul Bjorkman and living with him in his moving company warehouse, surrounded by objets d'art being stored by our primarily homosexual clientele. There were even a couple of Picasso forgeries we'd hung to give the place a homey look. I had begun to be bored with Paul and our unrelieved bohemian existence. In contrast, John O'Connell seemed decidedly engaging, a real change of pace which I figured I could use a bit of.

Although the moving business seems exotic at first, with its daily unfolding of bizarre and catastrophic episodes, it loses much of its charm before very long. The fact is that it's a grimy, ugly way to make a living, marked by constant bickering between owner and customer. Paul was forever being cheated out of money by people he moved who claimed that the job had taken too long, that he sent more men than they needed, that he overcharged them, etc. When I came home in the evening, he was not in a very pleasant state of mind after the multi-tensions of the day, which we knew would be repeated the next day, and the next, and the next. There is tension in every business, but the moving business differs in that you're at a disadvantage to begin with: people hate to move and they take out their anxieties, resentment, and paranoia upon the mover. If it hadn't been for the fact that Paul and I had a compelling sex life, I probably would have left him sooner, but you can disregard a lot of crap when you have a nightime of eroticism to look forward to.

Before Paul had gone into the Village moving business he'd held a number of respectable uptown jobs which later turned his stomach, so much so that he completely rejected anything above Fourteenth Street. That put me at a great disadvantage. Sometimes I'd want him to come with me to a certain movie, or a party being given by a person at the network, and he simply refused. He'd never heard of the movie and he didn't know the person, he just wouldn't go outside the radius of a few blocks, and after a while it got to be a terrible drag. I like people who are flexible, not threatened by strange surroundings or a new social scene. John O'Connell struck me as a man who would not be threatened, and as it turned out I was right. In looking back, I realize that I sacrificed the sexual mobility I had with Paul for the social mobility I wanted with John. What I really wanted was both qualities in the same person. Lots of luck.

John's client, Robert Fingerhood, turned out to be a pretty cool customer on television. He said he'd written his murder novel to rid himself of a lot of psychic pain, and to give a realistic glimpse into the daily life of a clinical psychologist (as though anyone cared). After the taping the three of us went to Sardi's for a drink, although as usual I stuck to ginger ale. I was hoping that Fingerhood would take off, leaving me alone with John, but he didn't seem about to, and it was I who finally said I had to be getting home.

"Can I drop you?" John asked.

"I live pretty far downtown. I'm sure it would be out of your way."

"Let me worry about that."

Fingerhood lived in the East Twenties, and we dropped him first. When we came to my block on Washington Street, John said, "It sure is dark around here. Where do you live?"

I pointed to The Green Hornet sign on the front of our building. "There."

"But that looks like some kind of warehouse."

"It is. It's a moving company and a warehouse. My husband and I own it."

I caught a fast glimpse at his expression. Yes, he was surprised that I was married. And disappointed.

"We have a little apartment on the second floor. Would you like to come up and meet my husband?"

John later told me that sheer curiosity made him say, "Yes." After all, who in their right minds would live in a fucking warehouse? Only us chickens. I rang the bell, but nobody answered. We had four different locks on the door, it was a very Rube Goldberg security arrangement. After much fumbling around, I managed to find the right key for the right lock.

"Wake up," I called out, as we came up the stairs.

Paul was dead asleep on an Early American rocker that one of our customers had given to us in exchange for a lacquered bureau. Asleep and looking very beat.

"This is a very interesting place," John said, glancing around. "Does your husband always use a dolly as a footrest?"

"Only when he's home."

We had just gotten a storage load that afternoon and the front part of our apartment was filled with cartons and barrels, not to mention the usual collection of junk that had been abandoned by various people we moved. Our workers were told never to abandon anything, because after a certain legal amount of time it was okay to auction it off—that is, if we didn't want it, and frequently we did. That's how we furnished our apartment, which consisted of one enormous room: with homosexual remains. And we all know they have snappy taste, right?

I touched Paul on the shoulder. "Baby?"

He shifted in the rocker, but did not open his eyes. "Huh? What? Who?"

"Perhaps you should let him sleep," John said.

"Perhaps you're right."

"I think that under the circumstances, I'd better be going."

"I'm sorry you didn't get a chance to meet my husband, but I don't like to wake him. He puts in a rough day. Why don't you call me at the network? We can have lunch."

"Fine. I'd love to. You were very nice to Dr. Fingerhood tonight. I appreciate it."

That "Dr." business should have warned me that John O'Connell took all the wrong things seriously, but what did I know then? I was only twenty-seven, not the mature thirty-two of today when I've learned to spot the ominous danger signals. Tempus fugit, all right. There's no denying that one.

"Loretta. When did you get in?"

John had just left, and I was putting my coat and purse away. "A few seconds ago. I brought someone home to meet you, but you seemed to be sound asleep. Did you have a rough day?"

"No rougher than usual. Who'd you bring home?"

"A literary agent. I booked one of his clients on the show tonight. Then the three of us went to Sardi's for a drink."

Paul eyed me suspiciously. Of all my husbands, he was the most jealous and not without cause. After all, I was married to Chip Kramer when I met Paul who at that time was the ladies' shoe buyer at Lord & Taylor. Yes, that was how the big romance started, over a pair of pointy toed black silk pumps. I don't know how women ever walked in those contraptions. We must have all been crazy.

"Have you eaten?" I asked Paul.

"Not since lunch."

"Neither have I. Would you like to go to the White Horse for a meatloaf sandwich?"

"That sounds good."

He stood up and stretched. Paul was very attractive, tall, husky, with darkish blond hair and a great moustache. He was wearing blue jeans and his favorite denim shirt that I had washed the day before, with Duz. He put on a suede jacket that had a pile lining. It was winter, but Paul never wore a coat. Then, giving me a big hug, he said, "Let's go, sweetheart," all signs of jealousy gone. His moods were subject to sudden change. To this day Paul Bjorkman still remains a mystery to me, a quiet, intense, brooding man, the Greta Garbo of the Village moving business.

The day I told him I was leaving him, he said: "There's a train going to Chicago at nine o'clock. Be under it."

"Do you want to?" John said.

"You know I do."

"Not by the way you fell asleep last night. Right in the middle."

"I'm sorry about that, but it was the liquor. I'm not used to drinking. Come on."

I started to take off my robe, or I should say, Josephine's robe, when there was a knock on the door. I could only think it must be Josephine, coming up to apologize for her behavior of last night.

"Don't let her in," I whispered to John, pulling the sheet up to my neck.

"Who is it?" he called out.

A man's garbled reply came back in return.

"Just a minute," John said, getting out of bed and going to the door. He still had on his blue terry-cloth robe. When he opened the door, an extremely thin man lurched in, carrying a bucket of water and wearing a wide belt across the middle of his drab gray uniform. There were metal attachments on either side of the belt, and hanging from one was what looked to me like a car's windshield wiper.

"*Jo napott kivanok*," the man said. "My name is Aladar. I come to wash the windows."

"On Sunday?" John said.

The man was so drunk, he could barely stand. "Leonard Stein tell me to wash windows today. He is my cousin."

John looked at him in dismay. "I suggest that you come back another time when you're feeling better. You're in no condition–"

The man unsteadily put his bucket on the floor, and some of the water sloshed over onto the poison-green carpeting. "When my cousin say today, he mean today. If you don't like, *isten lova baszja*. That's Hungarian for, God's horses fuck you. You too, lady."

He grinned at us. One of his front teeth was missing.

"Let him start washing," I said to John. "If he doesn't care whether he falls out the window why should we?"

"I'm nine floors up. He'll kill himself. Look at him. He's so thin that in his condition a strong wind could blow him away. Leonard Stein must be insane to send this drunk around."

"He probably gets him cheap."

John turned to Aladar. "Have you ever washed windows before?"

"For twenty years I wash the highest buildings in New York. Never have accident. Now I start."

"Maybe you were never drunk before," John said.

Aladar honored us with another toothless grin. "Always drunk." He pulled a pint of vodka out of his back pants pocket. "Good stuff. Gives energy. You want some?"

"No, thank you."

"You, lady?"

"I'll pass, too."

"First in this room I start. Go back to bed, Mister. Pay no attention to Aladar."

With that, he took a slug of vodka and got out on the window ledge, hooking his belt to some attachment on either side of the window, and began washing away.

"Let's go into the living room," I suggested. "I can't bear to watch him, not in my weakened condition."

The Pullman kitchenette was off the living room and John made scrambled eggs and toast for the two of us. I thought again of the parsley I used to sprinkle on his eggs when we were married. Aside from his drinking problem, John hadn't been a bad husband, just not a terribly exciting one. Paul, for all his silences, had a dynamism about him, a certain masculinity that John lacked. John was good looking, but not in the animalistic way most women find so appealing. Women wanted to mother John, they wanted to pursue and capture Paul. I had pursued and captured him, then I left him. He was too remote, just as John thought I was. I'm convinced that in each marriage I picked up a salient quality of my husband which I then brought to the next marriage as my own. The interesting thing was that it often turned out to be a quality I used to criticize and belittle. Perhaps because at the time I didn't have it and was somehow envious, even when it wasn't the most attractive quality in the world. I really don't know.

"I wonder what's taking him so long," John said.

I had almost forgotten about the window washer. "Let's go see."

The two bedroom windows sparkled in the early morning sun, the venetian blinds still rolled up tight. There was no sign of Aladar. John turned pale. "He's not here."

"Maybe he finished and left."

"Why would he do that? He knew there was another room. I never should have let him go out on that ledge. You saw how drunk he was."

"Now don't get excited, John."

"He's probably lying on the pavement below, smashed to pieces, the poor bastard."

"We would have heard the commotion. There would have been police cars, sirens. We would have heard *something*."

John grabbed the house phone. "I'm going to call the desk."

"Why don't we just look down and see if we can spot him?"

"You look. Not me. I'm calling the desk."

"*Ki csinalja eszt a zavart?*"

The muffled words came from the bed, where Aladar had pulled the sheets over his head. He was so thin we hadn't noticed him. Then a pillow moved and Aladar's face emerged. "Aladar take little nap. Now I wash other windows."

"I'm going to talk to Leonard Stein about this," John said, after Aladar had left the room. "He has no right sending his drunken cousins to wash my windows and sleep in my bed. Leonard Stein is going to hear from me about this."

"Oh screw Leonard Stein. I'm sick of the sound of his name."

"Except when you bring it up, like in connection with your air-conditioner. If you weren't so stubborn, Loretta, you'd get the damned thing fixed yourself and stop making such an issue about it."

I was in no mood for an argument, I was in the mood to make love. I would have bet anything that Billy was making love to Inger at that very moment, and I was sick with jealousy. They were probably drinking aquavit and planning their wedding. How could Billy forget me so easily? Was I that easy to replace? None of my other husbands seemed to think so, or they would have remarried, wouldn't they? Chip, Paul, John. None of them had found a suitable replacement for me, so how dare Billy? When I married him, my father (who still hadn't recovered from my Protestant and Catholic marriages) told me I was letting myself in for a lot of *shvartze* trouble.

"What kind of trouble is that?" I asked him.

"You laugh at your father because he's just a kosher butcher in The Bronx, but wait, you'll see."

"See what?"

"You'll see," he repeated.

"How will I know what it is when it happens, unless you tell me now?"

"You'll know."

My father's inscrutable nature had always driven me crazy, and never more so than just then. "What will I know, father?"

"You'll find out."

"Tell me something. Are you sure you're not Charlie Chan in drag?"

"You'll be sorry you didn't listen to your father," were

my father's last words on the subject of my marriage to Billy Ray.

When I saw my father for dinner later this evening, I was going to tell him that I was very sorry I hadn't listened to his warning two years ago, even though I still didn't know what he had had in mind. But whatever it was, I was sorry. Yes, father, you were right about Billy Ray, he's turned into a real no-goodnik. In reply, my father would say something like, "Maybe next time you'll listen to your father."

Every Sunday my father came down from The Bronx on the IRT subway to have dinner with me at La Chiripa, an ordeal that both of us secretly dreaded but pretended we loved. My father dreaded it because he was even more opposed to the decidedly un-kosher food at La Chiripa than he was to my offbeat friends. And I dreaded it because he never stopped complaining about either.

When I moved into Hotel Splendide, my father was convinced that I'd hit an all-time low. *Dreck*, was his name for Splendide. In fact, if it hadn't been for the respectability of my job, and my healthy salary of three hundred and fifty dollars a week, my father would be sitting *shiva* for me right now. The only thing that could make him more unsettled than he already was, would be for him to learn that I thought I was pregnant. That would be the end. He'd probably stab himself in the stomach with a kosher butcher knife, and beg God to forgive him for having such a disgraceful daughter.

"John," I said. "Do you want to make love?"

"Sure."

We were back in bed, minus our bathrobes. Somehow the room seemed much warmer, although the air-conditioner was still whirring away. It was probably going to be another sizzler and I dreaded the thought of returning to my oven of a room, but that wasn't the only reason I wanted to stay here with John. I needed reassurance, emotional support, love. Billy's letter had upset me even more than I realized yesterday. Now that I'd slept on it, the full reality of his request for a divorce came pounding home in a nightmarish way. Nobody had ever asked me for a divorce before. *I* was the one who'd always asked. *I* was the one who'd always left them. I even used to joke about it. "Nobody leaves me and lives." Very funny.

John O'Connell and I spent a happy half hour or so making love, and afterward when we were lying there, exhausted, I said, "I love you."

"No, you don't. You're just upset about Billy."

"I really do love you, John."

"Let's say that you're fond of me, and leave it at that. Okay?"

"I love you, I tell you!" I was practically shouting in desperation. "And you love me, too!"

He looked reflective. "No, I love Josephine, although God knows why. She's even more impossible than you."

That was the last straw. First Billy, and now John. Two rejections in two days. Loretta Silverman was slipping all right, but she wasn't done for yet.

"Where are you going?" John asked, alarmed by the way I had jumped out of bed, scooped up my clothes, and was heading rapidly for the door.

"I'm going home, you miserable son of a bitch. *Ver gershtaben.*"

Aladar was passed out on John's living room sofa, one of his hands dangling in the bucket of water. "*Isten lova baszja,*" he said in his sleep. Hungarian curses had nothing on Jewish curses. When I got out into the hall, The Naked Seven were standing there, waiting for the elevator. But I was The Naked

One. In true Hotel Splendide fashion, they didn't blink an eyelid at my lack of dress.

"You'll wait for that fucking elevator forever," I told them.

They sort of nodded and continued to stand there, while I walked down the two flights of stairs to my room. On the seventh floor I ran into Peggy who was coming out of the communal bathroom, her long hair swimming in black dye. Some of the dye had dripped down onto her forehead.

"Pretend you didn't see me," she laughed.

"Ditto."

My room was even hotter than I had anticipated. I threw last night's clothes on the bed, and in complete and utter desperation, shouted, "If it's the last thing I ever do in this world, I'm going to murder Leonard Stein!"

And thanks to Leonard's miserable soundproofing, I. C. Ring shouted back from his room, "Welcome home. How many orgasms did you have?"

Sunday Afternoon

IF the roof of Hotel Splendide had been of the tar variety, it would have turned to junket hours ago, that was how hot it was when I finally dragged myself up there, shortly after noon. I'd been coming up to the roof for a bit of socializing and sunbathing every Sunday and Monday, my two days off, since the summer began.

The Splendide Sun & Surf Club, that was how we resident-inmates referred to it, each of us wondering why we weren't at Easthampton, or Fire Island, or Martha's Vineyard, or one of those peachy places. Why *here*, with the gasoline fumes drifting up from the heavy traffic on Broadway, not to mention the garlic cooking odors drifting up from the ever-active La Chiripa kitchen?

It was a question that we asked ourselves every time we gathered on the roof and dreamed of happier days on white beaches with people we used to love. I think that, secretly, all of us wondered whether those halcyon days were lost forever, or maybe we wondered whether they'd ever been as halcyon as they now seemed in nostalgic retrospect.

Peggy was at one end of the roof, her newly dyed hair covered by a status scarf. My own hair, which I had just washed, was set in enormous wire rollers that I'd bought on sale at Woolworth's. Ordinarily, I would have sat under my Oster hair dryer, but the heat in my room made that convenience an impossibility (one more strike against Leonard Stein). Any other girl would have been ashamed to appear publicly with her hair in rollers, but my features were so perfect, so symmetrical, that I could get away with it. Another advantage of sheer beauty.

Peggy and the girl who designed towels and sheets for a prominent cotton goods manufacturer shared one moth-eaten blanket which had been pulled up against the slope of the hotel's only penthouse. Both Peggy and the designer were wearing huge black sunglasses, and maillot bathing suits. Peggy waved to me, and the designer said, "Would you sleep on a khaki sheet?"

"No."

"Why not?"

"Khaki reminds me of the army."

"Would you sleep on a striped black-and-white sheet?"

"No."

"Why not?"

"Black-and-white stripes remind me of prison movies."

"Everything reminds you of something. Would you sleep on a bright orange sheet? The Roof wants to know."

If you didn't stop her, she'd go on forever. I felt sorry for the cotton goods manufacturer if he based his line of sheets on the precarious taste of people who lived at Hotel Splendide. The designer took our opinions very seriously, and even now was making careful notes in the small pad that she always carried with her for just that purpose. Peggy raised her sunglasses and winked at me. The designer amused her. As I started to walk to the far end of the roof, I heard the designer say to Peggy, "Would you sleep on a solid black sheet?"

The roof was quite long, about one hundred and fifty feet, and when I got to the other end, there was Parker Mason stretched out on his Abercrombie & Fitch beach chair, looking very aristocratic and above it all. The chrome of the chair blinked and glared in the intense heat. Parker was plowing through the financial section of the Sunday *Times*, and it took him a moment to acknowledge my presence.

"Well, good morning," he said, with his usual smile of bland amusement. "Or is it afternoon?"

I threw Leonard Stein's miserable blanket on the brick floor of the roof. "Afternoon."

But he had gone back to the news of corporate earnings, losses, mergers, and stock market quotations. Looking over his shoulder, I noticed that the price of polystyrene was going up. As if there wasn't enough trouble in the world.

"Would you sleep on a bright orange sheet?" I asked him. "The Roof wants to know."

"Oh Christ, don't tell me that that nut is up here."

"Relax. She's way at the other end, and too busy giving Peggy the third degree to bother you. At least for a while."

"That woman is a menace. I'd rather sleep on a bare bed than any sheet she designed."

I considered that pretty whimsical of Parker, in view of the fact that, like the rest of us, the only sheets he slept on these days were the hospital white, Leonard Stein variety. Even the sheet designer slept on them. Once a week the maids at the hotel changed the linen. If you wanted more than a weekly change, it cost three dollars a shot. Leonard Stein didn't believe in missing any possible chance of raking in the old do-re-mi. I still wondered how much he was paying his drunken cousin, Aladar, to crap out in the bed of everyone whose windows he washed. My hunch was that Aladar owed him money, and Leonard was characteristically taking it out in trade. Leonard had even put his own father to work at Splendide as night desk clerk. There was a lot of speculation as to how Leonard's mother had managed to escape her son's relentless tyranny. Probably by dying.

I dropped my blanket alongside Parker's beach chair, and proceeded to remove my Vera shift, revealing a ruffled, turquoise bikini. Despite the fact that I'm thirty-two and have led a life of emotional torment, thanks to my four crazy husbands, I must say that I'm in very good physical shape and could give any young girl a run for her money. At the network, my secret nickname was "The Body," which I pretended I didn't know about. One of the bookers, the guy who specialized in comedians, laid that one on me after I'd been working there only a short while. What happened was that I came into the office one morning wearing a skimpy black knit dress that John O'Connell subsequently set fire to during his d.t. period. John had gotten it into his head that the dress, a bargain at Bendel's, had been sent by the devil to talk him out of his boozing. At first, he tried to placate the dress.

"How about if I cut down to a pint a day?" he would say.

But, apparently, the dress wouldn't go along with that.

"Hell, a pint's nothing," John argued. "Sixteen lousy ounces. That's only four martinis. Don't you think you're being a wee bit unreasonable?"

The dress, it seemed, did not. After much more back-and-forth conversation, John bellowed, "Well, if you and the devil don't like my drinking, screw the two of you." Then he marched into the bathroom where the fifty-piece symphony orchestra was tuning up for his arrival. A few minutes later, seemingly pacified, he emerged and promptly set the dress on fire with the Dunhill lighter I'd given him for Christmas. Before I could stop him, the dress was singed beyond repair.

The other talent coordinators at the network still asked me from time to time what ever happened to that "great little black dress" I used to wear. Not wishing to reveal the extent of my third husband's derangement, I told them it had been lost at the cleaner's. Although I try to keep up a cheerful façade, Loretta Silverman's life hasn't all been a barrel of laughs. No indeedy. Some of the things I've lived through would have destroyed a weaker woman, but I guess I take after my father in that respect. He's got his kosher meat business, and I've got my crazy husband business, and we just try to do the best we can with what we've been stuck with. Jewish stoics, like old J. C.

"Very nice," Parker said, admiring my turquoise bikini. "New?"

"No, I've worn it before."

"I never noticed it."

"You haven't been paying attention."

"I always pay attention to you, Loretta. It must be obvious by now."

His tone instantly perked me up. Nothing renews my enthusiasm for life faster than an unexpected bit of flattery, and in Parker's case it certainly was unexpected. He was the guarded type, careful never to go out on a limb, stingy when it came to dispensing compliments. Many of the people at Splendide thought that Parker was an embittered prick, with the soul of a cross-eyed iguana, and at times I agreed with them, but now that Billy was leaving me for Inger, I began to see Parker in a new light. If he was as embittered as people claimed, it would hardly be any wonder, considering that his wife had run off with the family dentist, taking their one child with her, a daughter whom Parker rarely spoke about. I met her once when she came in on a weekend from Bryn Mawr, an athletic girl with no discernible style. "Everyone at this hotel looks depraved," she said, to which I replied that we all were.

"Do you want any suntan lotion?" I asked Parker, who was once more buried in the stock-market quotations.

"I put some on already. Thanks."

Parker was attractive in a lanky, redhaired sort of way. His skin, though, seemed to be less sensitive than that of most redheads, who couldn't take the sun without the risk of being badly burned. Parker was wearing a pair of tartan Bermuda shorts and a baseball cap. Behind tortoise rimmed glasses, his eyes were the color of coffee that could use some more milk in it. Parker's coffee eyes and imperious manner had caused Josephine Jasmin to dub him, "El Exigente." All the resident-inmates had something bitchy to say about each other; that was one of the dubious charms of living at Hotel Splendide.

After I'd rubbed Bain du Soleil on every part of my body that I could reach, I lay down on the mangy blanket that I reserved for sunbathing purposes. A few feet away from me, riveted into the roof, was a small plaque that I'd never noticed before. It said, "This hotel was erected in January 1887." Which, no doubt, was the year that Leonard Stein bought the blanket that I lay on. The sun was incredibly hot, and in a few minutes I turned over on my stomach. That's when I saw the plastic picnic jug sitting in the shade under Parker's beach-chair.

"What's in it?" I asked him.

"Screwdrivers."

"Could I have one?"

"I thought you didn't drink."

"I don't, but I'm dying of thirst."

Between the heat and my hangover, I was feeling pretty awful. The sun was hell on hangovers, I could see that. No wonder I was never able to get John to go to a beach when we were married. I was only just now beginning to appreciate the tacit ground rules that all drinkers lived by to make themselves as comfortable as possible within the limits of their malaise.

Parker took a paper cup out of an old denim jacket that was slung over the back of his chair and filled it to the top with the orange concoction. Then he took out another cup and did the same. We touched cups.

"Chin chin," Parker said, taking a tentative sip. "It's not too strong for you, is it?"

"It's wet, and that's all I care about at the moment."

"Well, be careful. There's more vodka in it than you might realize at first."

First flattery, and now protectiveness. There was a decided switch in Parker's attitude toward me, which in the past had been characterized by a guarded sarcasm and sometimes not so guarded disdain. Even though Parker and I had gone to bed about half a dozen times, he'd never before shown any benevolence toward me, even in what should have been a tender moment. I remember one night when we had finished making love in his room and were lying in the dark, smoking mentholated cigarettes and thinking our own private thoughts, I said, "Perhaps I should go back to my own room." I didn't really want to go; what I wanted was for him to ask me to stay.

"It's your move," Parker said in the darkness, as though he were discussing a chess game.

"Perhaps I'll stay here."

Parker's reaction to that was to crush out his cigarette, pat me on the shoulders, turn over on his side, and go to sleep. Stalemate.

"That screwdriver really hit the spot," I said now, hoping to keep alive the sudden flare of rapport between us. "And I didn't even taste the vodka."

"Good girl." He had switched to the real estate section. "Help yourself to another, if you feel like it."

"Thanks, but not right now."

Stillness prevailed, shattered only by a ship's blast from the Hudson. An ocean liner packed with American vacationers bound for the summer tourist madness of Europe. Champagne kisses and sloppy good-byes. In the past, I would have wished I were on that ship, about to sail to exotic ports, but since moving into the hotel I had had no such urges. At Splendide, we manufactured our own brand of exoticism. Peggy once admitted that when she sunbathed on the roof she closed her eyes and pretended she was on the beach at Malibu where she'd spent her teen-age years. With Parker, it was Oyster Bay, his last summer site of marital happiness before disaster struck. Josephine Jasmin made wistful references to the beauty of South Carolina's resort area (she was from Charleston). As for me, I couldn't make up my mind where I was. Some days it would be the French Riviera (when I was still in love with John); Provincetown (breaking up with Billy); the west coast of Mexico (delirious with Paul); a hotel swimming pool in Las Vegas (gambling evenings with Chip). And meanwhile, here I sat on a parched and sooty rooftop, the New York air destroying my lungs.

"Parker," I said, my eyes closed to the sun, "I don't like to ask for free legal advice, but what would happen if I refused to give Billy a divorce?"

"What do you mean?"

"I mean, could he go ahead and divorce me without my consent?"

"He's in Sweden now, isn't he?"

"Yes."

"Does he plan to stay there awhile?"

"I don't know. What are you getting at?"

"The laws of Sweden, which I'm not familiar with offhand. If Billy plans to divorce you in Sweden—in absentia—then his ability to do so would depend upon the Swedish divorce laws. I'd have to look them up. Do you want me to?"

"Yes. I'd appreciate it."

"You sound pretty upset. What's the matter? Are you still in love with the guy?"

I'd been doing some heavy thinking, mostly about Billy's career. I likened it to Ringo Starr's. What if I had divorced Ringo in 1960 before the Beatles made it? Nobody would have predicted that the Beatles would be the musical smash of the century, back when they were playing in Hamburg. Not even their own mothers. Stockholm might turn out to be Billy's Hamburg, his first real professional break. The Swedes were supposed to be wild about Negroes. Naturally I was thinking about alimony, which I'd never before collected.

"Love has nothing to do with it," I said.

"Odd." Parker smiled. "I would have imagined just the opposite, but then I've only been married once. I don't have the benefit of your vast experience. Maybe by the fourth trip to the altar other, more compelling factors might enter the picture."

"There's no reason to be so snide."

"Isn't there?"

Tears came to my eyes. Every man I trusted was suddenly turning against me: Billy, John, and now Parker. What had I done to deserve such callous treatment? Who had I betrayed? When? Where? I couldn't understand it. Maybe I was losing my looks more rapidly than I'd imagined. Men took a particularly nasty delight in knocking women who were on their way down, I had seen it happen too many times to other women not to recognize the familiar signs of rejection. Was this the beginning of the demise of Loretta Silverman? I resolved then and there, my eyes swimming in tears, to buy a carload of the new moisturizer that *Women's Wear* had raved about in last Friday's issue. It was supposed to contain a secret ingredient that other moisturizers lacked.

"When I say that love has nothing to do with it, I don't mean that I wasn't in love with Billy when I married him," I explained to Parker. "I love Billy just as I loved all my husbands."

"But you don't love him anymore."

"No."

"And yet you don't want to give him a divorce."

"No."

"Witness dismissed," Parker said, looking thoughtful.

I felt like telling him to go fuck himself, but I somehow managed to control the urge. I needed Parker, and not just for legal advice. I could get that from any half-assed lawyer. No, I needed Parker for more emotional reasons. I might be carrying his child. If it turned out that I was pregnant, I had decided to tell Parker it was his. I guess I got the idea to do that last night when I impetuously told John the same thing. I had a hunch Parker might welcome the prospect of becoming a father again, his only daughter now being a very grown-up eighteen. It could give Parker a new impetus for living. It might even give him an excuse to love me. His image of Loretta, the ballbreaker, would be replaced by the image of Loretta, the little mother. Men were suckers for a pregnant woman. Take the worst bitch in the world, stick her in a maternity dress, and she automatically turns into a madonna.

Then something occurred to me. If I were pregnant, the child would legally be Billy's, even though I had not gone to bed with Billy in more than six months. The situation was ridiculous. *I* was being ridiculous, inconsistent. I had just told Parker that I didn't want a divorce, yet I expected him to take responsibility for a child that legally belonged to another man. It didn't make sense.

Working for Talk for so many years had seriously impaired my powers of logic, I could see that now. The world of television is so crazy and illogical, it's such a make-believe world, that after a while the most unlikely things seem possible. All you needed was the determination to believe them. For instance, I still harbored the unlikely illusion that one day, singlehanded, I would book Charles Lindbergh, Greta Garbo, Howard Hughes, and J. D. Salinger on the same show. If you believe that, amigo, you can believe anything.

"Confucius say, people who lie in sun never tell truth in shade."

I opened my eyes and there was I. C. Ring, looking enormously pleased about something. He was wearing a long green sari, carrying a straw mat, and smiling for all he was worth. I wondered what he was so happy about. I can't bear to be around happy people when I'm feeling confused, neglected, and miserable, and that's exactly how I felt at the moment. In fact, if it hadn't been for the consoling thought of my first and second husbands' lingering devotion to me, I don't know what I would have done. Good old Chip and Paul. I knew I could count on them.

"Would you sleep on an art nouveau sheet?" I. C. asked us. "The Roof wants to know."

"Would you take a fast boat to China," Parker said, putting down the Real Estate section, and picking up Sports.

Being an only child is not a great way to grow up, unless you happen to have been born with an extremely happy disposition. If you weren't, it's too easy to drift into melancholia and linger there in a fit of maudlin egocentricity. Not only are all your waking thoughts centered upon yourself, since you don't have any brothers or sisters to distract you, but so are the hopes, dreams, and fears of both your parents.

Maybe one of the reasons I get married so often is because I'm afraid to be alone. As a child I felt inextricably alone, and it frightened me. Although my parents paid a great deal of attention to me (too much, in fact), they were still my parents, adults, grown-ups, not my contemporaries. The one close friendship I had with a girl of my own age was abruptly terminated by her family moving to Arizona for her father's health when she was twelve.

None of the other girls at school interested me as she had, and pretty soon I started spending more and more time by myself. I read a great deal, and two afternoons a week I went to dancing school to study tap and ballet. Most of my reading at that time was about great ballerinas, like Pavlova and Markova, and the tribulations of their lives. Even then I fancied myself a tragic heroine, a concept that neither time nor the love of four husbands has managed to erase.

I became passionate about dancing school and dreamed of being a star of the ballet when I was eighteen. LORETTA SILVERMAN DANCES! Then one day, the owners of the school announced they were moving their operation to Queens, where they had rented much larger quarters. Since my mother flatly refused to take me to Queens twice a week, and there was no other dancing school in the neighborhood, that was the end of my career as a prima ballerina. Within one year I had lost my best friend and my hopes for a glittering future. My sense of desolation was so great that I decided then and there never again to become too dependent on anyone or anything, for fear that it might be taken from me just when I needed it the most. I'm not much of a believer in Freudian psychology, but I can't help wondering whether that fierce early decision of mine hasn't colored all my relationships with men. I fall in love, get the man, then I leave him. Before he can leave me?

It wasn't until I discovered boys at the age of fifteen that my life took a sharp swing upward, and I felt as though I was really alive for the first time since I was born. I remained a virgin until seventeen, through no fault of my own. Boys were shy in those days, at least the boys I knew, and they never did more than feel you up, and if they were courageous, dry fuck you. How we used to moan in frustration, and how simple it would have been to end that frustration, but nobody had the nerve even to suggest it. After an evening spent in the back seat of a car, I'd be nauseated for days, sometimes I'd even throw up: that was how sick I felt with all those sexual desires left cruelly unfulfilled.

The man who finally relieved me of my unwanted virginity was six years my senior, and it was obvious at first glance that he was nobody to be trifled with. Not only was he considerably older than the boys I usually dated, but there was an aura of glamour about him due to the fact that one of his brothers was a successful nightclub comedian. When Sidney came around to pick me up in the evening, he'd arrive in his brother's chauffeured limousine, which caused a minor riot in our neighborhood. The only place anyone there had ever seen such a spectacle was in one of those Katharine Hepburn movies of the thirties, when she played spoiled rich girl parts, and Eugene Palette was her apopletic father.

My family lived in a large, yellowish apartment building in the northeast Bronx, and when Sidney drove up in his brother's Cadillac, all activity on our street came to a halt. Everyone just froze in his tracks and stared. People ran to their windows to see what celebrity had arrived to grace our undistinguished neighborhood. Sidney told me that one evening, as he was getting out of the car, a teen-aged girl rushed up to him and asked if he were Tony Curtis (whom Sidney resembled).

"What did you say?" I wanted to know.

"I told her I was Gregory Peck."

Sidney and I went to nightclubs almost exclusively during our brief romance. After the nightclub we'd go to his brother's Fifth Avenue apartment, where Sidney had a bedroom, and make violent love. His brother was there only once, with a party of people, and paid absolutely no attention to us. Then, around three in the morning, Sidney would put me in the limousine and send me home to The Bronx where my mother was invariably waiting for me in the kitchen, her eyes swollen with tears. She'd be wearing her pale blue housecoat and drinking Ovaltine when I rolled in, somewhat disheveled, but feeling on top of the world. Sidney might not have been Tony Curtis or Gregory Peck, but he sure was a superstar in bed, and I've always been thankful that my first lover was not one of those incompetent fumblers that so many girls have the misfortune of getting stuck with the first time around.

In looking back, I realize that Sidney and I did just about everything sexually that there was to do, so he really sent me off to a knowledgeable start. The last I heard of him he had married an automobile heiress, and they were photographed skiing at Gstaad, Sidney looking as arrogant and handsome as ever, and his millionaire wife, sleek and adoring. I wondered whether he said all the obscene things to her when they made love that he used to say to me. For a non-talker in social situations, old Sidney became a real blabbermouth as soon as he took me in his arms—crude, but exciting too. I thought he was pretty wild, and each time he sent me home I couldn't wait to hear from him again. It would have been an ideal romance if it weren't for my mother who made a scene whenever I got in at some unholy hour in the morning.

"Where have you been? I thought you were dead. What do you know about his family? He's too old for you. Your father thinks he's on dope. What's wrong with Artie down the block? Did he try to make love to you? He's too handsome for his own good. What do I care if his brother is a famous comedian? Has he said anything about marriage? He's probably got a wife that you don't know about, he's just the type. If he ever tries to make love to you, kick him in the *kishkas*, hard. Thank God you're going away to school in a couple of months. That will be the end of Nightclub Sidney."

And, of course, it was. But only the beginning of Marathon Mike, my second lover, the romeo of the campus because of his incredible staying power that made Sidney seem pretty pallid in comparison. My college career (which lasted two years) was one long course in eroticism, disrupted only because of my return to New York during the Christmas holidays. It was on that trip that I met Chip Kramer, who introduced me to the wonderful world of television and later married me. If it weren't for Chip, I'd probably have married Marathon Mike, had a houseful of children, and played bridge every Tuesday afternoon. I might even have been happy. I certainly would not be living at Hotel Splendide, a resident-inmate of six months, with no relief in sight.

"Would you like a screwdriver?" Parker asked I. C. Ring, who was unfolding his straw mat.

"No thanks. I never touch the stuff."

Parker looked at I. C. with undisguised disdain. It was Parker who had changed I. C.'s name from Ling to Ring, simply because there was no "R" sound in the Chinese language. That was typical of Parker's sense of humor, which everyone at the hotel agreed had a decidedly sadistic bent.

"They're really cooking at La Chiripa," I. C. said, as another garlic blast hit our nostrils. "That's strong stuff."

"Are you having dinner with your father tonight?" Parker asked me.

"Yes, and it's a terrible strain on both of us. It starts with the food at La Chiripa. There are only three dishes on the menu that my father will eat."

"That's three more than I'll eat," Parker said.

"Yes, but with my father it's not a matter of taste, it's the kosher business. It gets pretty tedious after a while. All he does is complain about everything."

"It must be rough on him, having a ding-a-ling like you for a daughter."

If I weren't so basically good-natured, I would have told him what I thought of *his* daughter, the Virgin Mary of Bryn Mawr's tennis courts. Parker's ex-wife had undeniably done a first rate job on her. Poor old Park. If our child were a girl, she'd probably be born without a hymen, thanks to Lamarck's theory of acquired characteristics.

"You'd better start acting nicer to me," I told Parker, "or find yourself another laundry service. Those shirts you gave me last week were terrible. I've never seen such stains in my life. What do you do—roll around in your food before you eat it?"

"Put the blame on Josephine Jasmin. She threw her Veal Madrilena at me when I suggested that she try acting her age for a change."

"Speaking of the devil . . ." I. C. said.

There was Josephine walking toward us, accompanied by an extremely beautiful girl of about seventeen. Josephine was wearing what appeared to be a tea gown, vintage 1931, a pastel chiffon with long, billowy sleeves. Over her head she carried a pastel parasol.

Parker took one look at Josephine's getup and announced, "Here she is, folks, the Blanche DuBois of Hotel Splendide."

"I'd like you all to meet my daughter, Daffodil," Josephine said. "She just flew in from Berkeley."

Daffodil had long, straight blond hair, and large brown eyes, very similar to her mother's, but of an even more dreamy expression. Around her slender ankles she wore rings of paper flowers, and her bikini was so tiny that it made mine seem conservative in comparison.

"You never told me you had such a beautiful daughter," I. C. said to Josephine.

"All of my children are beautiful," Josephine replied, giving him a dirty look.

I. C. couldn't take his eyes off Daffodil, who appeared unmoved by his blatant attention. In fact, Daffodil seemed to be in a dream world all her own, high on something. If she wanted to get even higher, she certainly was in the right place. There was such a fantastic degree of drug traffic within the hotel that I often wondered how much money Leonard Stein had to pay the cops to keep them off his back. It must have been plenty.

"Are you a student at Berkeley?" I. C. asked Daffodil, his eyes still riveted on her.

"No, but a friend of mine is. He's an activist. You've probably seen him on TV, during the riots. He was the one without the beard or moustache."

"What do you do?"

Daffodil shrugged away the significance of this question. "I live with him and bake bread."

"What kind?" I. C. asked, hypnotized.

"Whole wheat. Soya date. Banana."

"That sounds fascinating."

Daffodil shrugged again. "It's okay. Sometimes I put hash in the dough."

"Do you get high?"

"Stoned."

"That sounds fascinating," I. C. said again.

Josephine appeared to be in an extremely agitated state, and had begun to twirl her parasol around and around. Her lips were tense, disapproving. She turned toward me.

"I tried to drop in on you last evening, Loretta. It was a couple of hours after I'd left you and John at La Chiripa. I wanted to apologize for my behavior, but you didn't answer the door."

"I wasn't there."

"Oh, Where were you?"

I felt an immense hostility toward her, mainly because of John's admission earlier that morning that it wasn't me he loved, it was Josephine.

"If you must know, I spent the night with my ex-husband."

"Which one?" Parker asked.

"Marriage is outdated," Daffodil said. "The law has no right to interfere with people's personal lives."

"My third ex-husband."

Josephine stared at me in stunned disbelief. "Loretta, are you trying to tell me that you spent the night with *my* John?"

"As I keep pointing out, dear, he was *my* John before he became your John."

"That's disgusting."

"How do you know what we did?"

"Ladies, ladies," Parker said. "Please. You know I can't stand arguments. Josephine, why don't you have a screwdriver? You, too, Daffodil."

"I don't drink," Daffodil said.

"Neither do I," I. C. said, excitedly, as though some great psychic bond had just been established between the two of them.

"After LSD, everything else is anticlimactic."

"I've never tried LSD," I. C. said.

"I'll turn you on."

"You will?"

None of us had ever seen I. C. in such a pitch of excitement. Ordinarily, he was the epitome of studied casualness, but Daffodil had really gotten to him in a spectacular way, and it was apparent that Josephine didn't like it one bit. What with all of her anxieties about losing her looks, I figured it must be tough on her to have such a young and beautiful daughter, but I didn't realize how rough the competition was until Josephine said:

"I. C. heard me knocking on your door, Loretta, and when you didn't answer, he came out to see if he could be of any assistance."

She paused theatrically, and gave I. C. a murderous look. I. C., in turn, glanced at Daffodil who still seemed to be in a dreamlike trance and not the least bit interested in her mother's mounting hysteria or I. C.'s obvious embarrassment.

"Josephine," he said, "*please*."

But there was no stopping her now. "I told I. C. that I was looking for you, Loretta, but either you hadn't returned to your room yet, or weren't answering the door. I. C. was very considerate. Or so I thought at the time. He invited me in for a drink, and, as everyone knows, I don't have much of a capacity for alcohol, and one thing led to another, and before I knew it—"

"For Christ's sake, Josephine," I. C. said. "Nobody's interested in your damn sex life."

"You certainly were. You couldn't wait to get enough details for your survey. I'm surprised you even had the graciousness to wait until afterward, before you started bombarding me with intimate questions." She turned regally to Parker, very much the Southern belle. "I'll have that screwdriver now, if I may."

After Parker had filled a paper cup for her, tears came to Josephine's eyes, and she said to no one in particular, "It's not very flattering to be used by a man in such a callous fashion, not when you're my age. In fact, it's quite inexcusable, ungentlemanly."

"How old are you?" I. C. asked, once more the detached survey taker.

"I'll be forty in September." The whine in her voice was getting worse by the minute. "You can add that to the rest of your statistics. I suppose that was the only reason you made love to me at all—in order to get a few more statistics for your dreadful survey. And now that you've gotten what you wanted from me, you've turned your attentions to my daughter. *Oh, Trusting Fool* is right. That's the story of my life. And as for you, Loretta, you're just as bad as I. C. You're both selfish and inconsiderate, all you ever think about are yourselves."

"Look who's talking," I said, wondering how John, *my* John, could be in love with her. "If I have to hear how you're losing your looks one more time, I believe I'll go mad. Why don't you just lose them and be done with it?"

"You're a vulgar, trashy person. I don't know how I could have ever considered you a friend."

"There are a few names I could call you, but I don't want to embarrass you in front of your daughter, so why don't we just drop it?"

But she wasn't having any. "Speaking of daughters, what are you hoping for, Loretta? A boy or a girl?"

Parker stared at me in astonishment, and I. C. was simply beside himself with curiosity. "Are you really pregnant, Loretta? What month are you in? Did you use a contraceptive on the fateful day? Which kind?"

"Why don't you shut up?" Parker said to him. "It's none of your business."

"But that's exactly what it is." I. C. looked genuinely offended. "*My business.*"

"I hope you're planning to have natural childbirth," Daffodil said. "It's beautiful that way. You can watch your own baby being born."

Peggy and the girl who designed towels and sheets chose this moment to join our seething little group.

"What's all the excitement?" the designer asked. "We could hear you at the other end of the roof."

"There's no excitement," Josephine said, viciously triumphant. "We're merely celebrating Loretta's pregnancy, that's all."

"Oh, are you pregnant? That's very interesting." The designer took out her familiar pad. "I'm doing a line of sheets for babies. Tell me, Loretta, would you want your baby to sleep on a mauve sheet with a border of daisies?"

"How would you like to disappear and take your lousy questions with you?"

"But The Roof wants to know."

"We only have your best interests at heart," Josephine added.

I could have shot her for having publicly announced my pregnancy predicament, that's how angry I was, and in a moment of almost lunatic rage I grabbed her parasol, broke it in two, and tossed the pieces over the side of the roof where they floated down to the rubble and grime of Broadway. In retaliation, Josephine poured her screwdriver over my hair rollers and burst into loud tears.

"This is more fun than the riots at Berkeley," Daffodil Jasmin said, as I. C. Ring stared at my bare stomach with x-ray curiosity.

Sunday Evening

IT was seven o'clock on the button when I went down to La Chiripa to meet my father who was due in half an hour. In his honor, I had changed into my most conservative summertime outfit: green-and-white mini culottes and white patent mules. My hair was pulled demurely back with a white barrette, and, all in all, I looked the picture of girlish innocence. It had only taken me an hour in Torrid Zone to achieve this casual effect with an array of cosmetics that would have warmed Charles Revson's heart had he actually seen me using them. I booked him on Talk a couple of weeks ago, and the next day I received a complete line of Revlon's makeup, with his card thanking me for being so nice.

The man who carried lizards in his pocket was at the bar drinking a Papa Doble and talking to Peggy, who had phoned me from her room when we got down from the roof.

"I've gone crazy," Peggy said. "Can you drop over for a few minutes?"

I was in the middle of washing Parker's stained shirts with New Oxydol Plus, which was supposed to contain an enzyme pre-soaker *and* a bleach, but I said okay. I like to feel that people can count on me in time of need. It gives me a sense of selflessness which I know to be utterly false. Still, I enjoy playing the role of the concerned friend. The fact that I'm motivated more by morbid curiosity than any deep desire to be helpful doesn't bother me in the least. Aren't most people?

"I've gone crazy," Peggy repeated, when I got to her room. "This time I really did it. I'm not kidding."

Poor Peggy. Her room *was* the smallest one in the hotel, with only a tiny washbasin in the corner in the way of accommodations. She was trying to get Leonard Stein to give her a larger room, but Leonard kept putting her off, which was his archetypal reaction to resident-inmates who were already settled, no matter how unhappily. Leonard's policy was that it proved to be less expensive to keep people where they were, rather than start shifting them around. Peggy had tried to make the room as attractive as possible by hanging Klee prints on the walls and keeping everything scrupulously clean, but unfortunately she'd ruined the effect by burning a large hole in the middle of the poison-green wall-to-wall carpeting. She had fallen asleep one night with a lit cigarette, which rolled out of the ashtray and onto the carpet. By the time the smell of smoke woke her up, the damage was done. That was one of the hazards of living at Hotel Splendide: periodic fire scares.

"What do you mean, you've gone crazy?" I said. "You are crazy. We're all crazy."

Peggy laughed, but in a very jittery way. "No, I've gone off the deep end, you have no idea how bad it is. I still can't believe this has happened, I've really flipped. Zachary has a lot to do with it."

Zachary was the man who carried lizards in his pocket and boa constrictors over his shoulder.

"Zachary has a lot to do with *what*?"

"He's part of the inner circle, the secret society, the magicians, the evil geniuses. I think they're trying to initiate me into their rites. I think he put them up to it."

"What rites? What secret society? What are you talking about?"

"I know I sound nuts, but these people are involved with the occult. You know, with mysticism, numerology, Tarot cards, the Rosicrucians, astrology, the Cabala, Madam Blavatsky, the path of the adept." Peggy was rolling a neat marijuana cigarette. "And I think they want to kill me. That's the crazy part."

In the next room someone was playing the guitar and singing "Tambourine Man" in a gusty voice. That was another hazard. You never knew what kind of noisemaker your immediate neighbor might turn out to be, nor when he'd choose to go into action. Before I. C. moved in, I had a nutty lady next door who used to play the organ in the middle of the night. She worked as a typist for the Salvation Army during the daytime and played at skating rinks on weekends. Her favorite song was "In the Good Old Summertime."

"What makes you think they want to kill you?" I asked, beginning to believe that she had gone crazy.

"It's something I feel, I can't explain it. Like they need a sacrificial victim. They're evil. They meet at Zachary's, in the jungle."

Zachary had converted his penthouse studio into an extravagant tropical jungle, complete with plants, birds, and reptiles, and he was continually being photographed by various newspapers and magazines standing amidst the fauna and foliage that had become his passion. Thanks to Zachary, the hotel received a great deal of free publicity, so much so that Leonard Stein let Zach use all the electric current he needed to pump water into his numerous fish tanks. Leonard knew when he was getting a good deal.

"What do they do at Zach's?" I asked.

"I'm not sure yet, because they've just started to take me into their confidence. Up until a few days ago I knew something was going on, but they'd never reveal themselves to me. Now they've begun to, and it's made me very paranoid. Do you know that I can't get into a taxi anymore? I'm convinced I'm going to be killed. I see ominous symbols everywhere."

"Like what?"

"Two-headed serpents, the hangman, burning crosses. I tell you, I've become absolutely paranoid. I got a call the other day to test for a hairspray commercial, and I didn't go because I was too scared to leave the hotel. I need the money, too. I'm practically broke."

"Maybe you should see a psychiatrist."

"I've thought of that. Zachary wants to send me to his, but I'm afraid he's one of them. Isn't that cuckoo? I think they're everywhere, watching me."

"But Zachary seems so . . ." I started to say.

"So harmless? Maybe he was before he got into the occult, but not any more. I suspect they have weird sexual practices, and that's one of the rites they want to initiate me into. Group things. With blood and pain."

"Zachary?"

"Don't laugh." Peggy was using a roach holder now for the remains of her cigarette. "He's into it as deep as any of them."

I remember Peggy telling me about her innocent enough

meeting with Zachary. It was right after she had moved to New York from Hollywood and divorced her husband, a stunt man. According to Peggy, not all his stunts were confined to the movie set. After they were married, he stopped making love to her and would disappear for days on end. When she asked him where he had been, he either refused to answer or would slap her. She put up with his abuses for about a year, then moved east where she promptly got a job doing a deodorant commercial on television. Zachary played her husband on the commercial (he was the one who smelled).

Peggy told me that, at that time, Zachary was a recent escapee from a long-standing suburban marriage, and fond of telling anyone who'd listen how his ex-wife wouldn't let him make love to her more than twice a week, because that was par for the course among the women she knew. When Zachary announced he was leaving, she relented and said he could make love to her as often as he liked, but by then he was no longer interested.

His reputation around the hotel as a lover was firmly entrenched, his preference being for very young girls. He went through them like a cyclone, and admitted that one of his techniques for meeting them was to ride up and down in the hotel's elevators as often as possible. "Would you like to see my jungle?" he would ask them. Since he was fortyish and respectable looking, they usually said okay, not dreaming there were any sexual strings attached. More than one beautiful young thing had fallen in love with him and threatened to kill herself when Zachary told her it was all over. Unfortunately, he had a habit of letting them move a few clothes into his apartment, so it was that much harder to get rid of them when he wanted to. One girl who really had it bad for him not only left half her wardrobe in his closet and still returned periodically when she needed a dress, but made it a practice to go up on the roof of the hotel and throw rocks at his skylight if she saw him with another woman. Zachary and his Lolitas were a standing joke at Splendide, and even Zach made fun of his own romantic escapades. He had always struck me as a bit of a buffoon but harmless enough, and I found it pretty hard to imagine him involved in anything more mysterious than running around with lizards in his pocket.

"I don't know what to say," I confessed.

"Maybe I should have myself committed to Bellevue."

"No, don't do that. It's supposed to be awful. Either go see a psychiatrist, or stop seeing these people, or both."

"I want to stop seeing them, yet I'm intrigued. If only I didn't think they were going to kill me. But you're right, I've got to do something. I can't go on like this. I haven't left the hotel in more than a week. Oh Christ, you haven't heard the latest. Zach's boa constrictor has disappeared."

"But Zach had him with him just last night at La Chiripa."

"That was last night. This morning when Zach went to feed him, he found the cage open and the snake gone. Do you know what you feed a snake?"

"What?"

"Mice." Peggy laughed her jittery laugh. "You cut them in two first. Sacrificial blood."

Sunday evenings were different from most at La Chiripa in that they tended to be a family affair, with many Spanish-speaking people coming to the restaurant for an early dinner. Sometimes there would be three generations at one table, noisy children, overweight wives and mothers, bored husbands, and restrained grandparents who often spoke no English. This Spanish middle-class contingent had about as much in common with the resident-inmates of the hotel as my father had with Andy Warhol, and neither group took any notice of the other.

To drum up as much family trade as possible, the owners of La Chiripa presented a special Sunday dinner, from appetizer to dessert, for the bargain price of four ninety-five. They even threw in a large pitcher of sangria at no extra cost. The sangria was so weak that the Spanish mothers gave it to their children as if it were lemonade. In certain ways I envied these people for whom the close-knit family unit was still very much a way of life. They weren't like me and my friends, fragmented and rootless.

Daffodil Jasmin was seated by herself at one of the booths when I came in. I caught her eye and walked over. "Mind if I join you?"

She was wearing a transparent blouse with nothing underneath it and, from what I could see, a short wool skirt. "Sit down. I'm waiting for my mother. We're going to dinner at some Middle Eastern restaurant down the street."

"That's right. I heard John say he'd take you both out tonight."

Daffodil sipped her Coke. "John's not coming with us. He and Josephine had a fight. She accused him of spending the night with you."

"But she spent the night with I. C."

"I know."

Daffodil's manner was so deadpan that it was difficult to tell what she thought about anything. There didn't seem to be the same levels of approval and censure that were typical of most older people, but I had encountered this non-attitude so many times among the kids I met at La Chiripa that I was used to it by now. I suppose that like most of her contemporaries, Daffodil didn't believe in value judgments and was content to let everyone do his own thing, whatever it happened to be. In contrast, I felt very square, part of an older, obsolete generation.

"How long are you going to be in New York?" I asked, trying to make conversation.

"I don't know. My mother wants me to stay awhile, but she's hard to get along with. She doesn't approve of me. The drug bit. It scares her. She keeps asking me what I'm going to do with my life." Daffodil shrugged her thin shoulders as though this were of no concern to her. "I'm going to groove on whatever I can. What else is there to do?"

I remembered my mother's frantic disapproval of me when I was Daffodil's age and used to come home late at night after a date with Nightclub Sidney. And I also remembered how annoyed I was by her interference and lack of understanding. I used to brush her criticism aside like a speck of dust. Had my attitude been much different from Daffodil's?

"Josephine wants me to leave Edward," Daffodil said. "He's the one I live with at Berkeley. Josephine thinks he's a bad influence on me."

My mother had thought the same thing about Sidney.

"I never took LSD before I met Edward. She blames him for it, which is silly. If it hadn't been Edward, it would have been someone else. All the kids drop acid."

"It can be dangerous."

Drinking is dangerous, my mother used to say. *It warps your judgment.*

"If you know your source and take it with the right person, it's a cool trip. But I can't explain that to my mother. You can't *explain* the drug experience. You have to experience it."

Drinking is only dangerous if you drink too much, I said to my mother. *I'm very careful. I never have more than three.*

I wondered, though, whether these analogies were meaningful. Now I no longer drank. Would Daffodil no longer take drugs in a few years? Or was she there to stay? If I were Josephine, I'd be concerned, too.

"One Coke, please," I told our waiter.

His name was Julio, and rumor had it that his wife had to be locked up periodically, because when she flipped she used to take a pair of scissors and cut off all of Julio's trousers at the knee. Naturally, this put quite a dent in his clothes budget, not to mention the anxiety of coming home and never knowing if he'd had anything to wear the next day other than what he had on his back. In many ways the people who owned and worked at La Chiripa were not too dissimilar to the people who lived at Hotel Splendide. Like us, they too were uprooted, homeless, and more than a little crackers.

"One Coke," Julio repeated, his mind obviously elsewhere.

"I'll have another one, too," Daffodil said.

"Two Cokes," Julio said, walking away in a daze.

I saw a dazzling blue ocean, the Pacific, a beachside restaurant, Paul Bjorkman and me in bathing suits wet from the water. We were greedily drinking two Cokes and laughing. It was our honeymoon, the second one for both of us. Paul had wanted to spend it in a small town he had discovered on the west coast of Mexico, and I ecstatically agreed. I still remember how self-confident I was that Paul and I would be married forever and ever. Foolish.

I had crossed off my first marriage as the kind of mistake any young girl could make, particularly if she was anxious to escape the ties of family and background. College, I then felt, was only a fleeting escape. Even if I got a job in Manhattan when I graduated, as I intended to, I knew I didn't have the strength of character to find an apartment of my own in the city, and the prospect of going back to live with my parents in The Bronx was more than dismal, it was horrifying.

Chip Kramer seemed like the ideal solution to my problems. He was handsome, charming, attentive, worked in what I then visualized as the glamorous world of television, and he wanted to marry me. To this day, I can't understand why. Because no sooner were we married than he proceeded to give me a hard time. We rented an apartment on West End Avenue, I marketed at Peter Reeves, and we had the usual collection of Waring blenders, lazy susans, and electric percolators that all newlyweds acquire from solicitous relatives and friends. The fact that Chip and I rarely saw eye to eye on anything didn't bother me as much as one might imagine. I was too busy enjoying my new status of being Mrs. Somebody, basking in the sense of independence I felt in terms of my parents. No longer would I be subjected to lectures from my mother about who I went out with and what time I came home, nor would I have to put up with my father's medieval views on virginity. I was twenty, grown-up, a respectable married lady with an apartment to decorate as I wished, a husband to cook for, children to think about having. Bliss. Little did I know then what a rude awakening was in store for me.

I spent the first year of my marriage in a pink-and-white fantasy world, floating on a cloud of gorgeous self-deception. I started to subscribe to the various women's magazines and promptly swallowed all their propaganda about the joys and duties of a young wife, what was expected of her, how best she could please her husband, why she should learn to prepare gourmet meals, participate in civic affairs, remain perfumed and coiffed at all times. I began to collect exotic recipes (I'd never made anything more exotic than scrambled eggs in my life), I planned intimate little dinners, with wine and candlelight. I bought languid at-home clothes to wear on these occasions. One evening when I served some ersatz French mess accompanied by an acid Rosé, Chip blew out the candles and said I was ruining his digestive system.

"Can't you ever make a plain steak and baked potato?" he asked. "I'm sick of casseroles with garlic and fancy names I don't understand. I'm sick of wine with dinner. I like milk. Skimmed milk. And I'm sick of having to wear a jacket to my own table every evening, just because you seem to think we're dining at the Pavillon. You're a sensible girl, Loretta, at least I always thought you were. Now do me a favor and knock off all this cuisine cooking. I was raised on simple, broiled food, and I never had indigestion in my life until I married you. *Simple, broiled food*. Plain vegetables. No sauces. That's the healthy way. You keep this up and we'll both have gout before we're thirty."

On the surface, Chip's objections might not sound invalid, but I soon discovered that darker demons were at work in the mind of my handsome, charming husband.

"Do you know why most people never feel quite up to par?" he asked one morning after he'd wolfed down a breakfast of Swiss cereal flavored with blackstrap molasses and two cups of rose-hip tea. "Because they're impacted with shit, that's why. Most people are constipated all their lives, but they don't know it. They think that just because they have one half-assed bowel movement a day, they're all right, but nothing could be further from the truth. They've got *tons* of impacted shit in them and it creates a highly toxic condition. Their systems are continually being poisoned by their own garbage, and the poor bastards aren't even aware of it. Enemas, I have decided, are the only solution. In order to be truly healthy, everyone should have at least one enema a week to clean him out. That's what I've begun to do, and if you're smart, you'll do the same."

"I appreciate your consideration, but I don't have impacted shit."

"That's what everyone thinks. You've got it, all right. You're no different from the next person."

"Yes, I am. I married you."

"It's your system," Chip finally conceded. "If you want to go on poisoning yourself, I guess I can't stop you, but believe me, Loretta, you're making a fatal mistake. And it wouldn't do you any harm to fast one day a week either."

"What for? I'm not overweight."

"I'm not talking about your weight. Fasting once a week is just as important as the enema. They both work together to rid your body of harmful poisons. From now on, I'm going to fast every Wednesday. Nothing but fruit juices for me on Wednesday, so you can spare yourself the trouble of cooking."

"Which day is your enema day?"

"Thursday. After the fast."

"I can hardly wait to hear what you've got planned for the rest of the week."

I felt cruelly betrayed. There was nothing in *Ladies' Home Journal*, *McCall's*, or *Redbook* to tell me how to cope with this bizarre turn of events. Blanquette du veau. Soufflé Grand Marnier. That's what they were good for, that, and giving instructions on how to do intricate needlework. Was I the only woman in the world whose husband hated wine and had an obsession with impacted shit?

I opened the new issue of *Redbook* and looked at the table of contents. The first article was entitled, "French Cooking for American Tastes." The second was, "If Your Baby

Is Premature." The third was, "Party Treats You Can Make Yourself." The fourth was, "Slipcovers That Are Fun."

I closed the magazine and decided to get a job.

Daffodil Jasmin and I were almost finished with our second round of Cokes when my father arrived. I looked up and there he was, coming through the door that opened onto the street. He was wearing a grayish wash-and-wear suit, almost the same shade as his carefully clipped moustache, and a white shirt open at the neck. I knew it would have short sleeves, because that was the only kind of shirt my father wore during the summer. I had offered to wash and iron his shirts, but he just laughed at the suggestion and said, "What's the matter with you? Are you crazy? Who washes and irons shirts when there are Chinese laundries everywhere?"

"There aren't any Chinese laundries in small towns in the Midwest."

"What's the Midwest got to do with it? You're living in New York City. Don't talk like a dope."

"I've got this Americana fantasy," I began. "It involves a tuna, noodle, and mushroom soup casserole."

I stood up halfway in my seat and waved at my father, then I quickly looked away. It always startled me to see him when he came into La Chiripa every Sunday evening, a stocky man of medium height, nearsightedly scanning the room for his only daughter. His lips were pursed in lines of disapproval, as though he carried with him the constant memory of my four disgraceful marriages.

"It's my father," I said to Daffodil. "You think you have problems."

The reason I am startled whenever I see my father is that he looks so much older than he is in my mind's eye. Shorter, too.

Like my husbands, he is frozen for me in nostalgic time and I never visualize him as being sixty-four, his present age, but rather somewhere in his forties before his hair had turned gray. I remember him and my mother as being very happy. She used to sing "I'm Just Wild About Harry" with a great deal of high-pitched conviction. I could still hear her wavery voice. *And Harry's wild about, he can't live without, Harry's wild about me.*

"Hello, father. How are you?"

"Hot." He wiped his forehead with a crumpled handkerchief that had an ink stain on it. "That's how I am."

We kissed each other self-consciously on the cheek and he sat down opposite me before noticing Daffodil.

"This is Daffodil Jasmin," I said. "Josephine's daughter. My father, Harry Silverman."

"Hello," Daffodil said, tonelessly.

My father's *hello* got lost somewhere in his throat as he focused on Daffodil's transparent blouse through which her small breasts were clearly visible. His reaction to Daffodil was pretty much on the order of Dean Rusk being confronted by an unclothed Raquel Welch on the Mohave Desert: utter confusion, embarrassment, lust, shock, ambivalence, etc. My father probably didn't even want to begin to think about girls like Daffodil, being as busy as he was still trying to make head and tail out of me. I wondered what he would say when I told him that Billy wanted a divorce. Probably something like, "Billy *who*?" At times I got the distinct feeling that although my father knew I had been married four times, it never really came home to him on some deep and meaningful level. That made two of us.

"How come you're wearing a wool skirt in the middle of July?" he said to Daffodil.

"What's the difference?"

"Aren't you hot?"

"No."

"I'm hot," my father said, trying to keep his eyes off Daffodil's blouse. "Doesn't the air conditioning in this place work?"

"It works," I said. "Just relax, and you'll feel it in a few minutes."

"They probably have it turned down low to save money. I keep mine on 'high cool' all the time. Have they fixed your air-conditioner yet, Loretta?"

"No, and my room is like an oven."

"How can you sleep? I don't understand it. You must *shvitz* plenty. You should eat oranges, like they do in the Turkish baths."

Since, in the past, my father had suffered so much on my account, I didn't think it feasible to tell him that I managed not to sleep in my room by virtue of sleeping in the rooms of various men in the hotel. I had never even told him that John O'Connell lived at Splendide. It just would have upset him unnecessarily. Any references to any of my husbands seemed to upset my father, and I'd asked John as a special favor to keep away from La Chiripa on Sunday evenings until around ten o'clock, by which time my father would have departed for the remote terrains of The Bronx, having once more survived another non-kosher dinner. "I'll make myself scarce," John agreed, and he had.

"Here comes my mother," Daffodil said.

I looked up, and there was Josephine approaching our table in her usual languid manner. She was wearing a sleeveless blue pants suit and thonged sandals, and looked at least ten years younger than her age. Ordinarily, I would have complimented her on her appearance, but after her vile behavior on the roof today, I'd washed my hands of her. She was a hopeless case, someone not to be trusted. I would never again tell her anything about myself unless I wanted her to broadcast it free of charge to whoever happened to be present. Thank goodness my father hadn't been there today. If he were ever told that I might be pregnant, I don't know what he would do, and I'm in no great rush to find out.

"Good evening," Josephine said, avoiding my eyes. "How are you, Mr. Silverman?"

"Hot. I hope your room is air-conditioned."

"How sweet of you to be concerned."

Undaunted by flattery, my father said, "You have a very attractive daughter, Mrs. Jasmin, but if you don't mind my saying so, you shouldn't let her run around dressed like that. She's liable to get into trouble."

"Daffodil knows how to take care of herself. That's more than can be said for your daughter."

"What did she mean by that?" my father asked, after Daffodil and Josephine had left.

"Nothing."

"What do you mean, *nothing*? She must have meant something."

"Well, if she did, I don't know what it was and what's more, I don't care." I picked up La Chiripa's menu which had a big grease mark over the *Beef Salteada*. "Let's order, shall we?"

"I guess we can't put it off any longer," my father said, a greenish cast coming over his features.

"I'll have the paella."

"Shellfish aren't kosher," he reminded me.

If there was one thing I didn't want to do, it was get into a harangue with my father about what was kosher and what wasn't. "What are you going to have?"

"The chicken with rice."

My father invariably ordered that, or the broiled lamb chops. Everything else on the menu horrified him because of its unfamiliarity, and he would make wistful references during the meal about how he wished he were at a nice dairy restaurant, eating a dish of chilled blueberries and sour cream. He still couldn't understand how I managed to have dinner here seven nights a week without developing severe stomach trouble. Neither could I.

After we had decided upon an appetizer and given our order to the dejected Julio, we did what we did every week—try to bring each other up to date on anything that might have taken place since the previous Sunday. Unfortunately, this presented several difficulties because in my father's case very little had happened, and in mine, I was usually reluctant to admit what it was for fear of upsetting my father. But we tried.

"Your aunt has a cold," my father said, helping himself to a black olive and a piece of wilted celery from the relish tray.

"That's too bad. How did she get it?"

He shrugged. "How does anybody get a cold? Who knows? Even the doctors don't know. She's taking antihistamines for it."

My aunt, a widow for many years, worked in my father's butcher shop cleaning the chickens and waiting on customers when it was busy. She was a somber, heavy-set woman who had been married for eight years before she let her husband make love to her. It was generally agreed in the family that that was why he died so young. Since my mother's death, my aunt had kept house for my father. She was very different, both in appearance and temperament, from my mother, a thin nervous woman who used to talk a lot. Even though I had disagreed with many of my mother's opinions, I still liked the fact that she voiced them vociferously. At least I used to know where I stood with her. "I don't like people who keep their thoughts to themselves," my mother would say. "Silence is for skiers." My father was like his sister, an armchair skier. Non-kosher food, antihistamines, air-conditioners that didn't work. He could cope with those verbally, but when it came to the grit things of life, the things that most deeply concerned the people closest to him, he might as well have been in Tibet. When I told him that I was divorcing Chip, he said I was crazy and then changed the subject to the World Series. When I divorced Paul and John, his only comment was that I never should have divorced Chip. I couldn't wait to hear what he would say when I told him about Billy's request for a divorce, which I planned to do as soon as he had something to eat and the air conditioning got to him.

"Why do we have to eat here every week?" my father asked for the millionth time, pouring us each a glass of the tepid sangria. "*Pishiks.*"

"Because I can't get a pass to go anywhere else."

"A pass? What are you talking about? You sound as though you're living in a lunatic asylum, instead of a hotel."

I was about to say that Splendide was a tricky combination of the two when my father went on.

"You make a good salary, you could live anywhere you wanted. You could have a beautiful apartment, instead of that one room with the gangrene carpet. I don't understand you, Loretta."

"I like it here. I have a lot of friends. I don't get lonely."

"Friends," he said contemptuously. "Girls who walk around half naked. And their mothers who don't know how to dress their age. What kind of friends are those? Who? The nut with the lizards in his pocket? That dizzy actress who's a dope fiend? Who? Tell me. Maybe that lawyer guy, Mason, maybe he's okay, maybe, I'm not sure. But if he were okay, why would he live in a crummy place like this?"

It took me a moment to realize that the "dope fiend" he referred to was Peggy. "For your information, father, a lot of very successful and distinguished people happen to live here. This hotel is internationally famous."

"I don't know what it's famous for, and I don't want to know. I know what I see, and I see a bunch of crazy-looking people wearing even crazier clothes."

"They're artists, father."

"If you hadn't divorced Chip Kramer, you'd never have ended up here. You'd have had a couple of kids by now and be living like a normal person. I still don't understand what made you divorce Chip."

"Forget Chip. That was eight years ago. I don't want to talk about him."

"I can't forget it. When you divorced Chip, that was the beginning of the end for you. Don't you realize that?"

"No. But speaking of divorces, I have something to tell you."

My father put down his fork and wiped his mouth. "I'm afraid to hear. You're getting married again."

"Don't be silly. How could I get married when I'm still married to Billy?"

"Billy?"

"Billy Ray, father. My fourth husband."

My father began eating again. "As far as I'm concerned, you were never married to him."

"What do you mean? Of course I was, *am* married to him."

"I don't recognize that marriage, that's what I mean. So please don't talk to me about it."

"But I have to talk about it. It's very important. Something has come up."

"I'm not interested."

"Please, father."

"I told you, I'm not–"

He stopped and stared incredulously across the room. "Am I seeing things, or is that that no good *shicker* you used to be married to?"

"You're seeing things," I said, as John O'Connell lurched drunkenly toward us and began to pump the hand of my astonished father.

"Well, well, Mr. Silverman, I can't believe my eyes."

"That makes two of us."

"Imagine running into you here. That's what I call luck, yes sir."

"What's lucky about it?"

"It's the luck of the Irish, yes sir. That's what it is."

John had a Papa Doble in one unsteady hand, and it was obvious that it wasn't his first. In fact, he was as drunk as I'd ever seen him during his d.t. period, and the only explanation was that he'd been drinking all day. Probably the argument with Josephine had set him off; it didn't take much to trigger his craving for alcohol. I could have shot him for not keeping his promise about staying away from La Chiripa on Sunday evening, yet I could tell by his remarks that he had no recollection of ever having made such a promise.

"It's a pleasure to see you again, Mr. Silverman, a real pleasure. How've you been?"

"Not bad," my father said, the look on his face contradicting his words.

"That's great."

John gave my father a clap on the back that made him gag, then he slid into the seat next to me and put his drink down on the table, barely missing the edge by an inch.

"Go away," I hissed, but I don't think he even heard me.

"Well, well," he said, grinning like the town idiot. "What's this, a nice little family reunion? That's what I like to see, family solidarity. You look wonderful, Mr. Silverman, yes sir."

"That's more than I can say for you."

"Wonderful. That goes for you, too, Loretta."

"Will you go away?" I hissed again.

"It's been a long time, Mr. Silverman, the longest saddest time of my life. I'll never forget the day your beautiful daughter said she was leaving me to marry that black guitar player. I sure was a sad sight that day."

"You're still a sad sight," my father said.

"I used to be madly in love with your daughter, Mr. Silverman. I want you to know that I wasn't the one who asked for a divorce. I never got a chance to tell you that, so I thought I'd set the record straight. It's important to set the record straight, yes sir."

"Now that you've set it straight," I said, getting angrier by the minute, "will you please *go away*?"

"But I tell you, Mr. Silverman, there's poetic justice after all, because now he's the one who's asking for a divorce. He's the one who's leaving Loretta to marry a Swedish girl named Inger. What do you think of that?"

"I don't know who, or what, you're talking about," my father said.

"Billy Ray. He wants to divorce Loretta. How do you like that for a switcheroo?"

My father looked at John the way an exterminator looks at a cockroach before he sprays it to death. "As far as I'm concerned, Mr. O'Connell, my daughter was never married to that *shvartzer*."

"But I was married to him," I said imploringly. "I mean, I *am* married to him. You can't pretend it never happened."

"Yes, I can. I not only can, I am. That's exactly what I'm pretending."

John gleefully slammed his fist on the table. "You tell her, Harry. You tell her that she never should have left me for that spade soul brother. I used to pretend it never happened, either. A lot of good it did me. A lot of good."

"I'll go one better," my father said, warming to his subject. "She was never married to you either, not you and not that *trumbenick* Swede who owned the moving company with one truck. In my religion, there is no such thing as divorce, so the only husband I recognize is her first. Chip Kramer, a nice Jewish boy."

"Nice?" I said. "That screwed-up health fiend? I never told you about the fasting and the enemas. That irresponsible gambler? You call him *nice*?"

"What enemas?" John said.

"That's the only marriage of yours I recognize," my father said. "So don't tell me about enemas or divorces, because I'm not listening."

"You never listen to the important things. All you want to talk about are air-conditioners that don't work, antihistamines, non-kosher food. What do I care about that crap?"

"Watch your language," my father cautioned.

"You're lucky she didn't say *shit*," John said.

"The trouble is, father, that you don't care about the things that really concern me. You've never cared. I'm trying to tell you that I'm unhappy. Don't you understand, father? I'm getting divorced for the fourth time. No one loves me. I'm miserable!"

"It's just indigestion. This lousy Cuban food is enough to give anyone indigestion. Me, I'm going home, I'm drinking some bicarb of soda, and what's more I have no intention of thinking about divorces, and even less intention of thinking about who your fifth husband might be. Because knowing you, Loretta, I'm afraid I already suspect the worst. A Chinaman? Right? At this very moment, he's probably sitting in a rice paddy in Vietnam, murdering one of our courageous boys."

"You never told me about any enemas," John said.

"Will you *go away*?"

"Look," my father said, "here he comes already."

It was I. C. Ring, coming through the door that led to the hotel. He walked directly to our table.

"I've got a piece of news that will kill you," he said to John and me. "Daffodil Jasmin hasn't been a virgin since she was eleven. She screwed her own stepfather! Boy, I tell you, the statistics are piling up like crazy. That gynecologist knew what he was doing when he told me to come to this hotel for his survey. He couldn't have picked a more decadent place if he resurrected Sodom and Gomorrah."

"How many of our boys did you kill in Vietnam?" my father asked, oblivious to I. C.'s sex communiqué. "Go ahead. Count. How many? Rotten Chinese commie."

I. C. smiled at me. "Who's the old nut?"

"My father," I said, regretfully.

After my father left, I hung around La Chiripa for a while talking to John and I. C., but the evening had collapsed. John was too drunk to make any kind of coherent conversation, and I. C. was too steamed up about how Daffodil had lost her virginity to want to talk about anything else. Between the two of them, I was so bored that I finally said good night and went upstairs to Torrid Zone.

It was twenty to eleven. The room was stifling, as I'd expected, and for a few minutes I just sat dispiritedly on my electric bed, trying to decide whether I should abandon my pride and call Parker in the hope that he would ask me to spend the night with him. After much consideration, I rang his room but there was no answer. I kicked off my mules and started to undress, wondering how I was going to get through the long night ahead. Then I remembered that on Sunday, Talk played re-runs of past shows that in the producer's eyes had been outstanding. I could watch the news at eleven, take a bath, and then watch Talk, which went on at midnight. It wasn't much, but it would keep me occupied until one thirty. Hopefully, I would be tired enough by that time to go to sleep.

Insomnia has always been one of my major problems. The analyst I went to after my second marriage collapsed said that my difficulty in falling asleep was connected with my fear of falling from high places, both of which were connected with my fear of falling in love. Dr. Maxwell said that if I could fall in love, I would have no problem falling asleep, and no fear of falling in general. "You're afraid of losing control," he explained, "that's why you can't fall in love. You don't trust anybody. You probably didn't trust your parents when you were a child. We'll work on that."

I liked Dr. Maxwell, but we didn't make much progress, I regret to say, and after about a year I lost interest and quit analysis. Dr. Maxwell had come to mind earlier when my father told me that my aunt had a cold. According to Dr. Maxwell, catching cold was a psychosomatic way of crying, which was why schizophrenics rarely caught cold—they were too estranged from their emotions to cry. At least my aunt wasn't crazy, there was that slight consolation. I'd been tempted to tell that to my father, but wisely refrained, knowing he would take it the wrong way. My sense of humor had always eluded him. In fact, my father once admitted that I was a total mystery to him, and that he'd long ago given up trying to understand me. He further admitted that he had a favorite daydream in which I was still married to Chip Kramer, and he was a proud grandfather who came to visit us every Sunday afternoon in our four-and-a-half-room apartment in Forest Hills with the sunken living room, wallpapered dinette, and air conditioning that worked. There I would cook a kosher dinner of pot roast and potato pancakes, after which he and Chip would sit down to a game of gin rummy while I served them tea and homemade apple strudel. My father didn't know it, but with his delusions he would have been right at home at Hotel Splendide.

The news on television was very boring—just the usual murders, strikes, and Vietnam atrocities. Nothing exciting there.

After my bath, I doused myself liberally with Jean Naté Friction Pour Le Bain, and then I put on one of several Pucci sleep culottes I own. This one was sleeveless, with swirling leaves in three different shades of green. Ever since moving into Splendide, I've become careful to look my best before going to bed. You may think this is strange, but as I mentioned before, the hotel is subject to frequent fires and I have no intention of running out in the corridor in the middle of the night wearing an old nightgown, my face greasy with cream. That's what happened to me the first week I was living here, and afterward I vowed *never again.* Out went all my old nightgowns, and in came the Puccis—five of them, in varying styles and colors. I even stopped creaming my face before going to bed, and to my surprise my complexion actually improved, so I suppose I have Splendide to thank for something.

I've often wondered what I would wear should a fire ever

break out when I was staying over in someone else's room, but luckily that hasn't happened yet. It's something to think about, though. I mean, what if he only had one bathrobe? Who would wear it? Knowing most of the men in this hotel, we'd probably burn to death fighting for possession of it. If chivalry weren't already dead, Splendide would smother it in a second.

According to the *TV Guide*, the following guests were to be on Talk this evening: Dr. Joyce Brothers, David Susskind, George Jessel, and an unknown singer named Cleo. I remembered the original show, which had been taped about a year ago. I booked both Joyce Brothers and David Susskind, neither of whom wanted to discuss beforehand what they would talk about on Talk. They said it was better to just let it flow, and since they were such old pros at television, I said okay.

I turned on my set just as the star was delivering his monologue and glancing even more conspicuously than usual at the cue cards for his joke lines. When he had finished giggling up the audience, there was a commercial break, and then he came back to introduce his first guest.

"This is a gentleman who really needs no introduction, folks, so won't you welcome him, please, the star of stage, screen, and Tel Aviv–Georgie Jessel!"

And out from behind the curtains came the old egomaniac himself, all decked out in his military uniform, the rows of medals on his chest blinking under the hot studio lights. Never at a loss for words, he launched into a schmaltzy description of his experiences during a recent trip to Vietnam to entertain American soldiers. The other talent coordinators and I always devised private nicknames for the guests we booked on the show. His was an unprintable one. It was harmless little games like these that kept our spirits soaring at the network, even during those weeks when our ratings faltered thanks to the fierce competition of Messrs. Carson, Bishop, and Griffin.

People are always asking me how I got started in television, which isn't surprising—their curiosity, that is. When I tell them that it was quite by accident, they become even more curious. It all began at the RCA Exhibition Hall in Rockefeller Center. I was home during a Christmas vacation from college and had decided to spend an afternoon in Manhattan seeing the sights, like any out-of-town tourist.

I looked particularly smashing that day, if I do say so myself. I was wearing a nubby wool coat trimmed with red fox, a Hanukkah present form my parents. On my head was a fluffy red fox hat, wet with snow. As I stood in the Exhibition Hall, watching myself on a television set, an extremely attractive man came up to me.

"Hello," he said. "My name is Chip Kramer. I work for You Said It! You know, the popular daytime game show."

Then he took a business card out of his jacket and handed it to me. The card said:

Charles Alan Kramer
Contestant Coordinator
You Said It!
KBC-TV

On the bottom of the card was a telephone number and an extension.

"So?" I said, smiling at him.

"So how would you like to be on You Said It!?"

"Me?"

This time he smiled, revealing perfectly capped teeth. Chip was easily my most handsome husband, with dark blue eyes and curly brown hair. He even had a cleft in his chin, the works. Compared to him, my boyfriend at college, Marathon Mike, looked like Woody Allen, and Mike didn't look like Woody Allen, if you know what I mean.

"Yes, *you*," Chip said. "How would you like to be a contestant?"

"I don't know. I'm not familiar with the show. I've never watched it."

He shook a playful finger at me. "B-a-a-d girl."

"I can't watch it," I amended. "You see, I go to college during the day."

"Which college is that?"

I told him, adding, "It's in Iowa."

"Oh." He looked thoughtful. "That means you'll be returning right after the holidays."

"No, I won't," I said quickly. "I mean, I won't be returning for a while. My mother is very sick and I'm afraid that if I leave her I might never see her again."

"I'm sorry to hear that. What's wrong with her? Or would you rather not say?"

"I'd rather not say."

"It isn't—?"

"We don't know yet."

He observed a moment of respectful silence for all cancer victims, then said, "Do you think you could leave your mother long enough to come up to our office? I'd like you to take a little test to see whether you qualify as a contestant."

"What kind of test?"

"Oh, it's very simple. A smart college girl like you shouldn't have any trouble. By the way, what are you majoring in?"

"Romance languages."

"Are you a romantic?"

Right then and there, I decided to marry him. I was a romantic, all right, but how could I have guessed then that such a gorgeous hunk of man would turn into an enema freak?

"Here's what you do," Chip said, getting businesslike. "You call the number on the card I gave you, and say you want to come up and see about being a contestant. Say that I told you to call. Okay?"

"When should I call?"

"Anytime during the day. The sooner, the better."

"I'll call first thing tomorrow."

"Great." His eyes wandered to a statuesque brunette, a few feet away. "I've got to go now. It's been very nice talking to you. Good luck on You Said It!"

"Won't I see you again?" I blurted out.

"Sure, if you make the show. I work with the contestants. By the way, what's your name?"

"Loretta Silverman."

"See you soon, Loretta."

I watched him walk over to the brunette, and although I couldn't hear his voice, I knew he was saying, "Hello, I'm Chip Kramer." My future husband, and he was picking up another woman. But I didn't even have time to be jealous because my brain was busy trying to solve several very penetrating problems, namely:

1) How was I going to explain to my parents why I wasn't returning to school after the holidays?

2) How was I going to explain to Chip that my mother wasn't a hopeless invalid?

3) How was I going to select a June wedding gown in snowy December?

I had become so immersed in my reflections that it took me a minute to realize the loud sound I'd just heard was the hotel's fire alarm. I leaped out of bed (as the star was introducing Joyce Brothers), wriggled into my mules, and ran out into the corridor, which smelled of smoke and confusion. People were scurrying from their rooms like rats, in varying degrees of disarray. One woman had on a hairnet, a burnoose, and no shoes. An elderly man was in his undershorts. Someone kept moaning that she couldn't find her glasses and couldn't see without them. Two baby-doll pajamas sped past me and down Splendide's winding staircase, bodies piled into the two creaking elevators, and Peggy, without makeup, said, "I can't take the elevator. I'm afraid I'll be killed."

We all wound up, minutes later, at the La Chiripa bar where Carlos began mixing Papa Dobles at a furious rate of speed, trying to make the most of this sudden, unexpected influx of customers. Parker once said that he suspected Carlos of starting all the fires, because it was so good for business. "Who started the fire?" everyone was asking everyone else. Then Zachary came in, one hand plunged into his lizard pocket, and said, "It was your ex-husband, Loretta."

"Which one?" Parker asked.

"It's the usual story," Zach said, wearily. "He fell asleep with a lit cigarette. According to the desk clerk, he was very badly burned. They've rushed him to the hospital. It sounds like it could be fatal."

"This was all I needed," Peggy moaned. "A fire. I see catastrophes everywhere, and now one has finally happened. The sacrificial victim. I suppose I'll be next."

"Oh, my God," Josephine Jasmin said softly. "Oh no, not John."

For once her eyes were conspicuously devoid of tears, but her mouth seemed to crumble. In a second she had aged ten years.

"He won't pull through," she said. "And he was such a

dear man. An unusual man. So tender. I don't know what I shall do without him."

"He's not dead yet," I said.

But she seemed oblivious of my presence. "I know what people think of me," she said to no one in particular. "That I'm a vain and frivolous woman, a fool, always worrying about my age. People make fun of me, they laugh. But it's not easy to be a woman approaching forty, in a world of twenty-year-olds. I have the same desires I did at twenty, but my body is no longer firm. . . ."

She stared off into space, as though she were quoting from something. "Armies have marched through it and left behind a holocaust. Their boot marks are still on the flesh that nobody wants any more. Except John Michael O'Connell. He wanted it, and now he's gone."

And then, as though reverting to her familiar, foolish self, she added, "Now *Oh, Trusting Fool* will never be published."

Daffodil tried in vain to comfort her, so did Zachary and Parker, but she didn't appear to notice them. Then she turned abruptly to me.

"If he dies, it will be on your conscience, Loretta."

I didn't say anything.

"John never would have gotten drunk tonight if we hadn't had a fight. The only reason we fought is because I accused him of spending the night with you. Why did you have to tell me about last night? Why did you want to hurt me? John doesn't mean anything to you. You don't care about him, you don't care about . . ." Her voice trailed off, as though she'd forgotten what she was going to say next. "The paths of glory lead but to the grave."

Later, after the firemen left the hotel and most of the

people at the bar had returned to their rooms, I said to Parker, "It's not my fault that John got drunk tonight."

We were Carlos' last customers, and Parker stared at me reflectively in the dark light.

"It's not my fault that John was unhappy, any more than it's my fault my father is unhappy. My father is always saying that I'm a disgrace to him, that I've ruined his life. On the roof today, you berated me for not loving Billy. John himself said that I've never loved anyone. I don't understand. Why me? Why do you all blame *me*?"

"Because you have the ability to hurt."

Monday Morning

ANOTHER night, another bed, another air-conditioner. This time it was Parker's. His long, lanky body lay sprawled diagonally across the mattress, face down, his nose buried in one lumpy pillow. "If it please your honor," he said in his sleep.

Billy used to talk in his sleep, but I never could make anything out of what he said, it sounded like an incoherent combination of musician patois and Southern colloquialisms. Billy, like Josephine Jasmin, had grown up in Charleston, but there the similarity ended, for where Josephine's parents were among the town's leading citizens (her father was a municipal judge), Billy's parents were menials. They both worked for the same high-powered family, his mother as a maid, his father as a chauffeur. Because they lived in, Billy, their only child, grew up within sight, if not grasp, of white luxury, and it had the usual embittering effect upon him, although he claimed it would have been much worse if it weren't for his early interest in music.

"It literally saved me," he said. "Without music, I don't know what I would have become. A crook, a rapist, a junkie. I always knew I'd be a musician. I always knew I'd get out of that town. My mother bought me my first guitar for my seventh birthday. She was a wonderful woman. Inspirational. She wouldn't let anything get her down, not even death. My father was killed in an automobile accident. It was the other driver's fault, he was drunk and went through a red light, but he was a bigshot in Charleston, a very prominent lawyer, so the whole thing was hushed up. I was almost fifteen when it happened, and I knew I couldn't go on living there after that, so I hitchhiked to New York and got a job as a busboy in a Village restaurant. I used to send my mother ten dollars a week, it was all I could afford. She died recently. I received a letter from the family she worked for. They buried her next to my father in the cemetery for niggers."

Billy told me this shortly after we were married and living in his borrowed loft with the mattress on the floor. Then, when we broke up and I moved to Splendide, I met Josephine and I've often thought how curious it would be if the man who crashed into Billy's father's car turned out to be Josephine's father. He must have been a lawyer before he became a judge. Yet I knew that the chances were unlikely. It would make too neat a story, and reality had a way of being much more untidy than that.

The ringing of the telephone did not seem to disturb Parker who went right on sleeping, oblivious to the outside world. I picked up the receiver and said hello.

"I thought you might be there," Josephine Jasmin said. "I have some very bad news."

Since Josephine's idea of bad news generally meant that

she'd discovered one more line on her face, I wasn't too alarmed. "What is it?"

"John is dead."

"*What*?"

"Yes, I know, it's awful. I just spoke to the hospital. He died during the night of third degree burns."

"I can't believe it."

"I know," she repeated, "it's awful, a real tragedy. He was only forty-one. You can imagine how I felt when I found out. I thought I'd never stop crying."

"I just can't believe it."

She cleared her throat. "Listen, Loretta, if you have no objections, I'd like to make arrangements for the funeral. John told me he had no family to speak of."

"That's right." I was still trying to digest the news. "Just a spinster aunt in Cleveland."

"I thought we'd have the service at Frank Campbell's. They're supposed to be the best. All the distinguished people go there."

I remembered the first night I spent with Billy, when I was married to John, and how I lied to him about a dream I had. I said that in my dream my husband had died, and the service was at Frank Campbell's. Except for the part about John stepping out of the casket and saying, "Fooled you all, didn't I?" the rest was coming true.

"Frank Campbell's sounds okay to me."

"They're supposed to do a beautiful job." She sounded as though she were talking about a catering service she'd just discovered. "I'm going to call them right now and see if they can accommodate us tomorrow. I'll let you know what happens as soon as I find out."

"Thanks."

She hesitated a moment. "Please forget what I said last

night, about your being responsible for John getting drunk. It was as much my fault as yours. I only said what I did because I was so upset."

I felt like saying that it wasn't my fault at all and that I didn't need her bogus forgiveness, but not wishing to start another argument, I replied, "Forget it," and thereby became friends with Josephine Jasmin all over again. Count on tragedy to bring out our most hypocritical selves. When Parker woke up a few minutes later, I told him what had happened. Parker had been fond of John, in his own undemonstrative way, but never one to indulge his emotions. All he said was, "I'm sorry to hear that."

"Josephine is taking care of the funeral arrangements."

"That's right up her alley. She'll have a field day. That woman dotes on catastrophes."

"You know, it's strange but I can't really tell how I feel about John's death."

"It's too soon."

"Is that what it is?"

"Sure, it hasn't sunk in yet."

"I guess I don't believe he's dead."

"That's what I mean. It hasn't gotten to you yet."

It had turned into quite a weekend, what with husband number four asking for a divorce, and husband number three burning himself to death. I couldn't help but wonder what was going on in the lives of husbands number one and two. Actually, I had no idea. The last I heard from Chip was this past winter when he sent me a postcard from Santa Anita where he was following the horses. The card had not been very informative, merely a brief message to the effect that he was well and thought of me often.

As for Paul, we'd been in touch only once since our divorce, and that was when I hired his company, The Green

Hornet, to move my furniture and personal possessions into Billy's bare loft, after I left John. Paul had sounded very solicitous when I called him explaining the nature of the move.

"I hope you'll be happy this time," he said. "And if there's anything else I can do, please let me know."

When the movers delivered the furniture, I saw that Paul had thrown in a wicker rocking chair as a gift, because he knew I'd always liked wicker. The thought of Chip and Paul still caring for me was more reassuring than I can say. They were part of me. By losing Billy and John, I felt as though I had lost part of myself, for what do our pasts amount to if there's no one else to remember them with us? My father's stubborn refusal to acknowledge any marriage other than my first had had the same effect upon me: one of irretrievable loss. My four husbands. They were my identity, my passport to the world, without them I felt like nothing. It was an unsettling realization and I instinctively moved closer to Parker for warmth and comfort. He had just started to kiss and caress me when there was a loud knock on the door.

"Who is it?" Parker asked.

"Open up, mister. I come to wash the windows."

"Oh, Christ," I said. "It's Aladar."

"Who?" Parker asked.

"The new window washer. And get ready for this—he's Leonard Stein's cousin."

"Come back later," Parker called out. "I'm busy."

More heavy knocking ensued, followed by muffled Hungarian threats. "Open up, mister."

"Maybe you had better," I said. "He's very insistent."

Parker reluctantly put on a paisley robe and opened the door, admitting an Aladar who was as unsteady as yesterday, the same bottle of vodka (or was it a new one?) sticking blatantly out of his back pants pocket. Looking at me, he said, "I meet you before in other room. Yes?"

"No."

"Yes, lady. Aladar recognize." He laughed his toothless laugh. "*Isten lova baszja.* And not always horses, hey, lady?"

"What the devil is he talking about?" Parker asked.

"I don't know. He's drunk."

As though on cue, Aladar took a large swig from the bottle, wiped his mouth on the back of his sleeve, and announced, "Now I go to work."

"Let's make love anyway," I said, as soon as Aladar had climbed out the window, and buckled himself in. "The room's dark. He won't be able to see us."

Parker seemed surprised by my suggestion, but pleased. As for me, I had never wanted to make love so badly. I needed the reassurance that only eroticism seems to be able to give me. I needed sexual attention to compensate for the loss of Billy and John, I needed a man to care for me, take me in his arms, tell me I was beautiful, desire me, devour me, lose himself in me, so I could lose myself too. I needed Parker at that moment as I had never needed anyone in my life, and my need swiftly translated itself into a kind of mounting excitement that I could feel right down to my toes. I was so worked up that I thought I'd come the second Parker entered me, but then it passed over, and then I couldn't seem to come at all, I just lingered on the edge of ecstasy, wishing he would never stop.

"Don't come yet," I said, anxiously.

My request must have made him anxious, too, because he suddenly erupted inside me with such spasmodic intensity that after it was over, he collapsed on top of me, sweating, and trying to catch his breath.

"I'm sorry," he said, at last, "but I couldn't control it."

I was dripping wet, and still excited. "I'm sorrier than you."

At that, a burst of applause greeted our stunned ears, and looking up we saw Aladar standing a few feet from the bed, hailing our performance.

"Very good fucking," he said, giving us one last round of enthusiastic applause. "I see you again, lady. *Jo regelt kivanok.*"

"We're glad that you approve," Parker said, as Aladar picked up his sloshy pail of water and marched out the door, humming to himself in Hungarian.

"Another little touch of quaintness at Hotel Splendide," I said. "A window washer who's a voyeur. Leonard Stein thinks of everything, except fixing my air-conditioner. I'm going to have a showdown with him this morning. I can't stand my room one more minute."

"How did you know Aladar? I've never seen him before."

"I met him yesterday morning, when he came to wash John's windows."

There was no point in denying that I'd stayed over at John's last night, since I myself had publicly announced that fact on the roof yesterday.

"I didn't know you'd been sleeping with John recently," Parker said. "I thought he was Josephine's exclusive domain."

"I wasn't sleeping with him. I just stayed over because my own room was so hot. John slept on the floor." It was only a half lie. "He likes to sleep on the floor. I mean, he used to like to."

"Are you really pregnant, Loretta?" Parker said, catching me by surprise.

"I'm not certain."

"When will you find out?"

"Soon. In fact, that reminds me I have to call my gynecologist today."

"Assuming you are pregnant, do you know who the father is?"

"Of course," I said, indignantly. "You."

"Me? Are you sure?"

"Positive."

"How can you be so sure it's me?"

"It's easy. You're the only man I slept with last month." I figured if he believed that, he'd believe anything.

"I see," Parker said, lighting his pipe.

"Is that all you have to say?"

"What would you like me to say?"

"It's not a matter of what *I'd* like. Don't you have any emotional reaction? I mean, it's not every day that a woman tells you you're the father of her unborn child."

"That's true."

"Then for Christ's sake, say something!"

"Debbie Reynolds."

"Parker, have you lost your mind?"

"Probably. Hasn't everyone we know?"

"That's not the question."

"What is?"

"The question is, how do you feel about the possibility of my being pregnant?"

"I think you'll make a wonderful mother, Loretta. You'll need a larger place, though. Maybe you can get Leonard to give you John's apartment. The baby could have the bedroom, and you could sleep in the living room."

"Parker, stop talking like a lawyer. I'm not interested at the moment in practical things like apartments. I might be pregnant. PREGNANT. With *your* child. You must have some feeling about it. Are you sorry? Glad? I mean, I could understand it if you got angry and said that you hated me. I could understand anything except this chilling detachment of yours."

"I'd like to oblige you, Loretta, by having a screaming fit of hysterics, but unfortunately I don't feel very hysterical at the moment. I don't feel angry, and I don't hate you. Why should I? Women get pregnant every day, I'm told."

"But you don't love me, either."

He tapped his pipe. "No, I don't."

"You bastard."

"Why? Have I ever led you to believe that I did?"

"Not exactly, but . . ."

His point-blank denial was like getting a bucket of ice water in my face. I couldn't believe that all these dreadful things were happening to me. Billy asking for a divorce, John burning to death, my father refusing to sympathize with my problems, and now, as the last wretched rejection, Parker crushing any hopes I might have had that he could deeply care for me and our child. I just wasn't used to being treated like this, not Loretta Silverman, child dancing prodigy, star of her high-school cheerleader team, Queen of the prom, college campus beauty, the girl other girls wanted to look like, copied, envied, were jealous of, the girl who ever since birth had the allure and fascination of a Hollywood love goddess, no, this simply could not be happening to Loretta Irene Silverman Kramer Bjorkman O'Connell Ray, the Ava Gardner of The Bronx!

"You stink," I said to Parker. "And to think I've defended you to other people in the hotel."

"Why? What did they say about me?"

"That you have the soul of a cross-eyed iguana. And they're right. Even an iguana is too good to be compared to you. I hate you. I hate all men. If I had the nerve, I'd become a lesbian."

"You and Josephine Jasmin."

"What the hell is that supposed to mean?"

He got out of bed and handed me a copy of *Lewd*, the latest underground freak newspaper. On the front page was a slightly blurred photograph of a girl going down on a man.

"Look at page eight," Parker said. "The belle of Charleston has an article there that might interest you."

Josephine's article was entitled, "The Female Prerogative," and basically contended that women should have no feelings of guilt or shame if they indulged in sexual acts with other women. The reason they shouldn't be ashamed, Josephine said, was because male insensitivity and emotional brutality were driving otherwise normal women into the arms of their female sisters, who were far more considerate and thoughtful than most men could ever be.

"I certainly agree with her about male insensitivity."

"I thought you would." Parker yawned, revealing a couple of interesting fillings. "I've got to go to work. You know, you have all my clean shirts."

"I'm through washing and ironing your shirts. No more. From now on, you can find yourself a new laundry service."

"Yes, Ma'am."

"When I think of all the New Oxydol Plus I've wasted on you, I could cry."

"Yes, Ma'am."

"And never try to talk to me again."

"Yes, Ma'am."

"And stop saying, *yes, Ma'am.*"

"Yes, Ma'am."

I hit him with one of Splendide's crummy ashtrays and he threw a pillow at me. Then we got dressed and went to my room, so Parker could collect his shirts. The last thing I noticed before we left his room was a book called *The Satanic Bible*.

After Parker had taken his shirts and gone to work, I collapsed on my electric bed, trying to gain the energy to shower, dress, and go downstairs to argue with Leonard Stein about fixing my air-conditioner. This time, I was determined to come out the victor, and it occurred to me that Leonard might be sympathetic to my wishes today, because of John's untimely death. Maybe he would act human for once in his life and feel sorry for me. Leonard knew that I was very fond of John, and whenever he was in one of his crummy moods, he used to say, "Why don't you two kids get married again? Come on. Look at the money you'd save on rent." Always the high priest of romance, that was Leonard Stein.

From I. C.'s room came the sound of familiar thrashing noises, and I tried to imagine who he was making it with. Whoever it was, they were really going at it at breakneck speed, and I could plainly hear every moan and groan, both his and hers, which didn't make me feel too good because of my own unresolved orgasm situation. That was about what I could expect from Parker Mason: no sexual satisfaction, and no emotional satisfaction either. Still, I had to admit that in a perverse way, he intrigued me. It was his stubborn resistance to my charms, his refusal to become involved with me, or let me hurt him. Once when he was drunk, he told me that just before his wife left him for the family dentist, she bleached her hair blonde and said, "I don't love you any more." The next day she was off, child and all.

"I couldn't believe it had happened," Parker said. "That she left me. That she didn't love me. I was stunned, dazed. I mean, she was my *wife*. I had no idea she was unhappy, or that anything was going on with another man. Sometimes I still wake up and expect to see her next to me in bed."

The thrashing on the other side of the wall had stopped, and then Daffodil Jasmin said, "No wonder my mother is jealous. You're sensational."

I couldn't hear I. C.'s muffled response, and in a few seconds the thrashing started all over again, this time even more energetically than before. "Oh, my God," Daffodil moaned. "Oh, baby, please don't stop, please." I had gotten so worked up listening to their bodies bang against each other, and imagining the sensations they felt, that when I heard I. C. say, "Now. Come now. *Now*!" I had an orgasm on the spot, and instantly felt much more optimistic about coping with Leonard Stein. There's nothing like a good orgasm (even the solitary variety) to set you up to face the hostile world with self-confidence and determination.

"Thanks, folks," I said, knocking on the wall that separated the two rooms. "Much obliged."

A few minutes later, I. C. came into my room with one of the hotel's towels wrapped around his slender waist. "What's up? What did you knock for?"

"I wanted you to know that I was here, in case you feel like toning it down a bit. I can hear every groan."

"Oh, that's okay. I don't mind, and I'm sure Daffodil couldn't care less. She doesn't have any inhibitions, that kid. What I'd like to do, is get them both in bed together."

"Who?"

"Daffodil and Josephine. Wouldn't that be something? A real socio-sexual comparison study of mother and daughter for my survey. Of course, I've got some pretty interesting statistics already. Like Daffodil uses an I.U.D. Got herself fitted for one when she was only thirteen. That's some precocious kid, I tell you."

"Just don't tell Josephine. She'll have a screaming fit if she finds out that you went to bed with her daughter. Didn't you see how jealous she was on the roof, when you were paying all that attention to Daffodil?"

"Don't worry about Josephine, I can handle that dizzy broad. But Daffodil might prove too much for me. She's got the energy of a dynamo. We've been going at it since last night, and she's still not satisfied. She keeps sticking those ammies in my mouth to pep me up. You should try them sometime, maybe we can try them together. I still intend to make it with you, Loretta. You fascinate me. I figure you'd either be sensational, or a complete washout, a dud. Nothing in-between with you, right?"

"You'll never know, Chinese Boy. I told you before that I have no intention of becoming one of your sexual-survey victims, so forget it."

"You'll change your mind," he said, as he was starting to leave. "By the way, if you use an I.U.D. like Daffodil, don't ride on motorcycles. Confucius say it might fall out. That's what happened to Daffodil when she was running around with the Hell's Angels. Just a friendly contraceptive tip from your friendly next door neighbor."

Just as I had taken off my Pucci sleep culottes and was about to get into the shower, the house phone rang.

"I've made the funeral arrangements," Josephine said. "We're all to be at Frank Campbell's at three o'clock tomorrow. Have you seen I. C. this morning? I just tried to ring him about the funeral, and there wasn't any answer. I also can't locate Daffodil. It seems peculiar to me that they've both disappeared at the same time."

"I haven't seen anyone this morning, except Parker, and that was one person too many. He turns out to be as big a bastard as every other man I know."

"You've always stuck up for him. What made you change your mind?"

"He has no feelings. He's cold as a fish. Here I am, pregnant with his child, and he acts as though nothing significant has happened."

"You didn't tell me that Parker was the father."

"I'm telling you now."

"At least you're going to have a child by the man you love." Josephine started to cry. "Look at me. John is gone. My daughter is a dope fiend. I have nothing, nobody."

"I don't love Parker. I hate him."

"If you don't love him," Josephine said, in between sobs, "why are you having his child? Not that I'm trying to discourage you from having it. Motherhood is wonderful. Difficult, but wonderful."

From I. C.'s room, came Daffodil's voice, screaming, "Fuck me, oh fuck me, fuck me, I'm going to come!"

"Is someone there with you?" Josephine asked.

"No, I'm alone."

"I could have sworn I heard a woman's voice."

"It must be on your floor. I didn't hear anything."

"The acoustics in this hotel certainly leave plenty to be desired." She blew her nose. "Well, I have to go now. I'm about to run over to Saks to see if I can find a little black dress for the funeral. I just realized that I don't own a single black dress."

A scream of tortured ecstasy now pierced my room, followed by Daffodil saying, "Oh it hurts, it always hurts afterward, damn it."

"Didn't you hear that scream?" Josephine asked, alarmed.

"What scream?"

"It sounded like someone was being killed."

"You're just all worked up because of John's death. No

one is being killed. Listen, I'll talk to you later. I have to go and bathe now. Good luck at Saks."

As soon as we hung up, Daffodil said, "Let's stay in bed all day and fuck our brains out. Okay?"

"Fuckee suckee fifty cents," I. C. replied in a hoarse stage whisper, just as my other phone, the outside phone, began to ring.

"What are you doing?" my father asked.

I could tell he was calling from his butcher shop, as he frequently did, because of all the female voices in the background, talking about flanken and chicken fat and which cut of beef was best for pot roast.

"I was just about to take a shower."

"Did you sleep last night?"

"Yes. Why? Didn't you?"

"Not a wink. I tossed and turned until it was time to get up. I've never had gas pains like that in my life. From now on, Loretta, we're going to eat at the Israeli restaurant on Broadway. I hear it's very good, and it's not far from that crazy hotel where you live. That's what we're going to do."

"John burned to death last night."

"*Traife* food gives me gas. I don't know why it doesn't give you gas. You weren't brought up on it."

"Father, I just said something. Didn't you hear me?"

"What'd you say?"

"That John burned to death last night."

There was a moment's hesitation. "John who?"

"John Barrymore."

My father laughed. "You know, sometimes I think you're really a dope, Loretta, even though you do make three hundred and fifty dollars a week. What are you talking about with John Barrymore? John Barrymore died a long time ago. I remember, I saw it in the papers."

"I was being sarcastic. Of course, I don't mean John Barrymore. I mean *my* John. John O'Connell. He fell asleep with a lit cigarette."

"Sure, the *shicker*. He's drunk and he smokes in bed. That's the kind of men you marry, Loretta. I'll never understand how that head of yours works. There are so many smart, sober, successful men around, you'd think you'd be able to find one of those for a husband, but no, not you. Irishmen who drink, Swedes who own moving companies with one truck, colored guitar players, that's who you marry. Where do you find them? Tell me. Is there a special place where they all congregate, like some kind of club for schlemiels? Your mother must have turned over plenty in her grave since you divorced Chip Kramer. And don't mention enemas to me again. I don't want to hear."

"I'm not mentioning anything to you anymore. It's just a waste of time."

"What kind of way is that to talk to your father? And speaking of a waste of time, who's the Chinaman with the dirty mouth? I don't like the look in his eyes, but I doubt that your father's opinion means anything to you at this late date."

"You don't have opinions. You have prejudices. You don't mean that you don't like the *look* in his eyes, you mean you don't like his eyes because they're a different shape than yours."

"Thank you for explaining it to me. If I didn't have you to tell me what I mean, I'd have to go through life in total ignorance, wouldn't I? So tell me, my wonderful, intelligent daughter, what does that Chinaman do for a living? Assuming he has a job, that is?"

"He's conducting a survey for a prominent gynecologist on the birth-control practices of unmarried women."

From the next room, I. C.'s voice came back: "Sexual practices, too," followed by Daffodil's girlish laughter.

"What was that?" my father asked.

"Nothing."

"I heard somebody say something."

"Well, I didn't."

"Okay, just do me one favor. If you should marry this survey conductor, God forbid, don't come and tell me about it. Keep it to yourself. I've had enough aggravation from you and your four *meshugena* marriages, I don't need any more. If there's one thing I can live without at this point in my life, it's a Chinaman for a son-in-law."

"I think I'm pregnant."

There was a horrified gasp at the other end of the line, and then dead silence.

"Aren't you going to say something?" I asked.

"Who?" he finally managed to choke out. "Who's the father?"

"A Hungarian window washer," I said, replacing the receiver on its hook.

After my shower, I put on a new bluish-green linen dress and tied a loose ascot of bluish-green silk inside the v-neck of the dress. I had brushed my hair the usual one hundred times, and it shone in all its auburn glory, barely skimming the silk ascot. My suntan was very effective against the colors of my dress and hair, and as I admired myself in the full-length mirror that hung on the bathroom door, I found it hard to believe that any man could remain immune to my obvious appeal for very long.

I was thinking specifically of Leonard Stein whom I intended to hypnotize, in just a few minutes, into fixing my air-conditioner. So as not to appear unmarred by John's death, I put on a pair of huge black sunglasses, which I rarely wore, in the hope that Leonard would think I had spent the night in tears. A spray of Cabochard, and I was off to tangle with the owner of Hotel Splendide in his own den, and this time I fully intended to emerge victorious.

The lobby of the hotel was at its typical Monday morning apogee. The psychedelic lights were going full blast, there was a painter carrying an unfinished canvas out into the street, a beautiful Negro model showing her portfolio to a man in cowboy boots, a couple of bushy-haired poets speaking to the Berlitz clerk in French, the lady with the Rheingold six-pack, the bellman who specialized in grass arranging something with Peggy, who waved at me, and another rock group checking in, The Candy Store.

Leonard Stein's office was at the far end of the lobby, tucked away in an inconspicuous corridor that might have housed nothing more interesting than a broom closet unless you knew what you were looking for. I knocked on the unmarked door and heard Leonard say, "Come in."

He was seated behind a long oak desk that had all kinds of papers, notes, telephone messages, leases, and ledgers scattered the length of it. Leonard was in shirt sleeves but he had a tie on, and was talking on one of his two telephones. I noticed that the office was refreshingly cool, thanks to a jumbo window unit that looked as though it could have air-conditioned Carnegie Hall.

"Now you listen to me," Leonard was saying into the receiver, "either you sign the lease I've drawn up, or else you move out. That's right. *Out*. If you want to pay our special, monthly rates, then you have to sign a year's lease. Now, I'm tired of arguing with you, Corina. You either sign, or I'm going to evict you."

He looked at me and rolled his eyes in despair. "Would I *what?* Would I sleep on a bright orange sheet? Yes, I suppose so, if it were clean. But you're going to be sleeping in the street unless you come to your senses. I've got a list of more than fifty people who are waiting to move into Hotel Splendide. Any one of them would grab your room in a minute, you have one of the most beautiful rooms in the hotel, and if you want to keep it, you come into this office today and put your signature on this lease. And I mean today, or out you go. I'm not kidding around, Corina. That's final!"

He slammed down the receiver, wiped his forehead with a handkerchief, and said to me, "I've been after that Corina to sign a lease for two months now. First she said she wouldn't sign unless I painted her room, so I painted it. Then she said she didn't like the paint job and she wanted me to scrape the floor, so I scraped it. Now she says she doesn't want to sign because she might go to Europe in the fall.

"You know what the trouble with you people is? You don't realize the headaches I've got running this hotel. All you think is that I'm making a lot of money with no effort. Do you have any idea the amount of service you get in a hotel like this? Do you know that the maids' salaries have gone up *twice* in the last year because of a union ruling? You think it's a picnic running a hotel, I suppose. You should know some of the things I've got to contend with, you wouldn't believe it.

"Just the other day one of our sculptors painted all her walls jet black. What am I going to do when she moves out? Do you know how many coats of white paint it would take to paint over those walls? I'm afraid to imagine. But I didn't reprimand her, because after all, that's what Hotel Splendide is noted for, isn't it? Artistic freedom? I let my tenants do as they please. Did you ever hear me tell anyone not to throw noisy parties, or that a musician shouldn't practice late at night if that's the only time he has available? How many other hotel owners would be as lenient as me? I'm sympathetic to artists,

I like to make them comfortable, but they've got to be sympathetic to my needs, too."

Leonard Stein was an extremely handsome man in his mid-thirties, who was reputed to have the largest penis on the Eastern seaboard. Recently he'd gotten a mod haircut in the style of many of his male tenants, and over his desk hung an interesting portrait of Leonard himself. Interesting because it had been painted by one of his tenants before he became successful, and the story went that the painter gave it to Leonard in lieu of one month's rent which he didn't have at the time. Leonard was supposed to have quite an extensive art collection in his home in Pelham, thanks to either the generosity of some of the painters who had lived at Splendide, or their unfortunate financial circumstances which Leonard lost no time in taking advantage of.

"How do you like my dress?" I said, giving him a dazzling television smile.

"It's very attractive. Where did you buy it?"

"At Bendel's."

"You must have a lot of money to shop there. They charge an arm and a leg."

"Television pays very well. Pretty soon I'll be as rich as you."

"I don't have as much money as people think," Leonard Stein said. "Now the bellmen want a raise. Everybody wants more money for the same amount of work. Tell me, Loretta, in all honesty, what do you think of your maid?"

"Evelyn's okay. I like her. I mean, she's a lousy maid, but she's a nice person."

Leonard pointed a finger at me. "You see? That's what I'm talking about. A lousy maid whose salary has just gone up *twice* in the last year. Why is she lousy?"

"She just moves the dust around, she doesn't particularly try to get rid of it."

He sighed the sigh to end all sighs. "What can I do? Do you know what it would cost me to hire top-notch maids? I'd have to go out of business. But you like her?"

"Yes, we get along very well, which is more than Peggy can say for the maid who cleans her room. Peggy can't stand her, she says she wakes her up all the time. Peggy likes to sleep late, and the maid insists on cleaning her room first thing in the morning."

"If your friend Peggy didn't sleep so late, maybe she'd get herself a job. She's two months behind in rent. I'll bet you didn't know that."

"No, I didn't."

"You have no idea how many people owe me back rent. Any other hotel, they'd be out in the street, but not at Splendide. Here, we're sympathetic, understanding. I like artists. They're temperamental, but they're interesting. They know they have a friend in Leonard Stein."

"The question is, do *I* have a friend in Leonard Stein?"

His eyes grew wary. "What's that supposed to mean?"

"You know what I'm talking about."

"I do?"

"Oh come on, Leonard, stop pretending."

"Who's pretending?"

"I'm talking about my air-conditioner."

He immediately became very busy shuffling papers around on his desk. "What about your air-conditioner?" he asked, after a few minutes of shuffling.

"It's still broken."

Leonard Stein stared out the window which faced grimy Broadway. Across the street, a man was picketing an Italian restaurant. "Unfair to labor, that's all you hear these days.

But who is labor fair to, that's what I want to know? Management has its problems too. I suppose you heard what happened to your ex-husband last night."

"Yes, I've been crying ever since Josephine Jasmin told me the ghastly news."

"*You've* been crying!" Leonard Stein leaped up from his chair, and began pacing the room. "Think what *I've* been doing. Think how that damn fire is going to affect my insurance rates. Think of all the unfavorable publicity. That was some winner you married, Loretta. One more fire because of pyromaniacs like that and Hotel Splendide won't even be able to get insurance. *She's* been crying!"

"I was only married to him, Leonard. It's not my fault he fell asleep with a lit cigarette."

"It's my fault, I suppose. You'd think anyone who drank as much as he did would know enough not to smoke in bed, wouldn't you? You should see his apartment, it's a disaster area. I figure it's going to cost me a thousand dollars to renovate it. A thousand dollars! Painters' wages went up twelve per cent this past winter. Unfair to labor. That's a good one."

"I repeat, I was only married to the man. Besides, I don't see what John's death has to do with your fixing my air-conditioner. Leonard, you don't know how hot it is in my room. I can't stand it any longer. I can't sleep."

"So you fix it."

"Oh, no. When I signed the lease, it clearly said that the hotel was responsible for the maintenance of all air-conditioners it supplied. I'm not paying to have it fixed. That's your responsibility."

"Okay, you twisted my arm. I'll fix it."

I couldn't believe my ears. "You will?"

"Sure," he said. "As soon as you get rid of the washing machine."

I should have known he wouldn't give in so easily. We were right back where we started: nowhere. "Look, Leonard," I began, "please don't ask me to get rid of the washing machine. I need it. It means a lot to me. It really does."

"But it's costing me a fortune in electricity. Besides, what do you need it for? There's a laundry right next door to the hotel, three feet away. You make a good salary, you just admitted it. You can afford to take your clothes to the laundry."

"That's not why I need it. I like to wash men's shirts."

He stopped in the middle of the room, and stared at me as though dumb-struck. "Men's shirts? Did I hear you say *men's shirts*? I think I'm losing my mind."

"Sometimes I do a handkerchief or two."

"Oh, my God. She's running a laundry business on my electric bill!"

"No, I'm not. I wash the shirts free of charge."

Leonard Stein threw his head back, his eyes pivoted on the flaky art nouveau ceiling. "I should have stayed in broadlooms. I didn't know when I was well off. This is the last straw. Men's shirts. Only at Hotel Splendide could something like this happen. The Algonquin, the Chelsea, the Royalton. They think they've got nuts living there, they should come over here and meet Loretta Silverman who takes in washing. On my electric bill! When I first saw that washing machine, I figured you were trying to save a little money by doing your own clothes, but it never occurred to me, it never crossed my mind, it wouldn't occur to anybody, it doesn't make any sense, it's ridiculous, *men's shirts*. This even beats Zachary and his jungle. Another electric current *shnorrer*, but compared to your washing machine, his fish tanks are nothing. *Bubkas*."

"I don't care what you say. I'm not getting rid of my washing machine. It's a Whirlpool, with permanent press cycles. I won it on You Said It! That's how I got started in television. Did I ever tell you? I was a contestant on a game show."

Leonard Stein sat down behind his desk, a broken man, and stared blankly off into space as I told him about the early career beginnings of Loretta Silverman.

When I got home to The Bronx after my first meeting with Chip, I didn't say a word to my parents about the possibility of my being on You Said It! I decided to play it safe and make sure that I was actually accepted as a contestant on the show before I broke the bad news to them: sorry, Mother and Father, but I'm not going back to college, I've got other plans.

Knowing my parents, I could well imagine the scene that would follow. Lots of screaming, crying, threats, supplications, and general hysteria. Like many people who have never been to college themselves, my parents regarded it as the promised land. Their reverence for a college education, *any* college education, knew no bounds, and they were convinced that the only people who didn't get one (if they could afford it) were the *goyim.* In my parents' minds, gentiles were handsome dopes whose main activity consisted of playing golf, drinking beer, and eating ham sandwiches with a lot of mayonnaise.

The next morning, I called the number on the card that Chip had given me and was asked by a Miss Ellis to come up the following day and take "a simple little test" to see whether I'd qualify as a contestant. Just as Miss Ellis thanked me for my interest and was about to hang up, I said, "Is Mr. Kramer around, by any chance?"

"Hold on a minute."

A few seconds later, Chip's voice greeted me. "Hello. Loretta?"

"Do you remember me? We met yesterday at the RCA Exhibition Hall."

"Yes, of course." But he sounded uncertain. "What can I do for you?"

"Nothing. I mean, I just wanted to tell you that I have an appointment to come up to your office tomorrow. Will you be there? My appointment's at ten o'clock."

"Yes." He sounded more uncertain than ever. "I should be floating around the general vicinity."

There was an uncomfortable pause, and I said, "Well, thank you, and I'll see you tomorrow. Maybe we can have coffee."

"Coffee?"

On impulse, I added, "I'm the girl who goes to college in Iowa."

"With the invalid mother."

So he did remember. "That's right."

"How's your mother feeling today?"

"Okay. I mean, okay for *her*. In other words, terrible."

"That's a shame. Look, I've got to go now, got to get over to the studio for a rehearsal. See you tomorrow."

And tomorrow, and tomorrow, and tomorrow, and tomorrow, I thought, dreaming of my wonderful future as the wife of Charles Alan Kramer.

"Who was that?" my mother asked, after I hung up.

"Nobody."

"Does this nobody happen to have a name?"

"It's just a man I met."

"So what's his name?"

"Chip."

"That's a name? It sounds like something you eat."

"It's a nickname. His real name is Charles."

"Charles *what*?"

"Never mind."

My mother looked at me suspiciously. "I know why you aren't telling me his last name. Because it's not a Jewish name. Is your mother right?"

"No, my mother is wrong."

"Then why not tell me? What's the big secret?"

"I just don't care to. But I will tell you this. I'm going to marry him."

"Well, in that case, don't you think I have the right to know the name of my future son-in-law?"

"Oh really, mother, what's the difference what his last name is? What if it's not a Jewish name? What if he's an Arab? Or a Negro?"

My mother sat down. "I knew we never should have sent you to school in the Midwest."

"What the hell does the Midwest have to do with it? I met Chip in Manhattan."

"I told your father that that college in Iowa was a mistake. I knew it, I told him, I warned him."

"Mother, you're not listening. I met Chip in New York, not Iowa. I mean, do you think there are more Arabs and Negroes in Iowa than in New York City?"

"Your father will have a heart attack when he hears about this. I feel sorry for his cholesterol count."

"Hears about *what*? What are you getting so excited about? All I said was that I met a man named Chip. Oh, forget it. This is ridiculous. I'm going for a walk. Okay, okay, I give in. His last name is Kramer."

My mother looked up at me, instantly alert. "Kramer. That could be Jewish. It also couldn't be Jewish. Kramer could be German. You're going to marry a Nazi, aren't you, Loretta?"

"Yes. His father was the commandant at Auschwitz. You should see their lampshades."

I dressed very carefully for my appointment at the network the next day. After much consideration, I chose my emerald green sweater dress which really brought out the green in my eyes, and a pair of sexy lizard slingbacks. The overall effect was one of sly sinuousness, and I felt convinced that Chip would be appropriately impressed. My coat with the red fox trim completed the animalistic image I wanted to convey. Stalk me, baby, I'm a tiger. Little did I know then about the lair we were going to wind up in, not that I should have been surprised because if there's one thing I can say about the life of Loretta Silverman, it is that it's rarely been dull.

When I got to the offices of You Said It! there were quite a few girls there before me, and all for the same reason, as it turned out. I instantly recognized the attractive brunette whom I had seen that fateful day at the Exhibition Hall, but to my disappointment there was no trace of Chip Kramer anywhere. His assistant was the Miss Ellis I had spoken to on the telephone, and she was the one who gave us the written test. She was right, it was a very simple test indeed, almost moronic, in fact, a kind of low-grade vocabulary quiz which I zoomed through in no time at all.

Miss Ellis wore glasses and was rather cute, with a twangy accent that I couldn't quite place. After she had collected our test papers, she disappeared for about ten minutes during which time I kept wondering whether or not Chip was going to put in an appearance. When Miss Ellis finally returned, she pointed to the attractive brunette, another girl with bangs, and me.

"Would you young ladies please remain here," she said. "Everyone else can leave, but if we can use you for the show, we'll be in touch. And thank you all very much. We really do appreciate your interest in being on You Said It!"

She had her little speech down pat, and I couldn't help but speculate how many times a week she went through it, nor how much she was paid for this rather peculiar occupation. After the dropouts had left, Miss Ellis turned to me.

"Loretta, we'd like you to be here tomorrow morning. Can you make it?"

"Yes. What time?"

"Nine o'clock. Wear something casual, like what you have on today. Nothing dressy, this is a morning show. Then I'll take you into makeup, we'll go to the studio, go through a rehearsal, and we'll do the show." She gave me a big professional smile. "Any questions?"

"Yes. Where is Mr. Kramer?"

A look of irritation crossed her face. "I really don't know."

"I was supposed to have coffee with him."

"Coffee?"

She said the word much as Chip had over the telephone, with the same kind of wonder, as though I were suggesting something definitely unheard of in the world of network television.

"Yes," I persisted. "I was supposed to meet him here."

"Mr. Kramer is a very busy man and a very, shall we say, unpredictable man. He's hard to keep track of, but if you wish to hang around for a while, there's a possibility he might show up. There's also a possibility he might not."

At that point, something told me that Miss Ellis' interest in Chip clearly went beyond the professional. Perhaps she, too, had her heart set on becoming Mrs. Charles Alan Kramer. I was just about to say that I would wait a few minutes, when the door to the office opened, and in walked my future husband himself, looking even more handsome than the day I met him.

"Hi," I said. "I'm going to be on You Said It! tomorrow."

For a moment I thought he didn't recognize me, then he broke out in a big smile. "That's wonderful, Loretta. I knew you'd make it."

"Are you going to buy me that cup of coffee now?"

"Sure. Come on." To Miss Ellis, he added, "Be back in half an hour."

"But–" she started to say. It was too late. We were out the door.

"She's a nice kid, but a little overly conscientious about her job," Chip said, as we swung down an office-lined corridor. "I thought you might like to see our commissary. We can have coffee there."

He could have suggested the broom closet, and I would have agreed. "That sounds fine."

The commissary was a very large, plain room that looked like an overlit cafeteria, with unadorned walls and an air of stark practicality, hardly the most romantic setting in the world for a first demi-date. Chip chose a corner table, and at the next table I recognized a well-known news broadcaster talking to the female co-host of a morning show for women. She appeared infinitely less attractive than she did on the television screen, and I mentioned this fact to Chip.

"Some people photograph better than others," he said. "Also, they know how to make up for TV. Are you worrying how you'll look?"

"I guess so, but it doesn't matter so much in my case. I'm not in the business."

"You'll look okay," he assured me. "You have good

features, more importantly, good cheekbones. They'll fix your eye makeup tomorrow."

"What's wrong with it?"

"The liner underneath the eyes. No good for TV. Makes you look like you have rings. Don't worry about it. That's why we have a makeup department."

"You know," I said, "I still don't have the vaguest idea what this show is all about. What kind of questions I'll be asked, what kind of prizes I might win."

"You might win anything from a trip to Tahiti to a washing machine."

"Now what would *I* do with a washing machine?" I asked, little dreaming that one day I would become the free laundry service of Hotel Splendide.

"Well, maybe your mother could use it. After she gets better, I mean."

"I'll take the trip to Tahiti. But you still haven't told me about the kind of questions I'll be asked. Or would that be cheating?"

"It'd be cheating. Besides, we don't let the contestants go on cold. You'll have a little rehearsal first, to get you acquainted with the nature of the show."

"Will you be there?"

"Sure will. I take you through the rehearsal, get you warmed up for the host of the show, and the real thing. Relax, Loretta. You've got nothing to worry about."

That's what he thought. Up until a few minutes ago, I had no idea that I'd be scheduled to appear on You Said It! as soon as tomorrow. I had no idea they worked so fast on television. I figured it might be a week, two weeks, even a month before I would make my first appearance on the show. Now there was no reason why I couldn't return to college in a few days, as originally planned, no reason at all except that if I did I might never see Chip again.

"Do you have time for a brief tour of the network?" Chip asked, after we had finished coffee.

I was totally unprepared for this suggestion, but delighted nonetheless, and I told him so.

"Sure your mother can get along without you?"

Something about the way he said that made me wonder if he'd ever believed the story of my mother's fatal illness. Perhaps he was more devious than he appeared, a much better actor than I would have imagined at first. Little did I know then that Chip's penchant for gambling and lying made him automatically doubt the truth of everyone's story, that his stake in life's game of chance would make him take chances few men would risk.

"My mother has a full-time nurse at home."

I could have sworn that he started to smile but then caught himself in time. "Good. Let's go."

We took a brief tour of the VIP offices where all the weighty decisions were made, looked in on a live soap opera at a studio across the street, and then came back to the executive building for a fast look at the sales, publicity, research, and news departments.

"This isn't much," Chip said, opening an unmarked door. "Just a storage room where our hand cameras are kept."

The shelves of the room were lined with small, identical cameras, and in the middle of the floor was a huge packing crate, marked "fragile," apparently containing more cameras. I couldn't imagine why in the world he had brought me here, until he unbuttoned my coat and brought his head down to the V of my sweater dress. Kissing my neck, he swiftly proceeded south to my breasts which were pretty available since I've never worn a brassiere in my life. All I had on under the dress was a flimsy, low-cut slip with elasticized straps which Chip lost very little time in slipping off my shoulders.

Motioning me toward the packing crate, he sat me down on it and removed my coat, then getting on his knees he started to kiss my unencumbered breasts through the wool of my dress. I became so excited that I instantly removed the dress. My slip had fallen down to my waist, leaving me completely naked from the waist up. Chip was quite a breast man and just couldn't seem to get enough of mine, and after a few minutes he began sucking on them with such a frenzy that I thought I would faint of sheer excitement.

And that's when it happened.

Zoom. Suddenly the door to our little retreat swung open, and there stood a KBC guidette in her pert uniform, with a slew of open-mouthed people lined up behind her. It didn't take much intelligence to figure out that she was obviously in the midst of conducting a guided tour of the network when she blundered across Chip and me.

"Chip," I whispered. "We're not alone."

His back was to the guidette and the people, but I was directly facing them all, half naked, with a man's mouth moving rapidly from one taut nipple to another.

"Fuck them," Chip mumbled, not stopping his activity for a second, not even bothering to turn around to see who was there, just as though he had spent half his life making love to women in full view of KBC's guided tours.

"But Chip."

"Don't pay any attention to them," he said, in between resonant sucks.

"I can't help it. I'm looking right at them. Chip, *please*."

But Chip Kramer, future first husband of Loretta Silverman, had nothing more to say on the subject. I suppose I could have stopped him, pushed him, kicked him, slapped him, or something, but I was as mesmerized as the KBC guidette, who, in her dilemma, began parroting the little speech she ordinarily gave at this point of the tour.

"The cameras stored in this particular room are Eyemo cameras, manufactured by Bell and Howell. They are hand-held, hand-wound cameras which have a three-lens turret, and they take one minute of thirty-five millimeter film."

As she spoke, her eyes never left Chip and me. Neither did the eyes of the people behind her. Twenty-five strangers from Columbus, Ohio were receiving a fast course on Eyemo cameras and nipple sucking, all at the same time. The interesting part was that nobody said a word to either Chip or me, and we didn't say anything either. I was too flabbergasted to open my mouth, and Chip's mouth obviously was elsewhere.

After the guidette had finished her speech, she said to the people, "Now we'll go and take a peek at KBC's research department, which I'm sure you'll all find very interesting."

At that, they marched out of the Eyemo camera storage room, carefully closing the door behind them. Then Chip looked up at me.

"Fucking voyeurs."

"You call that a story about how you got started on *television*?!" Leonard Stein shrieked.

"Well, I didn't exactly finish. I mean, you interrupted me. I never got to tell you how I went on You Said It! and won my wonderful Whirlpool washing machine. Which I have no intention of getting rid of."

Leonard Stein stared at the man picketing the Italian restaurant. "When I was in broadlooms, I was happy. The only trouble was, I didn't know it. If I knew then what I know now, I would have kissed my own crummy carpets. Would you believe that, Loretta?"

"Leonard, darling, I'd believe anything you told me, particularly if it was to the effect that you'll fix my air-conditioner."

At that, he seemed to snap out of his languor and revert to his old, normal, mean self. "The answer is the same as it was before, and I'm not going to repeat it again. Categorically *no*, until you get rid of the washing machine! And in the meantime, do me a favor. Don't tell me any more stories about how you got started in television. Okay?"

"*Isten lova baszja.*"

And with Aladar's Hungarian curse, I started to leave Leonard Stein's office, one rejection heavier. I went through the list again in my mind, all the men who had rejected me so recently, and in such a short period of time: Billy Ray, John O'Connell, my father, Parker Mason, and now Leonard Stein. It was too much to bear, far too much, without the warmth of at least one masculine shoulder to cry on. For some reason, my second husband, Paul Bjorkman, came to mind. It had been a long time since I'd seen him, almost six years to be exact, but I knew that if I could count on anyone to be sympathetic to my problems, it would be darling Paul who had loved me so much, who, I was certain, still loved me.

"I'll walk you out," Leonard Stein said. "I've got to go to the desk anyway."

As we stepped into the lobby of Hotel Splendide, a strange sight greeted our eyes. Josephine Jasmin and an underground filmmaker named Harry Brown were on their hands and knees apparently searching for something lost in the immediate vicinity of the plastic hairbrush sculpture. It looked like it was something pretty damned important, the way the two of them were crawling around on the poison-green carpet, sweating and searching.

"What is it?" Leonard asked. "Did someone lose a contact lens?"

"No," Harry Brown answered. "Pubic hairs."

Monday Afternoon

WHEN I got back to my room after the morbidly frustrating confrontation with Leonard Stein, I collapsed once more on my electric bed, wondering how I could gather the strength to go on. To say that I was at the depth of ultimate Gemini depression was the understatement of the last five centuries.

I, literally, felt like dying. I even thought of going up to the roof of the hotel and jumping off. That should give Cheap Leonard something to worry about in the way of adverse publicity. Or maybe I'd set the whole place on fire, and think gleefully of his insurance rates.

I wondered whether Leonard really did have the largest penis on the Eastern seaboard. Somehow it seemed inappropriate for a man as mean as he to be so well endowed. I tried to remember where I had heard that interesting little tidbit about Leonard Stein's private parts, and seemed to vaguely recall that it was Peggy who had told me, although where she'd picked it up, I could not remember.

What did it matter, though? Big penises, small penises, medium penises. In less than forty-eight hours, I'd been rejected by them all. Yes, there was no doubt about it, blunt denial had finally come to Loretta Silverman from every man she thought she could trust. Except, of course, from Chip Kramer and Paul Bjorkman, both of whom I somehow felt I could still rely upon.

With that slim hope in mind, I dozed off, anxious to escape from my misery. I was awakened a few hours later by a loud knock on the door. All I needed at this point in my deflated life was to see Aladar come lurching in, with his skinny frame and sloshy pail of water.

"Who is it?" I called out.

"Me. Josephine."

I immediately remembered I. C. and Daffodil on the other side of the wall. Since I'd returned to my room, they'd been strangely quiet. Perhaps they had gone out for something to eat, or perhaps they were simultaneously eating each other, which would account for their ominous silence. If Josephine came in and they started thrashing and moaning again, Leonard Stein was going to have something else to worry about: a double murder.

"Just a minute," I said, figuring that I had enough problems of my own, without trying to solve everyone else's. After all, Josephine was a big girl, even if she did go around acting like a demented teen-ager half the time.

"I bought a dress," she said, when I opened the door. "I thought you'd like to see it. It's not bad for a summer funeral. It's sleeveless."

"Come in. Torrid Zone awaits you."

"I see what you mean about this place being hot," Josephine said, sitting down on the bed. "It's worse than hot. It's stifling. Did you talk to Leonard about fixing your air-conditioner?"

"I sure did. That's where I was coming from when I saw you and Harry Brown crawling around on the lobby floor. What did he mean by saying that you were looking for pubic hairs?"

Josephine laughed. "It was really very funny. When I was leaving the hotel earlier to go to Saks, I stopped at the desk for my mail. There was a letter for me, postmarked Detroit, which surprised me because to the best of my knowledge, I don't know a soul in Detroit. It turned out to be from some lesbian who'd read my article in *Lewd* about women's sexual rights."

Josephine laughed again. Twice in a row. That was remarkable coming from her, since she generally appeared to be on the verge of tears and/or hysterics.

"This dyke had read the article in *Lewd* and loved it, simply adored it, said I was a fascinating, wonderful, beautiful woman. And as a token of her esteem, she was sending me a few of her pubic hairs, which she'd Scotch-taped to the letter."

All signs of amusement suddenly disappeared from Josephine's face, as she stopped and turned her head in the direction of I. C.'s room. Then I heard it, too. Faint, but distinct creaking bed sounds. Here we go, I thought. Disaster is about to strike. Leonard Stein, get ready.

"Finish the story about the pubic hairs," I said, hoping to distract her from what was taking place on the other side of the paper-thin wall.

"Oh yes, the pubic hairs." She started to smile again. "Well, as I was leaving the lobby of the hotel, I ran into

Harry Brown and showed him the letter. He thought it was very funny, particularly the part about the hairs—"

And then, the cry came. It was I. C. "Stop popping those fucking ammies in my mouth. I can't get it up one more time, I tell you, you insatiable cunt!"

Josephine jumped to her feet. "*I knew it! I knew it! You knew it, too!* You lied to me this morning when I asked whether you'd seen I. C. You knew all the time that he was in there with Daffodil, didn't you?"

"No, no. It's not Daffodil. It's someone else."

Josephine sat down, and looked at me shrewdly. "Who?"

Trying to think as fast as possible, I said, "Peggy."

"That bitch."

"Why is she a bitch?"

"She knows I went to bed with I. C. Saturday night. I told her so myself."

"Well, so what?" I was trying to make her see the lightheartedness of it all. "You went to bed with him on Saturday, and she's in bed with him on Monday. What's the big deal?"

But, as usual, Josephine wasn't buying lightheartedness. "If I didn't know that you spent last night with Parker, I'd figure you spent it with I. C. yourself," she said, bitterly.

"And what if I had? You don't have exclusive ownership rights on him, just because you screwed him once. Come on. Be reasonable. Relax."

Asking Josephine Jasmin to be reasonable was like asking Barbra Streisand to be the girl next door.

"I still don't like it," she pouted. "About Peggy, I mean. She always wants everyone else's man."

"That's not true."

"Yes, it is. Why do you think she's making it with Zachary? Because I once made it with him."

It was hopeless, her irrationality was absolutely hopeless. "Forget Peggy. Finish the pubic hairs story."

"There's not much more to tell. Just that as I was showing the letter to Harry Brown, the Scotch tape got loose and the pubic hairs fell on the lobby floor, on Leonard Stein's crummy carpet. It was Harry's idea to try to retrieve them. He said it wasn't every day in the week that a person received a stranger's pubic hairs in the mail. I suppose he had a point. And believe it or not, Loretta, we actually managed to recover three of them. Two are lost forever in the lobby of Hotel Splendide. It's funny that she should have been from Detroit."

Suddenly, Daffodil's voice came through, loud and clear. "If that's your attitude, I'm going back to my boyfriend in Berkeley, and the hell with you."

Josephine started to turn a distinct shade of deep mauve. "I KNEW IT. I KNEW MY DAUGHTER WAS IN THERE. THIS IS THE END. I'LL FIX THOSE TWO CHEATS!"

She was on her feet and at the door in a second, but I was right behind her. I grabbed her by the shoulder.

"Josephine, don't do it. Not today. Think of John. You loved him. You're in mourning. It wouldn't be fitting for you to go around behaving badly the very day after his death. It wouldn't be fair to the memory of John. It wouldn't be ladylike."

At that, she burst into tears and walked slowly back to my bed, and sat down on it once more. "I really did love him, Loretta. I still can't believe he's gone. He loved me, too, you know. He really did."

"I know he did. He told me so."

She brightened a little at that. "He did?"

"Yes. Many times. And he thought you were a very good writer, too."

"He did? Really?"

"Yes. Really. He was trying very hard to sell *Oh, Trusting Fool,* no matter what you might have thought of his efforts. He was doing his best."

This brought on a fresh flood of tears. "And now it will probably never be published. My literary career is finished. Through. Kaput."

Since it had never actually begun, I didn't know quite what to say to that. The Saks box lay next to her on the bed, unopened.

"Why don't you show me your dress?"

"Kaput," she repeated. "Now I have to start looking for a new agent. Good literary agents aren't so easy to come by. Sometimes I wish I were back in Charleston, eating she-crab soup. Sometimes I wish I'd never left Charleston. I'll bet you didn't know that jasmine is the state flower of South Carolina."

"Never mind Charleston. Show me your goddamned dress."

That seemed to snap her out of it, and she tearfully began to open the brown-and-white box. "Here it is." She held up a very simple, very attractive black sleeveless mini with a pleated skirt. "Should I try it on for you?"

"Yes, I'd love to see it."

Giggles, both I. C.'s and Daffodil's, started coming through the wall. Josephine was now in a black lace bra and black half slip, bordered in lace. For a woman of thirty-nine who had led a life of tribulation (not as much tribulation as Loretta Silverman, though), she was in surprisingly good shape, and I remembered John saying, only two days ago, that he preferred Josephine's voluptuous body to my rather slender one. He should turn over in his grave as soon as he got into it. The giggles grew louder. Throwing the dress down on my bed, Josephine walked over to the wall separating I. C.'s room from mine, and pounded loudly on it with one angry fist.

"Shut up in there. This is your mother, Daffodil. As for you, I. C. Ring, Chinese double-crosser, I hope you never come again in your life."

Dead silence from the other camp followed Josephine's outburst. Not a peep.

"They're probably stunned into immobility," I said.

"Screw the two of them. I'm in mourning." She started to slip the new dress over her head. "Look, it doesn't need one alteration. How's that for a perfect fit? It's a size nine."

It actually was a perfect fit. "It's lovely, Josephine. You'll be the star of the funeral."

"I still can't believe there's going to *be* a funeral. I keep expecting John to call me on the house phone any minute and ask me to have dinner with him. What are you going to wear tomorrow?"

"I have a black faille coatdress that I bought in Paris when John and I were married. It's a little on the warmish side for this time of year, but it's the only black dress I own, so what the hell."

"Must you always remind me that you were once married to the man I love? Loved, I mean. Sometimes you're even worse than Peggy in the bitch department."

"I'm sorry. It just slipped out. And I wish you'd stop calling Peggy a bitch. She really isn't. She's too paranoid these days to be bitchy. She can't even take taxis anymore, that's how nervous and unsettled she is. Last night when the fire broke out, she couldn't get into an elevator because she was so afraid she'd be killed."

"You'd be afraid, too, if you went to those crazy meetings in Zachary's jungle. Listening to Zach's interpretations of those Tarot cards is enough to turn anyone into a raving paranoic."

"What do you mean?"

"I went to one of the meetings, out of sheer curiosity. Zach uses the Tree of Life method. Here's what happened with his reading of Peggy. First of all, there were a lot of Sword cards. That's supposed to be bad. Strife and misfortune. Peggy had so many Sword cards that I thought she'd drop dead on the spot when she saw them. In the first triangle, which symbolizes the soul, the three cards all indicated loss, disorder, indecision, instability, and self-censure. 'You are definitely unhappy and confused,' Zachary said to her. I didn't stay for the rest, that was enough for me. How would you feel if someone you trusted, whose *methods* you trusted, told you something like that? No wonder she's become crazy. She'd better stop going to those Tarot card meetings, and try to get herself some work doing TV commercials. Leonard Stein is becoming fed up with her being behind in rent, and you know him. If you're rich and successful, you can owe him money for three years and the craven bastard won't open his mouth. But be down on your luck, and he zooms in like a vulture."

"Leonard Stein stinks. He refused to fix my air-conditioner today. He says he won't fix it unless I get rid of the washing machine. You know, I just realized that I lost two shirt customers this weekend. Parker and John. I wouldn't do Parker's shirts anymore on a bet. He's a heartless man. And I recently bought three boxes of Tide, with all those stain-killing XK enzymes, too. Oh well, I still have I. C., Zachary, and Harry Brown. Wait! I just got a brilliant flash."

Josephine had started to remove her funeral dress, and I saw by the label that it was a size eleven, not nine.

"What's the flash?" she said.

"Maybe if I agreed to do Leonard Stein's shirts, he'd let me keep the washing machine. You know how he likes to get things for nothing. I think I'll call him right now and suggest the idea. I'll bet anything he goes for it."

But just as I was about to call Simon Legree on the house telephone, it started to ring.

"Hello," said Annabelle, Splendide's super switchboard operator. "Is Mrs. Jasmin there?"

"Yes, she is. Just a minute." I handed the receiver to Josephine. "It's for you."

Of the three telephone operators who alternated at Splendide's obsolete switchboard, Annabelle was the one who kept tabs on all the regulars at the hotel. She had an absolutely uncanny way of knowing when so-and-so was in so-and-so's room, and more often than not, *why*. My father once tried to reach me when I was in bed with a Greek pop painter in his room. Annabelle didn't put the call through, because she knew that the painter would answer the phone and make my father even crazier than he already was. Instead, she discreetly rang the room herself and made sure that I was on the line before connecting me with my father. I later told her that she'd interrupted what had promised to be a couple of sensational orgasms, but Annabelle seemed unimpressed.

"You'll have more," was her comment. "Besides, your father sounded pretty upset about something."

"Oh, he was upset, all right. They delivered a carload of pork to his kosher butcher shop by mistake. He'll be talking about it for the next five years."

By now, the heat in Torrid Zone was staggering. I went into the bathroom to throw some cold water on my face, then I combed my hair, sprayed Jean Naté's deodorant under my arms, and dusted my nose with my new transparent powder, compliments of Revlon. Josephine was still on the telephone when I returned feeling slightly refreshed, but I noticed there was a strange expression of horror on her face.

"*Ears?*" she said, incredulously. "I'm not sure I understand, sir. Are you saying that you want me to select a pair of *ears* for Mr. O'Connell?"

Something told me she was talking to the Frank Campbell people about the service scheduled for tomorrow. The thought of going to that funeral had already started to make me sick. Funerals and bar mitzvahs were two events I could happily live without for the rest of my life (which, at the rate I was going, did not promise to be a long one, anyhow).

"And a toupee, too?" Josephine said, turning greener by the second. "Well, can't you select one? Mr. O'Connell had black, wavy hair. It was very thick, and he wasn't balding in the least."

The Frank Campbell man made some remark, which, unfortunately, I couldn't hear. Then Josephine replied, "But he wasn't graying, sir. He didn't have one gray hair in his head."

It went on like that, going back and forth from ears to toupees, until Josephine finally said, "Very well, sir. If you insist. I'll be right over."

Then she hung up. "Loretta, I need a drink. Do you have anything?"

"A little vodka. Peggy gave it to me."

"I don't care if that bitch did give it to you. Would you please pour me a vodka on the rocks? I think I'm going to faint."

I had never seen her so shook up. Never. I dashed into my kitchenette and poured the drink as fast as I could. Luckily, I had one tray of ice cubes in my low-boy refrigerator. In Josephine's condition, there simply wouldn't have been time to call a bellman for a pitcher of ice cubes, which were made in Splendide's own nifty ice-cube machine, located somewhere in the bowels of the hotel.

Josephine gulped down the drink in one swallow, and looked up at me, her dark eyes wide with dismay. "You don't know what I have to do, Loretta. I have to go over to Frank Campbell's and select a toupee and a pair of plastic ears for John. It seems that he fell asleep on his face, when he burned to death, and according to the cosmetician at Frank Campbell's, his hair and ears are completely gone. Apparently, in a case like this, those are the first to go."

A strong wave of nausea came over me. I ran into the bathroom and threw up last night's paella–rice, chicken, clams, shrimp, sausage, and all. I noticed there wasn't a shred of lobster in the toilet bowl, and thought once more of La Chiripa's paella made with empty lobster shells. Since I'd just spoken to Leonard Stein about my air-conditioner and gotten nowhere, I figured I might as well talk to Carlos about his lobster shells, and doubly get nowhere. This certainly was not the month for Gemini luck, that was for damned sure.

"You look like I feel," Josephine said, when I emerged from the bathroom after my little purge. "It's all pretty gory, isn't it? The cosmetician just told me they have an extensive selection of plastic ears, and that I should try to pick the pair that most resembles John's own ears. But the funny thing is, Loretta, that I can't for the life of me remember what his ears looked like. Can you?"

"Do you want me to throw up again?"

"Don't get angry at *me*," Josephine said, reverting to her old martyred self. "It wasn't *my* idea to pick out plastic ears. Do you think I relish the prospect of going through Frank Campbell's extensive ear collection all by myself? I wonder how many pairs they have. Incidentally, the cosmetician told me that they'll run about a hundred dollars a pair, and also, roughly, the same for a toupee. We have to have a conversation about money."

I could feel the nausea welling up again. "Must we?"

"You don't think I'm going to pay for everything, do you? The funeral itself will run about three thousand dollars."

"*What?*"

"That's right. You don't think they give away services at New York's most respected funeral institution for nothing, do you?"

"Why the hell didn't you tell me it was so expensive when you made the arrangements? Three thousand dollars! That's insane. Where are we going to get it?"

"I put a notice on the bulletin board downstairs, saying that I was taking up a collection for John O'Connell's funeral, and that anyone who cared to contribute should get in touch with me."

"I'll bet you've heard from a lot of people."

"This is no time for sarcasm, Loretta. Parker said I could count on him for a hundred."

"That should take care of the ears, anyway."

"I'm going to overlook your sarcastic remarks because I know that, deep down, you're as shook up over this as I am. You just have a peculiar way of showing it. Harry Brown said he'd throw in a hundred, too."

From the next room, I. C. Ring called out, "That's for the toupee," followed by Daffodil's suggestion, "Why don't you have him cremated, Mother?"

"You're in mourning," I reminded her, as the anger and jealousy began to show on her face. "Don't let them bait you. They're probably high as a kite, anyway."

"We're stoned out of our heads," Daffodil called back.

"Will you two kindly stop interfering in our conversation," I said, angrily. "Go about your own business, and shut up. No one's interested in your moronic remarks."

"Thank you," Josephine said, wiping a tear from her eye, with one of her ubiquitous perfumed handkerchiefs. "They're really inconsiderate as hell. I'm ashamed to say she's my own daughter." There was a moment's pause. Then, tentatively, "Loretta, I was just wondering . . ."

I had a hunch I knew what she was going to say. "What is it?"

"Would you come to Frank Campbell's with me? I'm not sure I can face this ordeal alone."

My hunch was right. "I'd love to help you out, Josephine, but I'm afraid I can't. Not today."

She immediately became suspicious. "Why not?"

"Because I have to go see Paul, my second ex-husband. He called me earlier and wants to talk to me about something. I said I'd drop by his moving company this afternoon."

"I fail to understand why your second ex-husband should be more important than your third ex-husband. Particularly under the circumstances."

"I figure that Paul must have something pretty important in mind to get in touch with me after six years, and I'm curious to find out what it is. Why don't you ask Zachary or Harry Brown to go to Frank Campbell's with you? They're both very visually oriented. They'll help you with the toupee and ears."

"That's a thought." Josephine closed the dress box and stood up. "I'd better go see who I can entice. I'll speak to you later, Loretta. I'll let you know all the gory details."

Just before leaving, she pounded on the wall that separated my room from I. C.'s. "Good-bye, children."

"Bye bye," they sang back in unison.

The minute she was out the door, the thrashing and

moaning started all over again. It was even beginning to wear me down, listening to so much sexual action and getting so little of it myself. Of all my husbands, Paul Bjorkman was the most sexually compelling, and I began to wonder whether my lie to Josephine, about his calling me, had not been prompted by some deep unconscious need to make love, to be loved, to wipe out the misery of the past two days. But first things first.

I picked up the house phone. "Leonard Stein, please," I said to Annabelle. "And by the way, Mrs. Jasmin has left here, in case anyone calls."

"Oh, I know that. She just went into La Chiripa."

For a stiff drink, no doubt, before facing the Frank Campbell ordeal. "You're right on the ball, Annabelle."

"I figure it's part of my job," she said, modestly. "Wait a minute. I'll ring Mr. Stein."

"Yes?" Leonard said, a minute later. His voice was always wary when he answered the telephone, as though he were continually prepared for impossible requests from his tenants, and/or frightening reports of the latest Splendide tragedy.

"It's Loretta Silverman. I have a suggestion to make."

"Yes?" He sounded more wary than ever.

"If I agree to wash and iron your shirts, free of charge, would you let me keep the washing machine? I really do a very professional job."

"I never want to hear about men's shirts again, not as long as I live. Do you understand?"

"Please, Leonard. I'll use an enzyme pre-soaker."

"Use your head, instead. Get rid of that damned washing machine, and stop talking like an idiot. I don't need you to wash my shirts. We have a maid at home who does all that. Good-bye. I'm busy."

Click. And he was gone. Back to his leases and troubles, and all the nagging mysteries of a hotel owner's daily life.

Leonard had inherited Splendide from his father, who'd bought it in the 1920s and converted it from an apartment house into a hotel. Nobody knew why the older Stein was now content to be his son's night desk clerk, although there were several theories floating around, the most popular of which was that he'd had a heart attack some years back and could no longer take the stress of actively running Splendide. His shift was from midnight to seven in the morning, when it was relatively quiet and peaceful compared to the frenzied hullabaloo of the daytime hours, and he would sit behind the long desk with a decidedly contented expression on his face, as though he still enjoyed being part of the institution he had started, if only in the most humble way.

Parker Mason, however, had a completely different theory. He claimed that Leonard drugged his father daily with a secret potion designed to render aged people helpless subservients and by so doing saved himself a night desk clerk's salary.

"Don't you see how glazed his eyes are?" Parker once said, referring to Stein, Sr. "He's very definitely under the influence of a strong drug."

"Maybe it's something he has to take for his heart condition," I replied.

"Leonard's the man with the heart condition. He doesn't have one."

No one seriously believed Parker's theory (not even Parker himself), but it gave us all pause for thought whenever Leonard went out of his way to be particularly lacking in compassion and understanding. Like the time he arbitrarily raised the rent of everyone in the hotel who couldn't afford it, but didn't touch his solvent, successful tenants, particularly if their success lay in an artistic realm. Somebody had once said that Leonard Stein was a combination of Jack Palance,

Ahab, and Menasha Skulnik—a real triple threat of a landlord.

My outside telephone began to ring. It was my father, still at his butcher shop.

"Hello," he said. "I would have called you back sooner, but I was busy. Loretta, are you serious about being pregnant?"

"I'm not sure yet. I have to speak to the doctor today."

"You shouldn't have scared me like that, if you're not sure."

"I know. I'm sorry. Look, father, I'll talk to you later. There are several things I must do now."

"Okay. I know you were kidding about the Hungarian window washer. You *were* kidding, weren't you, Loretta?"

"Yes, I was kidding." I felt very, very tired. It was a combination of the heat, plus my life. "I'll call you later this afternoon."

"That's all I need," my father said, while in the background a woman complained about last week's pot roast. "A grandchild by a Hungarian window washer. By the way, your aunt's cold is better. She sends her love."

"Tell her I send mine, too. And I'm really sorry if I upset you before, but I was very upset about John's death. The funeral is tomorrow. He lost all his hair and both his ears in the fire. They just burned right off. Did you ever hear of anything so terrible?"

"You mean, he's being buried without hair or ears?"

"No, he'll have them all when he's put in the grave. Josephine Jasmin just went over to the funeral parlor to pick out synthetic substitutes."

"What's a synthetic substitute?"

"Never mind, father. It's too terrible to go into. All I can say is, I'm glad I'm not much of a smoker."

"Me, too," my father said, a note of wonder in his voice.

"Hair and ears. *Zul gornisht helfen.* That's all I have to say."

After my father hung up, I called Dr. Oiseaux's office to tell him that I still hadn't gotten my period, but the nurse said he was in surgery. She suggested that I call back later in the day, any time after five.

"I want to talk to him about taking the rabbit test for pregnancy," I told her.

"How late are you?"

"I don't know. I've lost track."

"Have there been any signs of morning sickness?"

"Well, I did throw up a few minutes ago." I hesitated, not wishing to bring up the hair and ear business again. "Of course, it's not exactly morning. It's afternoon."

"You'd better talk to Dr. Oiseaux when he gets out of surgery."

I thanked her and hung up, seriously debating the wisdom of making the next phone call. On the other hand, what did I have to lose (that wasn't already lost in the disillusionment of the last two days)? Nothing, probably. But what if Paul said he didn't want to see me? Or told me he was getting married? Or worse yet, *was* already married? He could have gotten married without my knowing about it. After all, who would have to come to tell me the bad news? Nobody. Perhaps I'd been living in a dream world all this time, imagining that my second husband was still unattached and waiting patiently for me to come back to him.

Perhaps. And perhaps not. For even though my second marriage was the shortest of all four, there'd been a quality about it that the others lacked, a mysterious kind of intimacy, something primeval that I'd never understood, a meeting not of the mind, but of the genes, maybe that was finally the deepest meeting of all between a man and a woman: body chemistry that cannot be explained, the profound rationality of all our animal senses. I had a sudden, overwhelming need to make contact with Paul Bjorkman once more and find out if that chemistry still existed for me, for him. . . .

Luckily, I was saved by a knock on the door, and in came Evelyn, my lousy maid, wearing the poison-green Splendide uniform that matched Leonard Stein's carpets. Evelyn was a good-loooking black woman in (I imagined) her mid-forties. She had a lively sense of humor and knew all the hotel gossip, which she would fill me in on with great, unconcealed glee. I think the only reason she continued to work at Hotel Splendide was that the tenants, and their myriad capers, amused her so.

Despite Leonard Stein's complaints that maids' salaries had gone up twice in the past year, I doubted that Evelyn made much money at her job. She once told me she did a little hustling on the side, whenever the need for extra cash popped up. Like the time her younger brother broke his leg on a construction job, and there wasn't enough money in the family to pay for a good bone surgeon.

"I guess you've heard all about the fire by now," I said to Evelyn, who had ritualistically begun to take out the garbage.

"I sure did. You should see your ex-husband's room. You wouldn't believe it. It's one big cinder. He really did quite a job, that man. All that was left was a pair of cuff links. What was he smoking, anyway? A chimney stack?"

"Mr. Stein was telling me that it's going to cost a thousand dollars to renovate the room. He's pretty upset about the whole thing."

Evelyn paused on the threshold, my yellow garbage pail in her hand. "For once, I don't blame Scrooge for being upset. If he were smart, he'd get rid of every mattress in this hotel and replace them all with foam rubber. You've just got too many nuts living here, who fall asleep with lit cigarettes."

Then she was out the door and down the hall to the garbage disposal room, which looked like something from Dickens. When she returned, she was laughing.

"I just bumped into your friend Peggy. She was running to the communal bathroom like it was going to disappear any minute, and shouting that the evil geniuses were out to get her. Has she flipped, too?"

"You mean, like everyone else here?"

Evelyn nodded emphatically. "That's right."

"Yes, I'm afraid the spirit of Splendide has finally gotten to the poor girl. She's utterly paranoid at this point."

Evelyn had started to move the dust around with a limp rag. "You know, some days it's not entirely in your head. Some days they *are* all out to get you. And that's a fact."

"I know what you mean." I was thinking of my recent series of catastrophes. "I've had one hell of a weekend, Evelyn. These have been the worst three days in my whole life, and today isn't even over yet. I was just about to call my second husband when you came in."

"What are you calling him for? To tell him about your third husband's demise?"

I gave her a dirty look. "Don't be sarcastic."

"Who? *Me*?" She widened her eyes in mock incredulity. "Sarcastic? Not a chance."

"Oh, sure." I started to walk up and down the room, locked in deep thought. "I just have an urge to see Paul again. It's been six years since we were divorced."

"Is this the husband with the moving business?"

"If you call it a *business*."

Evelyn paused in her dusting. "He moves furniture, doesn't he?"

I paused, too. "Yes. His clientele is primarily homosexual.

At least it used to be, when we were married. Maybe all that's changed by now."

"How come? The homosexual part, I mean?"

Evelyn had resumed her dusting, and I, my walking. "It has to do with the truck he originally bought. It's a very peculiar-looking truck, and Paul named it 'The Greek' because it has a long, open rear end. The gay boys really picked up on that one, and word spread among them that when moving day rolled around, the company to call was The Green Hornet."

Evelyn looked at me with a kind of backhanded admiration. "You've led a pretty funny life, haven't you, Loretta?"

"Grotesque would be more like it."

"That's what I mean." She went into the bathroom to wash the tub, floor, and toilet bowl. There was no window in the bathroom, and when she came out, she was sweating heavily. "Aren't you ever going to get that air-conditioner of yours fixed? This place is murder."

I had no great desire to describe my unsuccessful run-in with Leonard on that score, so I merely said, "I'm working on it. I know it must be rough on you having to clean up in this heat. I'm sorry, Evelyn."

"Well, since your bed was made when I came in, I assume that at least you're not sleeping here."

"I try not to, because of the heat. I spent last night with Parker Mason. You know, the lawyer on the fifth floor."

"The nice-looking, red-haired fellow."

"That's the bastard."

"What's wrong now?"

"Everything. I think I'm pregnant."

"By Mr. Mason?"

"That's what I think. I don't even want to talk about it, Evelyn. It's all a mess. A mess! Not just the pregnancy part, either. I got a letter from my fourth husband on Saturday. He wants a divorce, so he can marry a Swedish girl named Inger."

"You're really getting it from all sides, aren't you?"

"It sure looks like it."

Evelyn had finished her cleaning chores for the day in room 701 and was about to depart. "Take it easy. Maybe you'll find out that you're not pregnant. Who knows? Maybe you'll even meet a nice man one of these years."

"Not in this crazy hotel, I won't."

She looked at me quizzically. "Then why do you continue to live here?"

"That's what my father wants to know, too. You might say I'm recuperating."

"From what?"

"My life."

After Evelyn had taken her cleaning paraphernalia and left, I very tentatively dialed Paul's number, which, to my surprise, I still remembered by heart. A man with a thick Puerto Rican accent answered the telephone.

"The Green Hornet Moving Company."

The name was funny enough all by itself, but with a Puerto Rican accent, it was even funnier. "Is Paul Bjorkman there?"

"Who's calling?"

"His ex-wife." Then I remembered that Paul had been married once before me. "Loretta."

"Just a minute, please."

There seemed to be a lot of commotion in the background, which was par for the course in Paul's business. That was one of the things I'd always liked about the Village moving companies. They operated on such a second-to-second catastrophe level that you didn't have time to contemplate your own personal catastrophes.

"That you, Loretta?"

It was definitely Paul's voice, but it sounded different somehow, more staccato. Paul had always spoken very quietly, slowly.

"It's me, all right. How are you?"

"Fine, fine, I'm just fine." His words sounded like a machine gun blast, that was how rapidly they tumbled out of his mouth. "How are you?"

"I'm okay," I said. "I was just wondering whether I could drop by this afternoon and see you for a while."

"Sure, sure, come on over. We're pretty busy here, though. I'm shooting an underground movie. It's called *A Day in the Life of a Village Mover*. But come on over, anyway, and lend moral support. We've having a ball with this flick."

Not only had his manner of speaking changed, but so had his choice of language. Definitely. The Paul Bjorkman I'd been married to would never have said, "ball" or "flick." An ominous feeling began to creep over me. Still, it was better than going to Frank Campbell's with Josephine to pick out plastic ears.

"I'll be there within half an hour," I said, little dreaming that plastic ears would have been beautiful compared to what was in store for me at The Green Hornet Moving Company.

You Said It! had a couple of surprises in store for me, too.

The first was Chip Kramer's distinct aloofness the morning I arrived at the network to make my first television appearance. He acted as though he'd met me once at the check-out section of a supermarket, and that was the beginning and end of our relationship. I felt pretty damned insulted by his attitude in view of the fact that after the KBC guidette and her entourage had left the camera room, Chip totally undressed me and put a fitting conclusion to the breast sucking foreplay.

Since I was then nineteen and had only gone to bed with two other men (Nightclub Sidney and my college boyfriend, Marathon Mike), I didn't have too much basis for sexual comparison, but even with my limited experience it was pretty obvious that Chip Kramer knew what he was about.

Unfortunately, I didn't have an orgasm. A wooden crate is not the most comfortable place on which to make love, and I kept thinking that I'd get a splinter in my ass. I was also unsettled by the possibility that the door to the camera room would open again any minute and another guided tour would come marching in. Neither of my fears was realized, I'm happy to say, but I still felt a great deal of anxiety throughout the entire time Chip was making love to me. He, on the other hand, seemed as totally relaxed and uninhibited as though he were home in his own bed. My first husband might have had a lot of serious faults, but lack of nerve was not one of them.

The second surprise waiting for me on You Said It! was meeting the handsome celebrity guest who would work with me, as a team, when playing the game on television. Chip introduced us.

"Loretta, I'd like you to meet the hottest new movie actor in Hollywood, Mick Donway. Mick, this is Loretta Silverman."

Mick and I looked at each other and burst out laughing. It was none other than Murray Derfler, who'd grown up three blocks away from me in The Bronx. We had gone to the same grade school and high school, Mick two classes ahead of me, and always very condescending because of his seniority. His arrogance used to infuriate me, particularly when I was my teens, since I was the acknowledged beauty of my high school and all the boys were killing themselves to get a date with

Loretta Silverman, professional virgin. All the boys except Murray Derfler, who I now noticed had had his hair straightened and lightened.

"What's so funny?" Chip wanted to know, as Murray, I mean Mick, and I were in hysterics.

I recovered first. "Mick and I are old friends. We went to school together." I figured it was strategic to omit any references to one Murray Derfler. "This is the first time we've seen each other in years. It's a funny coincidence."

"It sure is," Mick said, still laughing. "How've you been, Loretta?"

"Fine. Great. I've been going to college in Iowa for the last year and a half."

"You're looking wonderful. How are your parents?"

I was just about to say that they were okay, when I remembered my mother was supposed to have a fatal illness. "It's a long story," I said, trying to appear solemn. "I'll tell you later." I really didn't want to compound the lie I had told to Chip any more than was necessary. "How are *your* parents?"

Even though Mick had never dated me, our parents knew each other because they went to the same synagogue, and both our fathers used to play gin rummy at the local Liberal Party club on Allerton Avenue.

"Oh, Mom and Dad are all excited about my career," Mick said. "I'm in New York for the premier of my new movie. It's called *Save a Kiss for Katie*. I co-star with Debbie Reynolds. It was really a great break, getting this part and working with Debbie. She's a very warm human being."

Despite the fact that he'd changed his name, had his hair straightened and lightened, and actually *looked* like a movie star, he was still just as full of shit as when he was plain Murray Derfler who used to tell everyone at school that he was descended from a royal Egyptian family and that his parents weren't his real parents. His real parents, Murray used to insist, had been killed in Cairo when he was a child. They'd been killed in a political upheaval and he was subsequently sent to an adoption agency in the United States by a concerned uncle (who was also killed later), and it was at the adoption agency that the childless Derflers found him.

A lot of the kids at school used to call him Anastasia behind his back, although I think that in secret we admired his verve and imagination in making up such an outlandish story and fully expecting everyone to believe it. I guess it was inevitable that Murray Derfler should have become an actor and made his talent for fantasy pay off professionally.

"Congratulations on your movie," I said. "It all sounds very exciting."

"It certainly does," Chip added. "And I'm sure you'll get wonderful reviews. Now shall we go over to the studio and run through a rehearsal for You Said It!?"

There were two other couple-teams who would be on the show with us, and in each case one of the two was a celebrity of some sort. One of the other girls was a popular singer, and one of the men was a pro football player. The attractive brunette whom I'd seen that day at the RCA Exhibition Center was a contestant, and also a man I'd never before laid eyes on. We would all be competing for the prize merchandise, Chip explained as we went across the street to the studio they used for this particular show. Naturally, the celebrities didn't give a damn about the merchandise, they were there to plug something, like Mick and his movie.

You Said It! turned out to be a quotation game. The six of us were seated on a dais in front of a live studio audience and beneath the hottest, most blinding lights I had ever felt. It was hard to see the audience because the lights were so glaring, but you knew they were there and you knew damn well they could see you, which made it kind of nerve wracking. I found it interesting that, of the six of us, it was the three celebrities who seemed the most tense and keyed up. But then, it figured. They were on professional display, whereas the rest of us had nothing to lose except the prize merchandise. Chip then introduced us, by name, to the studio audience, and explained the rules of the game.

"The questions on this show will be asked of each team separately. Today we're going to start off with Loretta and Mick. You will both get the beginning of the first famous quotation, and then it will be up to the two of you to supply the ending of the quote, as well as the source. For instance, the host of the show, who'll be out in a few minutes, might say: There is nothing to fear but ———"

"Fear itself," I quickly answered.

"Franklin Delano Roosevelt," Mick said.

"You Said It!" Chip grinned. "Now if you answer correctly, as you just have, you get a chance at another quote. If you answer incorrectly, or not at all, we go on to the next couple." He motioned to the attractive brunette and the football player, who were sitting next to Mick and me. "However, each couple can only be asked three quotes in a row, and then Jason James, the host of the show, will automatically go on to the next couple to give them a chance to play You Said It! For every right answer each couple gets fifty points. If you only get one part of the answer right, like you know the end of the quote but you don't know the source, you get twenty-five points, and we go on to the next couple. The couple with the most points at the end of the show, wins, let's see . . ."

Chip glanced at some notes he had in his hand. "Today we're giving away to the highest scoring team a Whirlpool washing machine with permanent press cycles, or a trip to

Hawaii for two, courtesy of Pan American Airlines, or a matching set of Leed's luggage. Each member of the winning team has his and her choice of the three wonderful prizes we're offering today. For the other two couples, there will be prize compensations on a more modest level. But Jason James will tell you all about that when he joins us in a just a few minutes. Now, are there any questions from the contestants?"

The football player spoke up. "What if only one person from a team supplies both parts of the answer? Does the team still win fifty points? Or do both contestants on the team have to pitch in?"

"Good question," Chip said. "One person can answer, and the team will still get fifty points. Assuming, of course, that he or she answers correctly. The other thing I want to tell you is that you will have fifteen seconds in which to finish the quote and identify the source. Fifteen. That's all. Now, does anybody else have a question?"

We all looked at each other, but I was the only one with a pressing question. "Where's the bathroom?" I asked.

When I returned from the bathroom, Chip had disappeared and Jason James, host of You Said It!, was on stage, kidding around and warming up the studio audience with lots of corny folk humor. After a few minutes of making everyone feel jolly, it was air time. The eye of one of the cameras turned red, an engineer threw a hand signal, a record played a couple of fast, blaring bars from "Happy Days Are Here Again," and Jason James (who looked and acted as though he'd just swallowed five dexies), stepped briskly to the center of the stage.

"Yeah, yeah, yeah!" he said, with enough exuberance to choke a horse. "Welcome to You Said It!, the game show that makes everyone feel happy! We have six wonderful contestants with us this morning, all of them rarin' to go, rarin' to tackle our tricky quotes, and rarin' to win the wonderful prizes we're giving away—today—on You Said It!"

We were all seated behind mock desks, one couple to a desk, a microphone at our mouths. Our first names were printed on the front of the desk, facing the viewers, and between the two names there was a large, empty, square space which, Chip had explained, would eventually show the number of points we were scoring as a team. After Jason James officially introduced us to the television audience, he stopped for a taped baby food commercial, and I turned to Mick.

"Let's win this game, Moish."

"Mick," he corrected me, in his new Hollywood twang. "Of course, we're going to win. I'm a winner, baby."

As Chip had said, Mick and I would be given the first quotation, and when we were back on the air, Jason James said to us, "Okay, Loretta and Mick, are you ready to try for your first fifty points?"

"We're ready," Mick replied, smiling engagingly at the camera.

"Here we go! For your first fifty points, finish this quotation for me, and tell me who said it: "Scarlett O'Hara was not ———.' "

"Beautiful," I replied in one second flat. "Margaret Mitchell."

"You Said It! for fifty points," Jason James cried, beside himself with enthusiasm. "That was the first line of *Gone With The Wind*, folks. Okay, here's your next quote, Loretta and Mick: 'War is ———.' "

This time, Mick jumped right in. "Hell. General William Tecumseh Sherman."

"You Said It! Loretta and Mick are really rolling along. They now have one hundred beautiful points. And here is your third quote, for a total of one hundred and fifty points and a chance at the wonderful prizes we're offering today: 'Let them eat ———.' "

"Cake," Mick said.

"Marie Antoinette," I said, thinking of the movie with Norma Shearer.

"You Said It!" Jason James screamed.

Mick and I smiled happily at the camera. Old Murray Derfler and I were on our way to being big-time winners on the dopiest television show in the world.

The game went on. And actually it was pretty damned funny at times. The attractive brunette and pro football player were next in line for the tricky quote.

Jason James said, "Okay, here it is: 'Something is rotten in the state of ———.' "

"Nebraska," replied the brunette, obviously in a state of shock.

Dazed by this unexpected turn of events, the pro football player said, "William Shakespeare."

Jason James looked appropriately chagrined. "Gee, I'm sorry, folks, but you only guessed one half of it. Gee, that's too bad, but don't be too upset because you will both have another chance to play You Said It! And you do get twenty-five points for being half right."

Here are some of the other quotes that were used on the show that memorable day.

"Give me liberty, or give me ———."

"In the dark night of the soul, it's always ———."

"But that was in another country, and besides ———."

"Play it again, ———."

"I regret that I have only one life to ———."

"It is better to have loved and lost than ———."

"Walk softly, but carry ———."

"Ah, what a dusty answer gets the soul when ———."

"The only thing that's changed about sex in two thousand years is ———."

It was all over much sooner than I'd expected. Television time had surely fled, and Mick and I turned out to be the big winners of You Said It! that we had planned to be at the outset. But then a strange thing happened when the prizes were offered to us and we each had to make a weighty decision as to what, specifically, we wanted. Jason James asked me first.

"What's your heart's desire, Loretta?"

I felt like saying, "Chip Kramer," who had not been seen or heard from since taking the six of us through the warm-up of the show. The man I was going to marry, and he had neatly disappeared. Where was he? Would I ever see him again? Did he care for me at all? How many other unsuspecting women had he made love to in the Eyemo camera room?

"I'll take the Whirlpool washing machine," I said, stunned by the sound of my own voice, my own choice (I'd been planning on the trip to Hawaii for two).

Even Jason James looked surprised. "Marvelous, Loretta. A washing machine. That's very practical, very domestic. Are you, by any chance, planning to get married?"

Still operating by some weird instinct, I said, "Yes, Jason, yes I am. I'm marrying Chip Kramer in June." Then I laughed, idiotically. "I'm going to be a June bride. Congratulate me."

But Jason James was so startled that there was one second of dead air. Then he recovered. "Chip Kramer? Loretta, did I hear you say, Chip Kramer, the Contestant Coordinator of You Said It!?"

"You bet your life you did."

"Folks, this is a television first!" screamed the host. "This lovely young girl sitting here, who has just won a Whirlpool washing machine is going to marry the handsome Contestant

Coordinator of You Said It! Does that deserve a round of enthusiastic and well deserved applause? Does it?"

The glittery sign flashed on in the studio, and all the morons who had come to see the show duly started to applaud for all they were worth. Even Mick had stopped smiling at the camera long enough to give me a look of sheer admiration/envy/hate (how could I have topped him like this?).

"When did you two kids . . . meet . . . get together?" asked Jason James, who was now certain that he'd go down in television's hall of fame as a result of having accidentally fallen privy to this romantic escapade.

"We met in the RCA Exhibition Hall," I said, playing it for all it was worth. "Chip picked me up. I mean, he approached me and asked whether I wanted to be a contestant on You Said It!, and I said yes."

"Folks, are you hearing what I'm hearing?" Jason James asked. "Is this, or is this not the television romance of all time? To *beat* all time?"

The glittery "applause" sign went on once more.

"Where's Chip Kramer?" Jason James called out. "Are you backstage, Chip? Come on out, if you are."

What have I done, I said to myself, as a bewildered Chip emerged from behind the drapes. After we were married, Chip confessed that he'd been too bewildered at the time to be angry at me.

"I was just flabbergasted," he said, "hearing you announce our wedding plans, and not just on television but *network* television. Wow. I don't think I knew what I was doing when I walked out on that stage."

"Here he is, folks," Jason James beamed. "The future husband of Loretta Silverman. My congratulations to you both. Tell me, Chip, have you started to get the pre-wedding jitters yet?"

Chip looked at me as though he'd been hit over the head with a lead pipe. "Yes, Jason, I am a bit nervous, I must admit. It's not every day that a man gets married."

"We only have a few seconds left," Jason James said. "Chip, how about giving Loretta a big kiss for our millions of television viewers? How about that, folks?"

The applause sign flashed on. Chip kissed me to the sound of the heaviest clapping I have ever heard, and stuck his tongue so far down my throat that I nearly gagged. It was easily the most unfriendly kiss I'd ever received in my life.

Then we were off the air.

I left Hotel Splendide and took a taxi downtown to Washington Street, where The Green Hornet Moving Company was located. At first, I let a few cabs go by, hoping to find an air-conditioned one that was free, but after a couple of minutes of sweating in the intense heat, I gave up and hailed a yellow cab that had its windows open.

"They say it's going to hit a hundred today," the driver informed me as we swung down Broadway, the sun baking the windows and roof of the cab. "This has turned out to be one of the hottest summers I can remember, and it's only the middle of July. Think! We have at least another month and a half of roasting to death, and probably more than that. September is nothing to write home about when it comes to being hot. I guess you've got an air-conditioner in your apartment, though."

"I do, but it happens to be broken at the moment."

"You'd better get it fixed, lady. One hundred degrees today."

If there's one thing I can live without, it's cabdriver conversation, yet on some perverse level, I always provoke them to talk still more. By the time we got to Washington Street, near the docks, I practically knew the story of the driver's life, a soap opera like so many others.

"There it is," I said, pointing to Paul's five-story warehouse and moving company. "Where those men are loading the van."

"That truck has a funny shape."

"It sure does."

The Greek. So Paul still had it after all these years. It had been painted a bright yellow, and the Green Hornet name was now hand-lettered across the side in an artistic, antique script, but with its distinctive and unusual proportions, there could be no doubt that it was The Greek. I paid the driver and got out. Three Puerto Ricans were moving a storage lot from the warehouse into the long, high truck, moving and sweating under the glaring sun, white handkerchiefs tied around their foreheads like hospital bandages. On the sidewalk, between the warehouse and the truck, a fourth Puerto Rican was recording their movements with a movie camera. *A Day in the Life of a Village Mover.* This, undoubtedly, was the underground movie Paul had referred to on the telephone.

Then I spotted Paul himself, directing both the move and the movie. He was standing against the side of the building, wearing a familiar denim shirt and blue corduroy pants. He still had the same great moustache, and his dark blond hair was as thick and leonine as ever, but he weighed at least twenty pounds less than when we were married, and it did not become him. He was definitely too thin, not at all the healthy, hardy-looking man I remembered. When I got closer, I saw that he had three strands of love beads around his neck, and so did the cameraman, who was quite handsome.

"Paul. Hello."

My second husband looked at me sharply, his eyes very bright. Then he broke out in a warm, welcoming smile.

"Hey, Loretta baby, how are you?" He kissed me quickly on the cheek, and turned to the cameraman. "Juanito, did you get that part where Henry nearly dropped the bureau on the tailgate?"

"Man, I got it all. *Todo está seguro.*"

"You look sensational," Paul said to me, "absolutely sensational. How've you been? What's up? What do you think of this movie I'm directing? Pretty cuckoo idea, isn't it?"

He spoke just as he had earlier on the telephone, very fast, the words tumbling out of his mouth with an unnatural and disturbing rapidity. How can he have changed so much, I wondered? More importantly, *why*?

"It's sort of odd," I said, "your combining the moving business with the movie business. What prompted you to do it?"

He opened his mouth, as if to reply, then stopped and said instead, "What's Billy up to these days? Has he cut any good records lately?"

"Billy and his group are playing in Stockholm. They've been there six months now. I don't know if they've made any records lately."

Two of the Puerto Rican movers now picked up their straps, dollies, and pads and began to head back toward the warehouse as the third mover continued to load the truck. When Paul and I were married, I remembered him telling me that one of the toughest things about the moving business was finding a man who really knew how to load a truck so as to make the most of all available space and, at the same time, arrange and stack the customer's belongings with the least threat to their being broken or damaged en route.

"Get the refrigerators next," Paul told the two movers

going into the warehouse, while to Juanito he said, "Get a shot of them going into the warehouse, then switch to Henry in the truck. I'll tell you when they're coming out again."

"I got you, man."

"Juanito usually drives for me," Paul said, "but today we're going to let Henry do the driving. Juanito and I will follow behind in my car, so we can film them going through traffic. When you get right down to it, there's not that much difference between the moving business and the movie business, is there?"

I was about to say that there seemed to be a considerable difference to me, when Paul abruptly walked over to Juanito and had a hurried conversation with him that I could not hear. Then tenderly, affectionately, he brushed a strand of hair away from Juanito's eyes, did a fast little dance step on the pavement of Washington Street, and returned to me, wetting his lips with his tongue.

"Are you thirsty?" I asked. "It's so hot. I don't know how you can stand out here in this heat. Can't you take a break and we'll go get a Coke, or something?"

"No time, baby. Can't waste time." He wet his lips again. "I've got to finish this movie today." The door to the warehouse started to creak open. "Here they come, Juanito. Get that damn camera on them. Fast!"

The two movers emerged, this time each of them with a half-size refrigerator strapped to his back, the same kind of refrigerator that I had in my kitchenette at Hotel Splendide. Although I'd left the hotel only a little while ago, I was starting to miss it already, the familiarity of it, the womb-like warmth, the protectiveness of known surroundings, my crazy friends. I wondered how Josephine was making out with plastic ears at Frank Campbell's, whether Daffodil and I. C.

Ring were still going at it on the other side of the wall, what paranoia Peggy was experiencing.

I felt pretty paranoid myself at the moment, vulnerable and exposed, my heart anxiously pounding in my chest. Paul's attitude toward me today had come as a distinct shock. It was as though he'd never loved me, never known me, never begged me to leave Chip and marry him. I might just have been a vague acquaintance to him, instead of the wife he once was so sensuously involved with. I remembered the hours of love-making, and the hours afterward when we had slept locked in each other's arms, Paul breathing quietly in my ear. Why had I left him for John? John who was now dead. Why had I done it? Couldn't I stick with any man? And now Billy had left me. It was all such a mess. A *needless* mess? That was the part that hurt, that terrible possibility.

When I told Chip that I was leaving him for Paul Bjorkman, Chip had said, "Bjorkman? That's an odd name."

"It's Swedish. I mean, he was born in this country, in California, but he's of Swedish descent."

"Protestants make lousy husbands."

"How do you know? What the hell do you know about Protestants?"

"Plenty," Chip Kramer said, with his usual air of assurance. "And I'll tell you this. You'll be sorry you left me, Loretta, you really will. You'll live to regret it. Just remember—only Jewish men take out the garbage."

Chip turned out to be wrong in that respect, Paul had no compunction whatsoever when it came to taking out the garbage, but I did notice a couple of interesting differences between him and Chip, sexually, and at the time I passed them off as purely individual personality differences. But lately, I've begun to believe there is a distinct ethnic basis to them. For instance, Chip always wanted me to go down on him, whereas

Paul always wanted to go down on me. The reason I have since come to this ethnic conclusion is that in the six months that I've been living at Hotel Splendide, I have gone to bed with any number of both Jewish and Protestant men, and invariably the same sexual rule seems to apply. Jewish men have an absolutely frenzied need to be gone down on, and Protestant men have the same need to go down on you. Don't ask me why. In fact, if anyone ever figures out the reason for this fascinating phenomenon, I sure wish they'd drop a note to Loretta Silverman and let her know.

"Faster! Faster!" Paul was shouting to the two movers carrying the refrigerators. "Can't you go any faster?"

One of them stopped in the middle of the pavement. "If we go any faster, we're all going to have congestive heart attacks. Besides, my hernia hurts. I'm putting in for workman's comp."

"Faster!"

"I have a suggestion," I said to Paul, who was jumping up and down now. "After they get through loading the truck, why don't you reverse the reel? That way, they'll be seen taking the furniture back into the warehouse, backward. It would be very funny, especially if you speeded it up."

"We're only interested in realism around here, not stagey effects." He turned to the cameraman. "Juanito, as soon as Henry gets those refrigerators into the truck, run over with your camera and shoot the interior of the truck. Get a couple of good shots of the way the truck is now loaded. See where he puts the refrigerators. See what he's done with that long, oval mirror. The next thing the men are bringing down are the dummies."

"What dummies?" I said.

"Oh, they're mannequins. This guy we're taking out of storage is a dress designer. He's . . ." Again, my second husband seemed to drift off into oblivion, and again, he wet his lips, which were cracked and dry. "Are you still at the network, Loretta?"

"Yes, same job, but I make more money now."

"So what? All you do is pay more income tax. Do you know why New York State income tax is so high? I'll bet you don't know. It's all because of that damned Rockefeller. He's a Communist."

"Nelson Rockefeller?"

"Sure, he's stealing your income tax money. He sends it to Mao Tse-tung, in gold bullion. What do you think of that?"

"It's a very interesting theory."

But Paul seemed to have lost interest in Nelson Rockefeller. "Isn't that Juanito a handsome son of a bitch? He's a good cameraman, too. I'm a lucky son of a bitch to have found him."

I figured it was now or never. "Paul, it looks like I'm getting divorced. Billy has left me."

"Billy?"

"Billy Ray. My husband."

"How many times have you been married?"

"You know I've been married four times, Paul. You moved me into Billy's studio yourself. I mean, The Green Hornet did. Don't you remember? And you gave me that nice wicker rocking chair as a gift."

"Oh, yeah. Sure. Right. Hey, what time is it?"

I looked at my watch, a wedding present from John. "A quarter after four."

"That's funny. I seem to have lost a couple of hours." He pointed to The Greek. "What do you think of my new van?"

"I thought it was your old van."

"That's the point. You got it, baby. That's the whole point. It *is* my old van. But Juanito painted it, and did the antique lettering on it himself."

"He's a real triple threat, isn't he? A mover, a cameraman, and a hand letterer?"

Oblivious to my sarcasm, Paul replied, "Yes, he's wonderful, so talented, so handsome, I don't know what I'd do without him. I rely on him so."

The ghastly truth was beginning to dawn upon me, and I could hardly believe it. Paul, a homosexual! It was too much to absorb after all the shocking and traumatic happenings of the past two days.

"Are you and Juanito . . .?" I started to say, then stopped, too afraid to go on for fear of what his answer would be.

"Are we making it?" Paul asked. "Is that what you're trying to say?"

"Yes."

"Sure we are, baby. But don't look so surprised. You must have always known that I swung both ways."

"You mean, even when we were married?"

"Wait a minute." Paul shook his head. "Did those two guys go back to get the dummies? Where are they?"

"Of course, they went back. You sent them back. They're in the warehouse, getting them right now. What do you mean, *I must have known*?"

"Known?" He looked confused. "Known what?"

"That you made it with men, for Christ's sake. What's the matter with you, Paul? You can't seem to remember anything for longer than one second. Are you ill? I've never seen you like this. And you're so thin. Are you sure you're okay?"

"I'm great. Fine. Wonderful. Wunderbar. Now what the hell were we talking about?"

It was no use, hopeless. This was not the man I'd been

married to, not the man I'd loved, certainly not the man I'd ever undertsood. His primarily homosexual clientele. Why hadn't I guessed long before this? Had he gone to bed with other men while we were married? During the day, when I was at the network? It would have been convenient enough, what with our apartment being right in the warehouse. Other men. In my bed. And I'd never even *suspected.*

Paul took two pieces of bubble gum out of his pocket, and handed one to me. "Here. Make a bubble."

Dazed, I took off the paper wrapper and put the gum in my mouth. Then I looked at the wrapper which had a cartoon printed on it, as well as something called "Your personal fortune." It said, *The thrilling life of a circus performer will one day be yours.* I started to chew the dry, hard, sweet gum as the movers came out of the warehouse, each of them carrying two naked dummies by the neck. That was me, a dummy, only I had clothes on.

"I think I'll be leaving," I said to Paul, who was too busy watching Juanito shoot the dummy scene to hear me. "Paul, I've got to go."

"What?"

"I said I have to be leaving. I have an appointment."

"That's too bad. It's been great seeing you, though. Drop over any time you're in the neighborhood again."

He had never even asked where I was living. "I wasn't *in* the neighborhood. I live uptown."

"Yeah, well . . ." His voice trailed off. "Hey, Juanito, as soon as you're through with this scene, let's run up to the office for a few minutes. Give the guys a chance to catch their breath. I want you to shoot a few office interiors. You know, me at the desk, answering the phone, booking jobs, that stuff."

"I dig."

"I want the camera to follow me up the stairs. No cinematic editorializing. Just *follow* me as I go up."

"I'll be right behind you, man," Juanito said. "And when we get to the promised land, let's take another shot."

I turned to Paul in one last attempt at communication. "Oh Paul, you haven't begun drinking after all these years, have you?"

A bubble came out of his mouth, big and pink, only to snap and die an instant later. "Speed, baby, not booze."

Monday Evening

BY the time I got back to the hotel, it was after six. My meeting with Paul had been so depressing that, upon leaving him, I decided to go see *Bob and Carol and Ted and Alice* at one of those deliciously air-conditioned East Side movie houses. There was nothing like a good movie to take your mind off everything you didn't want to think about, and you must admit that in my case total amnesia would have been a blessing, if only I could achieve it.

I really loved *Bob and Carol and Ted and Alice*, particularly the scene at the end where all four of them wind up in bed in a hotel room in Las Vegas, and Robert Culp says something like, "Sure, first we're going to have an orgy, and then we're going to go hear Tony Bennett." I wished I were in Las Vegas at that moment, I wished I were Natalie Wood, or Dyan Cannon, anybody but Loretta Silverman, the girl who definitely did not seem to be succeeding at anything.

When I came out of the movie house into the oppressive summer heat, I took a cab to Hotel Splendide, wondering what to do with myself for the rest of the evening. My swollen breasts felt even more swollen than ever, as they strained against the clammy linen dress I'd been wearing since that morning when I tried to get Leonard Stein to fix my air-conditioner. The day seemed very long, so many catastrophes having been compressed into it. Husbands number two and three shot to hell, which naturally made me think of husbands number one and four. Chip was probably in Saratoga, playing the horses. When we were married, I used to give him a hard time because of his compulsive betting habits, but after today I realized it was certainly better to be a gambler than a dead man like John, or a faggot speed freak like Paul.

As for Billy Ray in Stockholm, well . . . I'd find out soon enough from Parker whether or not he could divorce me without my consent. But even if he couldn't, I had lost him anyway. He didn't have to *marry* Inger, he could just live with her. No matter how you looked at it, Loretta Silverman was manless for the first time since she'd discovered men.

When my cab pulled up to Splendide, I gave the driver a big smile and an extra large tip. "Pray for winter," I said, stepping out of the smothering car into the smothering lobby of the hotel. The first person I was saw Zachary, waiting for the elevator. He had a frog in a mayonnaise jar and seemed somewhat forlorn.

"I just came back from Frank Campbell's," he said. "You don't know what depression is until you've looked at a hundred plastic ears. Your friend Josephine will tell you all about it. She's in the bar. Me, I'm going upstairs and turn on. Wipe it all out."

I had planned to go upstairs, too, and change my clothes, but the thought of facing Torrid Zone struck me as too damned bleak, particuarly since I now had the excuse of joining Josephine at the air-conditioned bar and learning how she had fared at New York's most respected funeral institution.

"Is that a new frog?" I asked Zachary.

"No, that's Harold. He likes to go out once in a while. I do have a new iguana, though. Do you like iguanas?"

"I can't stand them. They remind me of Parker Mason."

"I never thought of it that way," Zachary said, disappearing into the elevator.

Before going into the bar, I stopped at the desk to see if I had any mail. There was a renewal notice from *Variety* and a message from Parker Mason saying that he had tried to call me at five after four, and would get in touch with me later. Probably to tell me the news concerning Swedish divorce laws. The way my luck had been running lately, it was bound to be grim news, which reminded me that I was supposed to call Dr. Oiseaux about taking a rabbit test. I ducked into the public telephone booth in the lobby and dialed his number.

"If those pills I gave you didn't work, that's a bad sign," Dr. Oiseaux said, in his heavily accented voice. "You'd better come in tomorrow for an examination and a rabbit test. Can you make it after work?"

I tried to remember who I had booked for tomorrow night's show, and whether I would have to hang around for the taping at eight. Oh, yes. Huntley and Brinkley, neither of whom would require any hand-holding, thank God.

"I can make it about six," I told Dr. Oiseaux. "Is that all right?"

"Six is fine, Loretta. I'll see you then."

"Thank you."

I hung up and thought of my agenda for tomorrow. A funeral at three o'clock, and a pregnancy test at six. There was something decidedly morbid about the coincidence of both events taking place the same day. One person, whom I had cared about very much, was leaving this earth. Another person, whom I would care about even more, was possibly going to enter it. I wondered whether it would be a boy or a girl.

"In case anyone wants me, I'll be at the bar," I told Annabelle, who had her hands full at Splendide's obsolete switchboard, which Leonard Stein refused to replace with a more contemporary model, for monetary reasons known to all us resident-inmates.

"Don't drink too many Papa Dobles," Annabelle called back.

I put on my sunglasses, which were in my purse, in an attempt to delude myself that it was dark in La Chiripa. Thanks to Daylight Saving Time, it wasn't, and I've always found it depressing to sit at a bar when it was still sunny outside. Josephine looked as though she found it depressing too, because she had seated herself at the very end of the bar, which was as far away from the windows as you could get. A couple of men I didn't know were at the other end, and the restaurant side was relatively quiet. La Chiripa didn't pick up much steam until at least seven or eight in the evening.

"Oh, am I glad to see you," Josephine said, as I slid onto a stool beside her. "It was even worse than I'd anticipated. What are you drinking?"

She was drinking a Papa Doble, and something told me it wasn't her first. Carlos Santiago, who owned the dump, stood behind the bar, waiting for my order.

"I'll have a Papa Doble, too," I said, forfeiting my usual ginger ale in respect for the day's cataclysmic events.

Carlos gave me the typically insecure and nervous smile he reserved for all unescorted women who might, potentially, cause trouble. I smiled back.

"Where are all the free hot hors d'oeuvres?" I asked, when he placed the double daiquiri before me.

His smile grew very painful, since the concept of free hors d'oeuvres, either hot *or* cold, was an alien to him as fixing my air-conditioner was to Leonard Stein. Carlos had never been known to give his best customer so much as a stale pretzel, let alone buy anyone a drink.

"If you don't want to serve hot hors d'oeuvres," I went on, "when are you going to start filling those empty lobster shells in the paella? You don't even have to fill them with lobster. How about cream cheese? Pickled herring? A little chopped liver, maybe? Think about it."

Carlos looked as though he were thinking about something other than lobster shells at the moment, namely how he wished I would disappear forever and stop needling him. Instead of answering me, he walked discreetly to the other end of the bar where the two men were sitting.

"I've never seen anything like it in my life," Josephine said, clutching her perfumed handkerchief. "But never. Even Zachary, who has a strong stomach, said afterward that he felt ill."

"You mean the plastic ears?"

"They were hanging on a big wall display. There must have been a hundred of them. Small ones, large ones, wrinkled ones, long ear lobes, short ear lobes, stickout ears, and different skin colors. There was even a black ear hanging there, amidst all the Caucasians. I guess they don't do much business with the black community."

"It sounds ghastly."

"It was so awful that I arbitrarily pointed to the first ear that wasn't too wrinkled and said it would do. Then came the toupee selection. For some reason, the cosmetician kept trying to get us to buy a toupee that had a sprinkling of grayish hairs mixed in among the black. You know, mostly at the sides. I told him that John didn't have a gray hair in his head, but he was very persistent. He said things like, 'It would be much nicer if the departed looked somewhat distinguished when he crosses The Great Divide.' "

"Did he actually use those words? *The Great Divide*?"

"More than once." Josephine dabbed at her moist eyes and motioned to Carlos for another round of drinks. "In referring to John's death, he also said, 'The departed will soon be joining The Grand Majority.' Do you believe it? If Zachary and I hadn't been so depressed by the ears and toupees, we would have burst out laughing. Except it wasn't the least bit funny. Poor John. Little does he know that he's going to be put into the grave tomorrow with plastic ears and graying hair."

"I've got a wonderful day tomorrow." I could feel the effects of the second drink, and realized that I hadn't eaten anything since the paella last night (which I'd thrown up this afternoon). "A funeral at three o'clock, and a rabbit test at six."

Josephine started to sob openly now. "I miss him so, Loretta. I miss him so much. I don't even have the comfort of my daughter's company. I haven't laid eyes on her since the fire last night. She's undoubtedly still locked up with that Chinese double-crosser, screwing and smoking her brains out. Or, I should say, what's left of them. Frankly, I wish she'd go back to her boyfriend in Berkeley. Her presence here inhibits me."

"How?"

"Oh, I don't know. I don't feel sexually free when Daffodil is around. I'd feel funny about going to bed with someone."

"But she's not really *around*. You yourself just said that you haven't seen her all day, so how can she possibly inhibit you? Besides, you don't have a man at the moment for her to inhibit you *with*."

"Thanks. Thanks for reminding me, for rubbing it in. Thanks a lot. Very kind of you, Loretta."

One of the men at the end of the bar got up to play the jukebox, and I realized that he was quite attractive. Tall, with sandy hair, and an aristocratic nose. He was wearing chinos, and a blue-and-white horizontally striped pullover that had a crew neckline. Most of the records on La Chiripa's jukebox were of the Spanish variety, all about *mi corazón, mi alma, linda linda, mi amor*, but he chose the Peter, Paul, and Mary version of "Leaving on a Jet Plane,"* which just happened to be my latest favorite song.

So kiss me and smile for me
Tell me that you'll wait for me
Hold me like you'll never let me go
I'm a-leaving on a jet plane
Don't know when I'll be back again. . . .

He saw me watching him as he walked back to join his friend at the bar, and he smiled at me.

So kiss me and smile for me
Tell me that you'll wait for me

I wondered whether he was married, or otherwise had someone waiting for him. Even if he did, it seemed apparent that he found me attractive, which immediately lifted my sagging spirits. Loretta Silverman might be manless at the moment, but she hadn't completely lost her touch when it came to the opposite sex—he was making that very clear.

"Are you flirting with that man?" Josephine asked.

"I sure am. Don't you think he's attractive?"

"I'm nearsighted. I can't tell."

"I never knew you were nearsighted. Why don't you wear glasses?"

"Vanity. Loretta, will you please stop looking at that man."

"Why? Are you jealous?"

"If you go to bed with him, I'll never speak to you again."

"So what? Who cares?"

"*Who cares*? What kind of remark is that? You're supposed to be my friend. You're supposed to care. Don't you have any sense of allegiance to your friends? Don't you realize what I've gone through today? What kind of person are you?"

"A flirtatious one."

I was trying to figure out what to do with the sandy-haired man. Should I go over and ask him for a cigarette? Maybe I should take a more direct approach, like just going over and asking him and his friend to join us. Carlos Santiago would have a heart attack. At times, I had the distinct impression that he secretly thought I was a call girl and used La Chiripa's bar as my headquarters for picking up men.

Because of Carlos' medieval Cuban mentality, he found it hard to believe that any young, attractive girl could have the kind of responsible, high-paying job that I had. It just didn't add up, in his mind. Women, to Carlos, were either wives and mothers who stayed home, or else if they weren't married and had to work, they were typists or switchboard operators like Annabelle. If a woman fit into neither of those categories, she was a whore. That was the extent of Carlos' great Batista-like insight into women, the stupid bastard.

"Look," Josephine said, triumphantly. "They're leaving. You didn't work fast enough."

She was right. Sure enough, the two men were paying the bill, getting up, and walking out, and the sandy-haired one didn't so much as give me a backward glance. Foiled again, I motioned to Carlos for a third Papa Doble. I was drunk and I didn't care, I wanted to get still drunker, I wanted to drown in alcohol, I wanted to be obliterated by it, wiped out, so I wouldn't have to think about the incredible number of rejections I had received, starting with Billy's letter Saturday night.

"What did your second husband want to see you about?" Josephine asked.

"He wanted my advice on a movie he's directing."

"Oh, is that all?"

"No, it's not all. It turns out that Paul is hooked on speed, and has fallen in love with one of his Puerto Rican moving men, who's now a cameraman. That's enough to give anyone a jolt, wouldn't you say? I still haven't recovered from the shock of it."

"But why should you care? You divorced Paul years ago. You're not emotionally involved with him any more. What's the difference to you what he's hooked on, or who he's in love with?"

"Never mind. You wouldn't understand."

I was too proud to admit the desperation of my search for one man who gave a damn whether I lived or died. One man. Was that asking too much? Apparently. For some peculiar reason, I remembered Paul once telling me that before he became a shoe buyer at Lord & Taylor, he was a male model, and before that, a public relations man for a rubber band manufacturer. If you took all four of my husbands and put their occupations together, the list would read like the classified employment section of *The New York Times,* of which my favorite fantasy job was "Skip Tracer."

"I never should have divorced Chip Kramer," I heard

myself say. "My father is right. That was my big mistake. So what if he went in for gambling and enemas? Are those any worse than the weirdo inclinations of my other husbands?"

"I wouldn't know, and frankly I'm not too interested in listening to you rave on about your husbands. That seems to be all you ever talk about. Husband number one, husband number two, bla, bla, bla, it's very boring. You have to realize, Loretta, that except for husband number three, I've never met any of the others, so it's hard for me to get worked up over them. Why don't you talk about Parker? That's who you should be expending your energies on. I can't stand the son of a bitch, but it's obvious he has a crush on you."

"It is? It's not the least bit obvious to me. I told you how he reacted when I said that I might be pregnant with his child. *Nada*. No empathy. No sympathy. I might as well have been talking about cheese blintzes, for all the good it did me. He's like Leonard Stein. He has a stone for a heart. That's why Parker understands Leonard's lack of compassion so well—because he's exactly the same way. If he cared anything at all about me, do you think he would have marched off to his law office this morning without so much as a word as to when he was going to see me again?"

"Don't be ridiculous." To Josephine, only her own problems were real; everyone else's were imaginary problems. "You know perfectly well when you'll see him again. Tonight. If you stick around here long enough. You know he always stops in for a drink after work."

"I don't mean seeing him that way: laying eyes on him. I mean, *being* with him. You're a woman. Don't you understand anything about basic female needs?"

Josephine stared morosely into her drink. "Of course I understand. I have the same needs. I can't live without a man, and there's nobody remotely in sight. Even I. C. has deserted me for Daffodil."

"Only temporarily. Daffodil will be returning to Berkeley soon, and then you'll get him back."

She looked at me with those big, dark, soulful eyes of hers. "Do you really think so?"

I polished off my third Papa Doble and started to do some rapid calculating. "Sure, unless I decide to go to bed with him myself."

Josephine stared at me, horrified, speechless, as Hotel Splendide's resident lawyer walked into the bar and sat down on the stool next to me.

"Good evening, ladies. Can I buy you both a drink?"

"I never knew the man who couldn't," Josephine said.

Parker was wearing the cream-colored suit he'd put on that morning when we went from his room to mine so he could collect his clean shirts. The shirt he'd chosen to wear was a brown-and-white check with French cuffs, and it was obvious that I had done an excellent job of washing and ironing it because even now, hours later, it still looked fresh and spotless, thanks to the fact that I had pre-soaked it in Axion before sticking it in the washing machine.

"I've changed my mind," Josephine announced. "I don't think it would be wise for me to have another drink. I think I should eat dinner. I'm getting drunk. Are either of you hungry? I dread dining alone."

"I couldn't eat a thing now," I said.

"Neither could I," Parker added. "Maybe in about an hour."

"I can't wait an hour." Then she spotted some people entering La Chiripa and heading toward the restaurant side. "Oh, there's that nice Italian couple. Have you met them? He's a poet, and she does translations. Maybe if I go over and say hello, they'll ask me to join them for dinner."

"Maybe," Parker said, sarcastically.

"What is that supposed to mean? That my company is undesirable?"

Parker shrugged. "All I said was *maybe*."

"Yes, but your intent was perfectly clear."

I was sorry I had made that crack before about going to bed with I. C., and yet Josephine Jasmin had the kind of personality that simply begged for abuse. It wasn't that I didn't mean what I'd said, just that it hadn't been necessary to make her even more miserable than she already was. The combination of John's death and Daffodil being holed up with I. C. Ring was pretty rough news, no matter how stoically you tried to look at it. And if there was one quality Josephine would never be accused of, it was stoicism, in any way, shape, or form.

"I got a message that you called me earlier," I said to Parker, after Josephine had gone to join the Italian couple. "Was it about the Swedish divorce laws?"

"Yes. Look at this."

Parker took a sheet of paper out of his pocket and handed it to me. It was a xerox copy, with the caption *Sweden Law Digest*, and read as follows:

> *Foreign Divorce*. Cases of divorce or separation between aliens, may, in principle, be tried in Sweden if the defendant is domiciled there. Divorce or separation may not be granted unless legal in the country of which the spouses are citizens, and there is a ground for divorce or separation according to the law of that country and Sweden (Act of 1904).

"The defendant," I said. "But *I'm* the defendant, and *I'm* not living in Sweden. That means Billy can't divorce me, doesn't it? Oh, Parker, this is terrific."

"Technically, it's terrific, but . . ."

"But what?"

"You see, the way the word *domicile* is legally used in such cases, it doesn't merely mean that you would have to be living in Sweden, but living there *with intent to reside.* Now, of course, you're doing neither, but the question is, is it possible that Billy plans to reside in Sweden, more or less permanently?"

"What difference does that make? He's not the defendant. I am."

"I know, but I suspect that if your husband does plan to stay in Sweden, and he gets himself a good lawyer, he can technically wiggle out of that clause."

"How?"

"I suspect that if Billy goes through the motions of setting up permanent residence in Sweden, it can be established that you, as his legal wife, are planning to reside there, too, even though you've never set foot in the country. Then, after a period of time, he can begin divorce proceedings. It might be sticky, and it might take awhile, but chances are that if he's persistent enough, he'll eventually be able to divorce you."

"It's not fair."

"Lots of legal loopholes aren't, but they exist just the same. I'm sorry, Loretta. I wish I could be more encouraging, but the fact is that Swedish divorce laws in general have become very lenient in recent years, and the courts there try to make divorce more easily obtainable than the law books indicate. So you see, the whole emotional trend in Sweden is toward relaxing the strictures of divorce, rather than enforcing them."

Why didn't Parker love me? That was all I could think of. *Why*? The hell with Billy Ray and Swedish divorce laws,

I no longer cared, I was beyond caring. Josephine had been right (for a change), Parker was the man I should be expending my energies on, not my four husbands, certainly not Billy who was thousands of miles away and in love with Inger. Billy was from hunger, but Parker was here and I was hungry. So naturally, as soon as he started to show a positive interest in me, I turned off. The story of Loretta Silverman's life: Don't get involved. *Run.*

"I'm sorry about the way I left things this morning." Parker put his hand on my hand. "I was inconsiderate. I admit it. I can imagine what you must be going through with this pregnancy uncertainty. It must be awful."

"I'll survive."

He tried again. "Look, Loretta, I'm really sorry if I sounded callous this morning, but you took me by surprise when you told me the baby was mine. I was quite stunned and I guess I reacted defensively. Inconsiderately. I apologize."

I wanted to say, "I'm glad you've explained. Thank you. Because I was very upset by your attitude."

Instead, I said, "Forget it. It doesn't matter."

But it did matter, it mattered very much to me, I just couldn't admit it. Run.

I'm a-leaving on a jet plane
Don't know when I'll be back again

"Loretta, if it turns out that you are pregnant, I'll take care of all financial responsibilities. I want you to know that."

At that moment, my life was at a turning point.

"I don't need, or want your help any longer."

Well, I had rounded the turn, the wrong one, as usual. A moment ago, all I could think of was: *Why didn't Parker love me*? Now, a moment later, all I could think of was: *Why did*

I ever divorce Chip Kramer? But if Chip were here, saying that he still loved me, would I be saying, "Sorry, baby, but I'm no longer interested"?

Somehow I did not think so. Chip had been my first love, and that surely counted for something, for a great deal. I'd been foolish to divorce him, to think that I could find something better with someone else. Of course we had had our problems (what couple didn't?). The real problem, though, was that I hadn't tried to work those problems out. I hadn't tried at all.

"Loretta, I'll marry you, if that's what you want," Parker said, as La Chiripa's crucifixes and saint statues watched over us.

"What I want to do is get on with my story."

After You Said It! was off the air, Jason James insisted upon taking Chip and me to Sardi's for lunch, to celebrate our forthcoming wedding. At the last minute, he invited Mick Donway to join us.

Chip looked uneasily at his watch. "It's only eleven-thirty. Will they be open this early?"

"They're opening up right this very minute," Jason James said, oblivious to Chip's attempt to squeeze out of this untenable situation as gracefully as possible. "Come on. We're wasting time. I can taste that Dom Perignon already. How about you, folks?"

Off camera, Jason James spoke pretty much the same as on camera, all speeded up and boyishly enthusiastic, although I would have guessed that he was easily in his early forties. When the four of us got to Sardi's, the maître d' gave Jason a very warm hello and Mick Donway, an obeisant smile, and led us to one of the more prominent tables in the uncrowded dining room. At one table I recognized Gig Young talking to an attractive woman in sunglasses, and at another table was Otto Preminger who looked like he was talking business to an unidentifiable man with a deep suntan. When the champagne arrived in a silver ice bucket, Jason proposed a toast.

"To the bride and groom, who never would have met and fallen in love if it hadn't been for You Said It! On behalf of the entire network, I want to extend my best wishes to them."

"I'll drink to that," Mick said, looking at me with what I had detected was growing resentment, ever since my dramatic television announcement a few minutes before.

After we had tasted the champagne, which was delicious, Jason said, "What I don't understand, Chip, is why you didn't tell me the exciting news about you and Loretta prior to the show. We would have had more time to make a fuss over the forthcoming wedding while we were on the air."

"Loretta wanted to surprise you," Chip said. "Didn't you, darling?"

Trying to appear as modest as possible, I said, "That's right, darling. I thought a surprise announcement would be more fun."

"You sure as hell surprised me," Mick murmured.

"You surprised everyone," Jason said, "including our millions of television viewers all over the country. This should shoot up our ratings like crazy. Not that we've been doing badly up until now, but a thing like this has real gut appeal for all those frustrated housewives and creepy shut-ins out there who watch our show every morning."

Chip looked up, suddenly alert. "You know, you're absolutely right, Jason. Loretta's announcement sure will have a beneficial effect on our ratings. I'll tell you a secret. What I just said a minute ago wasn't true—about Loretta wanting to surprise you with the announcement. The truth of the matter is, that at first Loretta didn't want to say a word on the air about our wedding plans. She's basically a very shy girl. Frankly, I talked her into it. Didn't I darling?"

"Yes," I said, confused by this turn of events. "Yes, darling, you did."

Suspicion flooded Jason James' face. "What are you getting at, Chip?"

"Oh, nothing. I just thought I'd get it straight whose idea it was to make that announcement."

"Okay," Jason said. "You've gotten it straight. So what?"

"So I think an idea that boosts our rating deserves some kind of reward. Like a big raise. I think Carlton will agree."

"Who's Carlton?" I asked.

"The producer of You Said It!" Jason James answered, getting angrier by the minute. "Very neat of you, Chip. Very clever. My compliments."

"Don't mention it."

Two bottles of Dom Perignon later, Jason said to Chip, "I guess I can't blame you for wanting a raise. Anybody who makes your lousy dough deserves a raise. Maybe even a promotion. Maybe you'd like my job. Maybe that's what you've been aiming for all along. How about it, wise guy?"

"Now, now, Jason. Mustn't be hostile. Mustn't be angry. It's bad for your image."

"Fuck my image."

"Why don't we order?" Mick said, nervously. "I'm starving. Do you see our waiter?"

Jason James snapped his fingers, and a waiter appeared with the menus. I ordered Eggs Benedict. Jason ordered fettuccine Alfredo. Chip ordered a small steak, rare. Mick ordered Beluga caviar and toast points, explaining, "I'm on a diet. Hollywood, you know."

Jason poured himself another glass of champagne. "Hollywood, my ass, you fucking faggot. You can't act your way out of a paper bag. I saw your last picture, that over-budgeted Western, where you play the young gunfighter. You don't even know how to hold a gun. You Hollywood actors really kill me. Where'd you get your training, amigo? On Muscle Beach, with the rest of the queers?"

"I don't have to take that crap from you," Mick said. "You're probably a hung-up actor yourself. That's why you're so hostile."

"Stop lisping. I might be a hung-up actor, but at least I'm not a fucking faggot like you."

"I resent your calling me a homosexual. I resent it very much."

"I'm not calling you a homosexual. I'm calling you a fucking faggot. There's a big difference."

"Why don't you can it?" Chip said to Jason. "Come on. You're smashed out of your head. Let the kid alone."

"You keep your nose out of it. This is strictly between Lover Boy and me."

Our waiter arrived with the food, and it was only when I started to cut into my Eggs Benedict that I realized how drunk I was, and looking around the table, I realized that everyone else was equally drunk, if not more so. Three bottles of champagne? Who wouldn't be drunk? All I'd had for breakfast before leaving The Bronx that morning was one cup of black coffee, and gauging from the way the others were unsteadily going at their food, I had a hunch they hadn't had much more.

"Tell me, Mick." Jason was back at it again. "What do you think of our two lovebirds here? Getting married and all. What's your feeling about such heterosexual bliss?"

"I'm all for it." One of Mick's toast points missed his

mouth, and a few specks of Beluga caviar landed on his pale orange shirt. "Marriage is wonderful. There's a girl I'm going with in Bel Air—"

"What's his name?" Jason asked, motioning to the waiter for more champagne.

"I've tried to overlook your insults, but it's becoming quite impossible. One more word out of you and I'll—"

Champagne from Jason's glass bubbled and spilled over onto the tablecloth. "You'll *what*?"

Mick backtracked. "Look, mister, I didn't come here for a fight. I accepted your invitation because Loretta and I are old friends, and she's getting married, and—"

"Don't you ever finish a sentence?" Jason asked.

Then I heard my own voice cut in. "Chip and I aren't getting married. It was all a lie. I made it up to try to trap him into marrying me, that's what I did."

Jason James stopped eating, his forkful of fettuccine in mid-air. "*You made it up*?" He stared at me in astonishment. "Why, you miserable tramp, do you realize that you've lied to millions of television viewers on *my* program? Do you know what you've done? Do you have any idea what this means? How am I going to explain this to our producer? To our audience? You've made a fool out of me. A schmuck. And on network television. When I think of the Nielsens!"

"I resent your calling Loretta a tramp," Chip said. "She may be a liar, but it's obvious that she's a nice, decent girl."

Mick laughed. "She's decent, all right. Loretta Silverman, the virgin of Christopher Columbus High School. You couldn't get into her pants, for love or money. Boy, you should have heard the pathetic stories about the poor bastards who tried."

"Well, we all know you weren't one of them," Jason said. "That's for damned sure. Fucking faggot."

"I repeat for the last time that I am not a fucking faggot. I mean, I'm not a homosexual."

"Sure, you're a *non*-fucking faggot. Someone as meticulous as you. You're probably afraid to get shit on your prick."

"Get up," Mick said. "I'm going to knock you on your stupid ass."

Jason tried to get to his feet, but Chip pushed him back in his chair. Then he grabbed his steak and slapped it in Jason's face. The blood from the steak dribbled down Jason's chin and onto his dark, conservative tie. It took the host of You Said It! a moment to recover from this unexpected assault, and when he did, he dumped his entire plate of fettuccine Alfredo over Mick Donway's head. Not to be outdone, Mick, half-blinded by pasta, rubbed caviar into my freshly washed hair, and said, "That's for giving the basketball team at Christopher Columbus a hard time, you bitch-tease."

Drunkenly, I picked up my Eggs Benedict, English muffin, ham, Hollandaise sauce, and all, and slipped it into Chip Kramer's jacket pocket. A piece of parsley that had been sitting on top of the Hollandaise missed the pocket and landed on Sardi's floor. In the distance, I saw our waiter, stiff with horror. Even Gig Young had stopped paying attention to his attractive luncheon companion and was staring at us, openmouthed. Otto Preminger and the man with the suntan applauded us, laughing.

"I wouldn't marry you on a bet," I said to Chip. "Any man who's so low that he would cash in on a girl's sincere and vulnerable feelings, just to get himself a fast raise, doesn't deserve Loretta Silverman."

Then I poured my glass of champagne over his head. A minute later the four of us were thrown out.

"And when I think of all the money I've spent in that joint," Jason James said, as we found ourselves stranded on

West 44th Street. Cursing, he turned and walked off in the direction of Broadway.

Mick brushed a strand of fettuccine out of his hair, and hailed a taxi, sobbing.

"Okay, lunatic," Chip said to me. "What happens now?"

"Now we go to The Bronx, so you can meet your future in-laws."

"I thought you just said you wouldn't marry me on a bet."

I gave him my ever-popular Ava Gardner smile. "Never believe a Jewish girl who eats ham and eggs."

When we got to my parents' apartment in The Bronx, my mother was waiting for me at the door, hysterical with excitement.

"Mrs. Ginsberg just told me about the TV program. I had to hear it from a stranger. Why didn't you tell me yourself, Loretta? Why? I could have watched it too." She gave Chip a sharp look. "Who's the *trumbenick*?"

"This is my husband-to-be. Charles Alan Kramer. Chip, this is my mother."

"The Nazi!" my mother cried. "And you bring him into an orthodox Jewish home. First, you go on a television show that you don't tell your parents about, and now you shlep in a German war criminal. Wait until your father hears about this, that's all I have to say. Wait!"

Chip cleared his throat. "I don't know what all this is about, Mrs. Silverman, but I'm not German. I'm an Austrian Jew, and I was too young to be in the war. I'm only twenty-five."

My mother just stood there with the same open-mouthed expression that Gig Young had had back at Sardi's. "What's that in your pocket?" she asked Chip, when she finally pulled herself together.

He took out the squashed, gooey remains of my Eggs Benedict. "It's a long story, Mrs. Silverman, A very long story."

"Something funny is going on here." My mother picked a few specks of Beluga caviar out of my hair. "It's a good thing you chose the washing machine, Loretta. You both look like *schmutz.*"

Chip winked at me. "I see that your mother has made a very speedy recovery."

In the hysteria of our expulsion from Sardi's, I had completely forgotten that my mother was supposed to be a helpless invalid. I opened my mouth to try to explain, but Chip stopped me.

"I know," he said, as he took me in his arms and made our engagement official. "Never believe a Jewish girl who eats ham and eggs."

"Are you saying you don't want to marry me?" Parker asked.

Outside, it had started to grow dark at last, and I felt comforted by the deepening envelope of darkness, protected from the glare of daylight which exposed one's secrets. Both the bar and restaurant sides at La Chiripa had started to fill up. That was comforting, too. People huddling together for mutual solace, yet it was not solace that I sought, quite the opposite.

"No, Parker, I don't want to marry you."

"But I thought—"

"That I did? That I would? Well, I don't and I won't."

"What about the baby? You said it was mine."

"You're the father, if that's what you mean. But the baby will be mine. Mine alone."

"Why?"

"I'm not in love with you."

"That's funny. I had the distinct impression you were."

So had I, until he'd asked me to marry him. "It's all changed."

"You mean, now that you've gotten what you thought you wanted, you suddenly don't want it any more."

"Perhaps." I felt a terrible bitterness start to set in. "Perhaps you've hit the nail on the head. Anyhow I'm no longer interested in you."

"You seem to derive a great deal of satisfaction out of saying that. Do you want another drink? Because I definitely want another drink. I need one."

I was so drunk with bitterness and self-reproach that another drink couldn't possibly matter. Ten other drinks. A million. Parker ordered drinks from Carlos who had continued to watch me with growing apprehension. What was he so afraid of? Did he think I was going to wreck the place? La Chiripa. It meant, "a piece of good luck" in Spanish. Some good luck. Some Hotel Splendide. Carlos Santiago and Leonard Stein had the same mordant sense of humor when it came to choosing names for their respective establishments.

"I guess you're still in love with the guy," Parker said.

"Who?"

"Billy."

"I told you yesterday on the roof that I'm not in love with him, and I tell you the same thing today. I just don't like the idea of his divorcing me to marry someone else."

"Sure, it's okay for you not to give a damn about anyone, but when the tables are turned, you don't like it much, do you?"

"Does anyone?"

Then, to my relief, Peggy and Zachary came in and

joined us. Peggy was wearing a geometric black and white sari, and Zachary had the boa constrictor around his neck, the snake's forked tongue flicking in and out against its owner's skin.

"I see that you've found the dear little reptile," I said to Zachary. "Peggy told me he was missing. Where did he finally turn up?"

"On the wall behind the refrigerator, dear. I had just about given up hope of ever seeing him again, too."

At the other end of the bar, I noticed Harry Brown with a group of people who were all involved in various aspects of movie making. Corina stood next to them, asking a Belgian art critic if he would sleep on a puce sheet.

"*Je déteste puce*," he said loudly.

The Naked Seven had their usual two tables pushed together on the restaurant side and were ordering dinner. A few tables away, Josephine Jasmin was eating paella with the Italian couple she had joined earlier. Only three people were missing: I. C. Ring, Daffodil, and my third husband, John O'Connell.

"Parker just asked me to marry him," I drunkenly informed Peggy and Zachary.

"Don't tell me we're going to have a funeral *and* a wedding all at once," Zachary said. "That reminds me, Loretta. I just left a couple of dirty shirts outside your door. I wonder if you could be sure to have the green one washed and ironed by tomorrow. I need it for the funeral."

"She won't wash my shirts anymore," Parker said. "I have to take them to the laundry from now on. She won't marry me, either."

"She can't marry you," Peggy said. "She's already married. You *are* married, aren't you, Loretta? I mean, I know I've gone crazy, but there are certain things I do remember.

It's very important to remember certain strategic facts, if they cart you off to Bellevue. Like, Richard M. Nixon is the President of the United States, Spiro T. Agnew is the Vice President, William P. Rogers is the Secretary of State. Little things like that really impress the authorities. They figure you're not as nuts as they'd imagined at first."

"Technically, I'm still married, but it looks like it won't be for long," I said. "My fourth husband wants a divorce so he can marry a Swedish girl named Inger. She probably has naturally blond hair. When Billy and I were married, he used to insist that I put on a blond dynel fall before he'd make love to me. Then he'd come all over the fall. It's a good thing dynel is washable, or I would have been in serious trouble with so much sticky sperm in my hairpiece. I wonder how Inger likes having to wash her own hair every other minute."

"You ought to publish your memoirs," Parker said. "You're a real reservoir of sexual detail, aren't you, Loretta? I've never known anyone with as sordid a background as you, although sometimes I think you've made it all up. It's hard to believe that one person could have had so many kinky experiences."

"Are you calling me a liar?"

"I'm merely suggesting the possibility that you might be stretching the truth a little."

"I never lie. I just happen to have led a very full life, that's all."

"Full is right," Parker said. "Full of morbidity."

"I wonder where I. C. and Daffodil are," Peggy said, trying to change the subject. "Has anybody seen them?"

"They're in I. C.'s room, screwing their brains out," I said. "They've been at it all day. You can hear every moan and groan from my room. Even Josephine heard them this afternoon, when she stopped in to see me. She wanted to show me the dress she'd bought for the funeral. She was pretty upset, and I can't say that I blame her. It must be rough on her, competing with such a young and beautiful daughter as Daffodil."

"Please, dear," Zachary implored me. "Josephine told me all about I. C. and Daffodil when we went to Frank Campbell's for the plastic ears. I don't care to hear another word on the bloody subject."

"Plastic ears?" Parker said.

"It's a very gruesome story," I told him. "I'd rather not talk about it now. What I think we should talk about, though, is the collection that Josephine is taking up to pay for John's funeral. She has to raise three thousand dollars."

Peggy and Zachary stared at me, stunned.

"I'm giving a hundred dollars," Parker said.

"Harry Brown has signed up for a hundred, too," I said. "How about you, Zach?"

"Okay, but I think it's highway robbery."

"I'm broke," Peggy announced.

"I know. I wasn't going to ask you. I suppose I should give five hundred, since he once was my husband. If I give five and Josephine gives five, that's a thousand dollars. Then three hundred from Harry, Zach, and Parker. It's almost half the total amount. And there's still I. C., Corinna, and God knows who else will come through. Maybe the Italian couple. They knew John. I hope Josephine has the brains to bring it up over dinner."

"Oh, oh," Peggy said. "She's done it again."

We all turned and watched Josephine take a bill from her purse, throw it on the table, and rush out of the restaurant, crying, as the Italian couple stared at her, retreating back in dumb amazement.

"They probably can't figure out what hit them," Peggy said.

A feeling of irritation came over me, irritation mingled with bitterness, defeat, fatigue, misery. I felt as though I had lived through this evening many times before, that we had all stood in the same place, saying the same things, drinking the same Papa Doble, that Josephine had predictably rushed out crying in the midst of dinner, throwing her money on the table, and worse, I knew that tomorrow night we would all be back, repeating, repeating. . . .

For the millionth time, I asked myself why I didn't move out of Hotel Splendide, get a nice apartment somewhere, fix it up, become really involved with one person, rather than this dormitory-style group involvement, which claimed us all. If I married Parker, he would want to take an apartment, it could be a chance, a beginning, an attempt at something private, substantial. But I didn't want to marry Parker, I didn't want to marry anyone at the moment, I liked the looseness of the group, its lack of demands, its flexibility, its obscene offer of detachment. I needed that. Even though I'd been married four times, I wondered now whether I had ever really been involved with anyone in my life beside myself.

"I propose a toast to Loretta Silverman," Parker said, drunkenly holding up his glass. "To Loretta, the one-woman United Nations sex symbol, who is making a big mistake by not marrying Parker Mason."

"Why is it a mistake?"

"Because you've never been married to a Pole, right? Well, I'm Polish. You didn't know that, did you? You goofed. My last name is really Mazurki. You could have added me to your ethnic list of husbands. Now it's too late. Too bad. Chin chin, everybody."

Somebody started to play "Leaving On a Jet Plane," and

I started to tap dance up and down the long La Chiripa bar. The movement felt wonderful. Leaping. Flying. I knocked over a couple of peoples' drinks by mistake, and I was laughing, singing with the record, I was free, happy for the first time since I returned from work Saturday evening to find Billy's letter waiting for me. When I tap-danced past Parker Mason, I threw my drink right in his Polish face, and kept on dancing until Carlos Santiago picked me up by the shoulders and threw me out of the bar.

"Don't ever come back to La Chiripa!" he shouted, as he not so gently deposited me in the psychedelic lobby of Hotel Splendide.

"I've been thrown out of better places than this," I said indignantly. "I've been thrown out of Sardi's."

I sat in an inflated plastic armchair in the lobby for minutes, sobbing in sheer humiliation and anger at being publicly evicted from La Chiripa.

"*Qu'est-ce qui passe?*" the Berlitz desk clerk asked me.

"*Rien de tout.*"

After awhile I decided to go upstairs and go to sleep in Torrid Zone, since there didn't seem to be much other choice. When I got to room 701, Zachary's bundle of dirty shirts was waiting for me in front of the door. Wearily, I picked them up and wondered whether it would lift my morale if I did a little washing and ironing before going to bed. Just as I put my key in the lock, the door to I. C.'s room opened and out walked Daffodil Jasmin, wearing a dreamy expression on her face and the same minuscule bikini that she'd had on yesterday on the roof (had it only been yesterday?).

"He's gorgeous," she said to me, as she sailed off toward the elevator. "Positively gorgeous."

Torrid Zone felt much the same as earlier, the heat of the day having been baked into it, the air heavy and thick. I put my head out the window and was greeted by a breezeless, starless night. Down below a scattering of cars occupied the hotel's parking lot, and from where I stood, seven floors above, they looked like tiny plastic cars in one of those tacky games for children.

My outside telephone began to ring. For a moment I contemplated not answering it, that's how depressed and uncommunicative I felt, but habit finally prevailed, and I picked up the receiver.

"You were supposed to call me back," my father said. "Did you see the doctor?"

"No, I'm seeing him tomorrow. He's going to give me the rabbit test."

"What will you do if it turns out that you're pregnant? Have you thought about that, Loretta?"

"What's the point in thinking about it until I know for sure?" Then on impulse, I added, "Parker Mason just asked me to marry him."

"And?"

"I said no."

My father sighed. "I'll tell you something. I'm not sure whether I'm happy about that, or unhappy. I'm so confused about you and all your marriages that I can't think straight on the subject any more."

"That makes two of us."

"You'd better try to get a good night's sleep. You've got to go to work tomorrow. At least you have a good job. That's something."

Tomorrow I had to start trying to book Norman Mailer and Tiny Tim for Talk. There were worse jobs. "Maybe one of these days I'll get to be associate producer."

"What's wrong with what you're doing now?"

"Nothing, but it's only natural to want to move up the ladder. I would have moved up long before this if it weren't for the fact that they're prejudiced against women. It's very hard for a woman to get an executive job in television. I'm lucky to even be a talent coordinator. You don't know how they discriminate against women."

"She's making three hundred and fifty dollars a week, and she complains about discrimination. I've never made three hundred and fifty dollars a week in my life, and I'm not a woman."

My father's ability to sidestep logic with ballroom ease had always fascinated me. "I'll speak to you tomorrow, but I'm not seeing Dr. Oiseaux until six, and I probably won't know the results of the test until the next day, and maybe even the day after that."

"I just hope you can sleep in that hothouse room of yours," my father said before he hung up.

I went into the kitchen to see about washing Zachary's shirts, but when I turned on the water in the sink to make sure it was hot, I discovered it wasn't. Tepid. Luckily, I still had some All-Temperature Cheer left. Cheer was one laundry detergent that worked equally well in hot, medium, or cold water.

After I had turned on my wonderful Whirlpool washing machine and made sure that Zach's shirts were whirling around in all those beautiful, cleansing suds, I went into the other room and flopped down on my bed. I felt dizzy from the Papa Dobles, dizzy, depressed, deflated. The prospect of sleeping alone in Torrid Zone was not very appealing, but what choice did I have? Parker hadn't even come to my rescue after I'd been thrown out of La Chiripa, that was how much he cared about Loretta Silverman.

I contemplated phoning him at the bar and saying that I'd changed my mind, that if he still wanted me, I'd marry him after all, but it seemed like quite a heavy sacrifice just to get one night of companioned, air-conditioned sleep. Then I remembered my next-door neighbor. *Why not*, I asked myself? I. C. had been after me ever since he'd moved into the hotel, and his air-conditioner was just as good as Parker's any day in the week.

I promptly got undressed and put on a fresh new pair of Pucci culottes, washed my face, brushed my hair, and dabbed some Cabochard behind my ears and on other strategic pulse points. There would be plenty of time tomorrow morning to throw Zachary's shirts in my Whirlpool dryer before I went to work. Thanks to the dryer's special tumbling feature, "Finish Guard," I knew that the shirts would come out wrinkle-free.

"Hooray for American technology," I said to I. C. when he opened the door. "Can I come in?"

I. C. had one of the hotel's towels wrapped around his lean waist and seemed surprised to see me. The room reeked of marijuana smoke, but was delightfully, deliciously cool.

"You know you're always welcome in my little den," he said, with a very un-enigmatic smile. "To what do I owe the pleasure?"

"I'm lonely. Everyone has abandoned me."

"Me, too. Daffodil is going back to Berkeley tomorrow. She says Hotel Splendide is too hectic for her. She misses the relative calm of all those campus riots."

"Josephine will be pleased to hear that she's leaving. You and Daffodil really upset her this afternoon. She heard you making love."

"Everything upsets Josephine, but I don't want to talk about her."

I sat down on I. C.'s unmade bed. Looking at the pillows, I felt as though I could still see the impression of Daffodil's head on one of them. I. C. was watching me, waiting. I gazed up at him in my most beguiling manner.

"I don't want to talk about Josephine, either. That's not why I'm here. You see, I've come to a decision. I'm ready to answer some of your questions for the survey, providing you promise to answer one of mine."

I. C. sat down beside me on the bed and began to kiss my bare shoulder. "What's the question?" he huskily asked, his Oriental eyes looking up at me with months of longing.

"Tell me, I. C., is it true that if I go down on you, I'll be hungry in a couple of hours?"

Tuesday Morning

HEARING the pleasant sound of the air-conditioner, I knew that I had awakened once more in someone else's room, which made three mornings in a row that I'd successfully managed to avoid the perils of sleeping in Torrid Zone. Sunday morning, I woke up beside John O'Connell, Monday, Parker Mason, and now . . . I. C. Ring, lover extraordinaire.

I. C. was still asleep on the other side of the bed, breathing gently, the hotel's drab, green blanket wrapped around his wiry body. Only a sheet covered me as I opened my eyes to greet another hot, sunny day, the day of my unfortunate third husband's funeral. I wondered how Josephine had slept, and whether she had as yet worked herself up to the pitch of hysteria she was bound to indulge in this afternoon at Frank Campbell's. It wouldn't surprise me if she fainted dead away, right in the middle of the service, very much the delicate

Southern belle, and I made a mental note to buy one of those half-pints of brandy at the local liquor store, in case it was necessary to revive her. If that did happen, she would probably look at me reproachfully and say that I should have used smelling salts. No matter how you tried to help Josephine Jasmin, she would figure out a way to make your efforts appear inadequate.

I checked my watch. It was early, only a little after seven. Then I remembered that I had to iron Zachary's green shirt before going to work. It seemed a millennium since I'd last been to my office at the network, answering telephone calls from agents and publicity people, getting my notes together for the eleven o'clock bookers' meeting with the producer and associate producer, going to lunch with a celebrity guest I'd booked for that evening's show, or possibly one I was trying to line up for a future show. For a moment I couldn't remember who I was having lunch with today, and then it came to me: Andy Warhol.

The producer had seen Warhol's latest underground cinematic effort, *Lonesome Cowboys,* which he described as "Sex beneath the cactus." Because of the pornographic nature of the movie, we would not be able to show a film clip, but the producer thought that Warhol himself might be interesting on Talk, providing he had something provocative to discuss within the limits of television censorship. Since nobody on our staff knew the elusive Mr. Warhol, it would be up to me to draw him out at lunch and decide whether he should be on the show.

I'd made reservations at Max's Kansas City for one o'clock. Ordinarily, I would not have been in any great rush to meet the king of pop art, but because of the funeral later that afternoon, he seemed like the ideal luncheon companion. If anyone should appreciate the grotesque plastic ear arrangements, it would be Andy Warhol, although as I had long ago discovered, you could never predict people's reactions. Some celebrities with a reputation for great poise and charm often turned out to be inhibited, confused, reticent clams when you asked them about themselves. And vice versa. It was the talent coordinator's job to warm up the repressed ones and channel the unbridled enthusiasm of the personality boys and girls.

I had seen Andy Warhol floating around Hotel Splendide several times, and I knew some people who knew him, which should make for a fast rapport. Also, one of his former superstars used to live directly beneath me until a few months ago when she burned up her room, much like John O'Connell, but unlike John she escaped with her life, a head of badly singed hair, and outraged curses from Leonard Stein.

I quickly reviewed the rest of my luncheon appointments for the week, my brain still somewhat woozy from the marijuana I had smoked with I. C. last night before we made love.

Tomorrow I was having lunch with Lillian Hellman, whose autobiography, *An Unfinished Woman*, had just been published. I'd made reservations at Quo Vadis, and I could taste those eels in green sauce already.

Thursday, my lunch date was Bill Buckley, at Le Veau d'Or.

Friday, Senator Eugene McCarthy, at The Spanish Pavillion.

And Saturday was salad day with Vidal Sassoon and his wife, Beverly, at The Palm Court of The Plaza.

When I first became a talent coordinator on Talk, I was overwhelmed by the roster of celebrities I would be dealing with every working day, but the glamour wore off once I was confronted with the actual personality. So few were as wonderful or witty as their press agents would lead you to believe. I wondered whether Lillian Hellman would want to comment on the women's liberation movement, inasmuch as she was considered one of the originally emancipated women back in the thirties. I wondered how Andy Warhol first hit upon his idea for exploiting the Campbell's soup can. I wondered whether I. C.'s explanation for his rather unbelievable virility could possibly be true.

"But what happened to your pubic hair?" I said last night, when I. C. removed the towel that was wrapped around his waist.

"I shave it."

"Shave it?! But why?"

"It's an ancient Oriental sex technique, Loretta. The body energy that would normally go into growing pubic hair goes instead into my genitals. That's why my penis stays hard for hours. That's why we Chinese are known to be such notoriously good lovers."

"I never heard that. Do Japanese men shave, too? Or is it only the Chinese?".

A look of distaste crossed I. C.'s face. "The Japanese have become very Western in their outlook. More and more they copy Caucasian customs, and soon will be as decadent as the Americans they try to emulate."

"But you're an American. You were born in Los Angeles. You told me so yourself."

"My Chinese heritage is deeper, older, wiser, it goes back farther than the place of my birth. Chinese men used to have to satisfy many women in the days they kept concubines. I'm referring to the aristocrats, of course, and it was considered a disgrace if a man did not have the necessary potency, the necessary staying power that was expected of him. My father told me all this when I was very young, so even though I dress and live like an American, in my heart I am Chinese through and through."

"What's your father's occupation?"

"He's a dog psychologist in Beverly Hills. That's a thriving business out there. His toughest case to date has been a Great Dane who thought he was a toy poodle. Xavier liked to wear pink ribbons in his hair, and jump on people's laps and try to cuddle up. But my father finally cured him. He told Xavier's owner to feed him the amount of food you would normally feed a toy poodle. One week of living on a couple of ounces of meat a day, and Xavier decided that it wasn't so bad being a Great Dane."

After that I. C. and I made love, and then I answered the questions for his survey, as agreed upon earlier. He gave me a sharp look when I said that I no longer took the pill because it completely screwed up my system.

Q. Which brand did you use?
A. Porusil.
Q. Are you positive?
A. Yes. Why?
Q. What I mean is, are you positive that you weren't taking Dorucan?
A. Now wait a minute. With Dorucan, you take white pills for fifteen days, then pink pills for the next five days. But with Porusil, you only take white pills. Right?
Q. Right.
A. I was taking Porusil. Why? Is Dorucan supposed to be better?
Q. Oh no, absolutely not. It's just the opposite. Porusil is far superior. That's why I was curious.
A. Well, I have a new gynecologist, and he's opposed to all brands of the birth control pill, so I'm back to a diaphragm again.
Q. Again?

A. That was the first contraceptive device I ever used. It's not so terrible, although there are certain disadvantages to it. Like when I left Chip Kramer to marry Paul Bjorkman, Chip took a scissors and cut both my diaphragms in half and tossed them in the garbage can. He did it right before my eyes, before I could stop him.

Q. Why did you have two diaphgrams?

A. One was for weekdays and one for weekends.

Q. What did you do then? Go to your doctor and get another diaphragm?

A. No, I decided to try the coil, but it wouldn't say in. My system kept ejecting it, so I had to give up on that and go back to a diaphragm.

Q. Why didn't you try Porusil?

A. I'd heard too many ghastly stories from women who had taken it and experienced a lot of unpleasant side effects. I also heard of women who died because of the pill.

Q. They must have been taking Dorucan.

A. Well, maybe some were. I don't know. I always thought one brand was pretty much the same as the other.

Q. That's where you're wrong. The incidence of discomfort is significantly higher among Dorucan users than it is among those who take Porusil.

A. I'm not just talking about *discomfort*, which is bad enough. Like getting blinding headaches, or being dizzy and nauseated in the morning, or gaining so much weight and becoming so water-logged that you can't fit into your clothes. I'm talking about women who have died of blood clots, or been permanently paralyzed from the waist down.

Q. There has never been any conclusive evidence that embolisms or paralysis are directly connected with Porusil.

A. I'm beginning to think you own stock in the company.
Q. [laughing] Hardly. But because of this survey, I've had an opportunity to speak to a lot of women who are on the pill, and you're the first one I've met so far who's so violently opposed to it. And yet, you did take it yourself finally. What made you do that?
A. When I left John O'Connell for Billy Ray, I packed so fast that I left my diaphragms behind. I was going to get another one, but Billy suggested I try the pill for a while. He said maybe it wouldn't bother me.
Q. And?
A. Except for some occasional morning nausea and vomiting, it was okay.
Q. But you said earlier that it had *completely* screwed up your system.
A. I was referring to something else. You see, after I left Billy and moved to Hotel Splendide, I kept on taking the pill without too many side effects. Then I must have had an attack of amnesia, I still can't figure it out, but I forgot to take my pill for two days in a row, and the result seems to have been instant fertility.
Q. What do you mean, *seems to have been*?
A. The final verdict hasn't come in yet. That's what I was trying to get at before. The reason the doctor couldn't conclude whether or not I was pregnant before this is that Porusil plays havoc with your menstrual cycle. The rabbit test isn't effective for the first few months after you've gone off the pill. So I've had to wait until now to find out whether I'm pregnant or not. And if I am, and if I decide I don't want the baby, it's probably too late for an abortion. Now do you understand why I hate the pill?

I. C. put down his list of questions and said, "Josephine tells me that if you are pregnant, you think Parker Mason is the father."

He waited for me to say something, but all I could think was that Hotel Splendide was just one vicious ring-around-a-rosie of gossip and intrigue. There was absolutely no privacy, nothing was sacred, yesterday's confidence was destined to be tomorrow's public knowledge. And yet I had always known that about the hotel, it was foolish to be surprised, let alone outraged, and I realized once more what an infantile, fishbowl kind of life we resident-inmates led (watched over by our keeper, Leonard Stein), while we pretended to be grown-up, and sophisticated, and independent. No doubt by tomorrow everyone would know that I had gone to bed with I. C. Ring, what we had done, talked about, felt toward each other. My own feelings about I. C. were nebulous, but not uninspired. I liked him better than I would have imagined, it was possible I'd grow to like him even more. My father's prophetic words of Sunday evening came rushing back.

"I have no intention of thinking about who your fifth husband might be. Because knowing you, Loretta, I'm afraid I already suspect the worst. A Chinaman. Right? At this very moment he's probably sitting in a rice paddy in Vietnam, murdering one of our courageous boys."

"No, father, he's in bed with your only daughter, giving her endless, Oriental orgasms, and asking her questions for his gynecological survey."

When I ignored I. C.'s question about Parker being the father of my child, he then urged me to tell him about my four marriages, which I did. I also told him which positions I liked best in bed, and my insights into the way men of different ethnic groups made love. He seemed particularly intrigued by this last topic, and said he'd never before heard anyone define lovemaking techniques by ethnic group, although he could see where I might have a point or two.

"You're a real little fund of information, Loretta. I thought I'd never get you to spill all. What made you change your mind?"

I could have said, "Your air-conditioner," but why be cruel? Besides, it wasn't solely that, it was also my horror of sleeping alone, of not being loved or desired. When nobody loved me, I felt like nobody. When nobody desired me, I felt totally undesirable, worthless. That I. C. desired me was plain enough, yet his self-control was extraordinary compared to most men. He understood the timing of love-making, the not rushing it, or allowing himself to lose control until he decided that I had had enough for the moment. Only then would he reach a climax, and even in that he was different from most men. I had the feeling that his orgasm was strictly incidental to satisfying me as much, and as often as he could. No wonder Daffodil had said he was "gorgeous." No wonder Josephine was so upset about losing him to her daughter.

After I had filled out I. C.'s verbal questionnaire, we made love again and it was even better than the first time, it lasted even longer, I felt more aroused, in fact I had never felt so aroused in my life. It was his attitude. He seemed to derive most of his satisfaction from satisfying me, he would watch me as we made love, which at first made me feel self-conscious, those eyes never leaving my face, but after a while I got used to it, there was something oddly exciting about the demoniac way he observed my every reaction, something almost obscene about his gaze, I can't really explain it, but no man had ever looked at me quite like that before, and perhaps it appealed to my narcissistic, theatrical bent. In being made love to by I. C., I was at the center of the stage at all times. He asked nothing for himself other than my pleasure, he wanted nothing else.

Once when I tentatively took the lead and tried to caress him, he pulled back, urging me not to worry about him, but to concentrate upon myself, indulge myself.

"You can come again," he said to me at one point, as I lay there, exhausted and sweating.

"No, I couldn't possibly."

His eyes seemed to burn into mine. His voice was soft, sinuous, different from his usual bantering tones. "Sure you can. I know you can. You know you can, too. Come on. Try."

Hypnotic. Maybe that was it, his voice, I mean. And I would try. And succeed. Which apparently delighted him, excited him, aroused him. His smile (or was it a leer?) seemed to indicate a great conquest, an erotic triumph beyond his most optimistic dreams, yet he would not be satisfied even with that, no, he wanted still more triumphs, demanded even more conquests, more proof that I could be tuned by him, as though I were a delicate instrument that only a master artist like him could possibly understand and appreciate. And in his arms, I became exactly what he wanted me to be: a more than willing, more than satisfied sexual slave.

"I'll wake you in the middle of the night," were his last words to me before we both fell asleep.

"You don't have to."

"I want to. We'll make love again."

"I'm too tired."

"Sleep awhile, then we'll see."

"Aren't you tired?"

"Temporarily. It will pass."

"You're amazing, I. C. I don't know how you do it."

"What?"

"Keep it up. Most men would have been dead hours ago. I mean, you were with Daffodil all day. And now me."

"It's a matter of attitude. I like to make you happy. Are you happy?"

"Yes." But I wasn't. I was something else. Sated. Flattered. Confused. There was a detachment to his love-making that I didn't understand. "Very happy."

"Good."

He kissed me on the forehead, an innocent, childlike kiss, and it occurred to me that not once, during all the love-making, had he kissed me on the mouth.

"Good night," I said.

"Loretta?"

He had turned out the small lamp next to the bed, and now it was pitch black. "Yes?"

"How many times did you come tonight?"

"I don't know."

"Think."

"I can't. I don't count."

"But you did come a lot?"

"Yes, of course. Why do you ask?"

"Sometimes women fake it. You weren't faking, were you?"

"Don't be silly."

He hesitated, his curiosity not yet satisfied. "Did you come more than three times?"

"Yes."

"More than five?"

"I. C., I really don't know. I'm not an adding machine."

"I know you're not, darling Loretta. Go to sleep. I'll wake you in the middle of the night. Will you come for me again?"

I was so worn out that I could barely talk, let alone think. "Yes, yes," I murmured, drifting off to sleep. "Yes, yes . . ."

In the middle of the night, I felt a hand on my shoulder

and I turned instinctively toward the body beside me, half-blurred by sleep but languidly receptive to another sexual encounter with the energetic I. C. Ring. The few hours of rest he'd had seemed to have refreshed him to an almost athletic pitch of activity. Up and down, in and out, sideways and crossways, this way and that way, until I was so exhausted that I dozed off right in the middle of everything.

"Loretta?"

I could hear him, but only from a distance. "What is it?"

"Don't you want me to make love to you?"

"I'm too tired. I have to sleep some more."

"I'll go down on you."

"No, I'm too tired."

"Don't you want to come again?"

"Not right now. I couldn't. Really."

"All right." He sounded defeated, disappointed.

"I'm sorry."

"You're a wonderful girl, Loretta."

Then I slept until awakened by the morning light and thoughts of that day's work schedule. Lying there in I. C.'s bed, I kept remembering Zachary's shirt that had to be ironed before I went to the network, yet try as I could, something prevented me from jumping out of bed with my usual enthusiasm, and going back to my own room to do all the things that had to be done if I were to get to the office on time. In order to be prepared for the eleven o'clock meeting with the other talent coordinators and the producer of Talk, I had to type up notes on Huntley & Brinkley, my guests for that evening's show. I also had to have something to report about booking Tiny Tim and Norman Mailer for later in the week.

The thought of it all made me suddenly weary. When I'd left the network Saturday evening, I was a different person, self-confident, optimistic, proud. Between then and now

I'd undergone such severe setbacks that I wondered if I would ever again be the same Loretta Silverman.

On that depressing note, I dove back into the deep forgetfulness of sleep.

When I woke up the second time, I. C. was talking on the telephone at the other end of the room. His back was toward me, and he was talking very softly, so softly that I wondered whether he was afraid I would hear what he was saying. Naturally, that aroused my curiosity and I promptly closed my eyes again, and lay very still.

"She insists it was Porusil," he said into the receiver. "What happened was that she forgot to take it two days in a row, and as a result, she's pretty sure she's pregnant."

There was a pause, and then I. C. said, "No, the gynecologist told her that the Porusil had screwed up her menstrual cycle so badly that the rabbit test is not necessarily accurate in cases like this. You see, if it weren't for the damned doctor, she'd probably have started taking it again, instead of reverting to a diaphragm. That seems to be happening with a lot of women I've spoken to—the doctor's condemning attitude, I mean. I definitely think it would be wise to make a written complaint to the AMA."

There was another pause, followed by I. C. saying, "I also think it's perfectly obvious why our sales figures have dropped drastically for the last quarter, although compared to ours, Dorucan's figures must be a nightmare, what with all that damaging publicity about blood clots and blurred vision. I'll have a complete report for Research and Sales very soon, but in the meantime it looks ominous. There's been a definite resurgence of the diaphragm and the IUD in recent months, no doubt about it. My report will contain a comprehensive breakdown of the factors responsible for our recent decrease in sales."

Then he hung up.

And I stood up. Naked, hysterical, and betrayed (again!), the truth of I. C.'s real occupation having just been revealed to me in all its blinding, ghastly simplicity.

"You're not taking a survey for a gynecologist," I shrieked. "You're a spy for a pharmaceutical company!"

Then I burst into painful tears. When I'd confided all my intimate secrets to I. C., my feeling was that if he did make professional use of them, at least it would be in a bonafide medical book, but to discover that I had been tricked for crass, commercial reasons, was the last straw, the end of any illusions I might still have retained about the opposite sex. It was hopeless. No matter where I turned, all I encountered was rejection, mockery, and insidious deceit. Wasn't there a single man on earth I could trust and rely upon? A minute later, one name came to mind: Chip Kramer. A light flickered in the long tunnel of darkness. Of course. Dear Chip. He was the only one left, the only man I had ever loved, and it struck me as bitterly ironic that after leaving him six years ago, and beginning my odyssey through the labyrinths of the masculine world, I should now, three marriages and countless affairs later, find myself back where I had originally started.

I stopped crying and made a mental note to try to locate Chip as soon as possible; if necessary I'd comb the earth, but I'd find out where he was, and I would rush to his side and tell him that I'd been a fool. I'd fall on my knees, I'd beseech him, I'd say that I didn't care if he was hooked on enemas, or gambled away all his salary, just so long as he took me back and forgave me for ever leaving him. Only then could I be happy again. With this seductive plan in mind, I was able to face I. C. Ring, the Benedict Arnold of Hotel Splendide, and ask him what time it was, my own watch having stopped.

"Ten after ten," he smilingly informed me.

"Oh, no. I'm late. I should have been at work over half an hour ago. I have an important meeting at eleven."

I started to get into last night's culottes as I. C. disappeared into the kitchenette and came out with a tall glass of orange juice, which he handed to me.

"For the road," he said. "And no hard feelings."

I gave him a dirty look, but drank the juice. I hadn't realized how thirsty I was, and it tasted wonderfully refreshing after the hot and heavy love-making of last night. It disgusted me now to think that I had made love to someone as low and conniving as my next-door neighbor, because of all the men I had ever known, I. C. headed the list when it came to immorality, indecency, and rank insincerity.

"I'm not washing your shirts anymore," I said.

"Now, Loretta, don't be like that."

"I'm like that. You can go to the laundry next door."

"Come on, Loretta. I would have told you about the pharmaceutical company sooner or later. What the hell. It's only a job."

"Don't ever speak to me again, you Chinese traitor."

"I'll see you at Frank Campbell's," he said cheerfully, as I marched out, slamming the door with an angry bang.

Two unpleasant surprises were waiting for me in the corridor. One was the sudsy stream of water that gurgled out from under the door of my room, and the other was my daily copy of *The New York Times* which lay next to the door, as it did every morning, having been delivered by the bellman who made book. The *Times* was somewhat soggy from all that water coursing over it, but that wasn't what bothered me. It was the story at the bottom of page one.

GAMBLER CAUGHT KIDNAPPING RACEHORSE
SOUGHT MILLION DOLLAR RANSOM

I opened the door to my room and went in, the *Times* under my arm, my heart heavy with defeat. The room was flooded ankle-deep with water, Leonard Stein's poison-green carpet was soaked and made a squishy sound as I walked barefoot across it and into the kitchenette, where, sure enough, one of the pipes attached to my wonderful Whirlpool washing machine had burst open, causing this terrible catastrophe. It wouldn't have surprised me if the pipe had been there since the hotel was erected in 1887, in fact nothing could surprise Loretta Silverman anymore.

The shirt that Zachary had wanted to wear to John's funeral continued to roll around in the washing machine like a bad joke. Saturday night, a fire. Today, a flood. It was all very biblical, very Old Testament, but definitely. I sat down on my electric bed, hoping to be mercifully electrocuted, as I read in the *Times* how one Charles Alan Kramer had tried to kidnap a racehorse named Clean Kid from his Saratoga Springs paddock, how he'd been apprehended by the horse's trainer, and was now awaiting prison sentence, which, according to the *Times* account, might be as much as five years in a state penitentiary.

I let the paper drop to the watery floor. It was hopeless to try to go to work, to attempt to get dressed in these soggy surroundings. Just as I was about to call my office to say that I wouldn't be in, the house phone rang. It was Peggy.

"Now I'm really crazy," she said. "I can't sleep in my bed. I'm afraid. I was wondering if I could sleep in your bed."

"No."

"But the evil geniuses are out to get me."

"I have a piece of news for you," I said. "They've *gotten* you."

As soon as I hung up, the phone rang again. This time it was Josephine, agitated as usual.

"Where have you been? I've been ringing you all morning. Daffodil has flipped out."

"She's not the only one," I said, thinking of myself and Peggy.

"No, you don't understand. She's on a bad acid trip. I don't know what to do. I'm frightened."

"Where did she get the stuff?"

"From Zachary."

"Why don't you call him? I don't know what to do. I've never taken acid."

I. C.'s buoyant, lilting voice reached me from the next room. "That's-what-you-think."

"Zach isn't in," Josephine said. "I've tried him."

"Call Peggy. Maybe she knows."

"That bitch."

"Look, Josephine, I'm sorry about Daffodil, but I have my own problems. My first husband is about to go to Sing-Sing for five years."

"That's all you ever talk about. Your husbands. When are you going to find a new subject to bore us all with?"

"The day that you stop being a pain in the ass. Meaning, probably never."

"It's no picnic being the mother of a drug addict," Josephine said, hanging up.

Using my outside phone, I dialed the network and asked for the associate producer of Talk. It was while telling him that I couldn't possibly make it to the office today that the walls of my room started to move. First they moved in, then out, then in again, I saw cracks I had never seen before, I saw my left hand getting much larger than my right hand which held the telephone receiver.

"Several emergencies have occurred today which require my immediate attention," I said to the associate producer.

"Would you please break my lunch date with Andy Warhol, and tell him that I'll call him tomorrow."

Then I laughed hysterically and hung up, just as the LSD that I. C. had slipped into my orange juice caught me firmly, frighteningly in its tenacious grasp.

Being under the influence of LSD made my senses so acute that I could smell and taste various dishes I had cooked during the time Chip and I were married . . . the intricate and exotic casseroles and ragouts I prepared before Chip gave me a lecture on the value of simple, broiled foods . . . the simple, broiled steaks and chops I used to prepare afterward . . . how miserable I was . . . how we found we had nothing to say to each other . . . how, out of sheer boredom, I finally decided to get a job.

Lying there in my electric bed, in a roomful of water, with the walls of Hotel Splendide moving in and out, I remembered the job. Assistant Contestant Coordinator for a TV game show that was on a different network than the one Chip worked for. My starting salary was seventy-five dollars a week. I'd never had a job before.

Then I was five years old and it was my first day in school. The teacher's name was Miss Greene. The shirt that Zachary wanted to wear to the funeral was green, too. Leonard Stein's carpet was green, brilliant green grass, through which I could see to the bottom. Worms hid there.

Chip went to the track more and more as the years of our marriage slid by. We spent as little time as possible in each other's company, we made love less and less, and eventually not at all, yet we stayed together. Worms hiding in the deep green grass.

Until I met Paul in Lord & Taylor's shoe department.

I bought a pair of avocado slingbacks and went to bed with Paul, all in the same afternoon. Avocado was green.

I loved Paul immediately.

I had hated Chip for so long.

I was glad he was going to prison.

Chip had never loved me. He never even liked me. He didn't like anyone. Was Chip Kramer a real person, with real, human feelings? Or was he a robot who couldn't think beyond the daily double at Belmont?

What was his favorite color? (I didn't know.)

His favorite actor or actress? (Didn't know.)

His favorite anything? (Didn't know didn't know didn't know.)

Didn't know Chip. Never knew him. He had a mole on his back, directly to the left of his spine. I could see it very clearly, it looked like a truffle. That was what I knew about him. That and the fact that he took an enema every Thursday morning. And didn't want to have children.

"I'm not cut out for fatherhood."

Paul wanted children, but by then I was too wrapped up in my career. During my marriage to Chip, I had progressed from Assistant Contestant Coordinator to Contestant Coordinator, to Assistant Talent Coordinator to Talent Coordinator. And Chip had been fired from You Said It!

The hotel phone began to ring but I ignored it, because there were so many people in the room. Standing in front of the window were rows of Orientals from another civilization, wearing elaborate, brocaded costumes. They were staring at me.

"Hi there," I said waving.

They didn't answer, or smile, they just stared, then they disappeared.

I heard I. C. talking in the next room, and simultaneously

heard a Bob Dylan record being played somewhere down the hall, heard my father berate me when I told him that I was leaving Chip to marry Paul Bjorkman. I felt dizzy, and I had a strange sensation in the corners of my throat just below my ears, my mouth felt very dry, I knew that if I tried to get up and walk, I wouldn't be able to, maybe I could walk on the water like Jesus. I was no longer afraid of anything.

I WAS FREE.
FOREVER.
NOTHING COULD HARM ME ANYMORE.

Someone knocked on the door, and the Orientals solemnly appeared next to the window, the room lit up like the Christmas tree at Rockefeller Plaza, I felt sorry for my father, I heard Zachary's shirt going round and round in my washing machine, then the door opened and in came Aladar with all his window washing equipment.

"*Jaj de nedves itten*!" he said, observing the flood.

I asked him to turn on the radio because I couldn't walk.

"I remember you, lady." He looked around. "Nobody else is here?" He looked in the closet and underneath the bed. "No. Nobody. You all alone this time."

"I'm alone, but I can't walk."

He turned on the radio to a Viennese waltz. The Orientals disappeared and in came Marie Antoinette, Austria's gift to France, wearing one of her milkmaid costumes, very white and virginal, very bucolic. She was carrying a staff. Le Petit Trianon.

"Let them eat merde," she said to me.

I could see inside her eyes, DuBarry was hiding there, all curled up, flashing her diamonds, emeralds, and rubies, and she was arguing with Louis XV.

"More, more," she kept saying.

"Non, non," he kept replying.

"She's speaking English," I said to Aladar, "but he's speaking French."

"Who you talking about, lady?"

"Don't you see them?"

"See who?"

"*Them.* DuBarry and Louis."

Aladar looked under the bed again. "Nobody here."

Marie Antoinette had disappeared, taking the others with her. I started to talk very fast.

"I've had four husbands and I see everything in fours. Look around this room. Look. There are four walls, and over there are four pictures on the wall, and four chairs, the bed has four corners, you have two arms and two legs which make four, two ears and two eyes which make four—" (DuBarry flashed four emerald rings at me) "—the name *Aladar* has six letters in it, and *Loretta* has seven. Six and seven are thirteen. Take thirteen apart. It's a one and a three, right? Well, one and three make four."

"You crazy, lady."

"I just read a book called *The Crazy Ladies*. There are four girls in it. The world is filled with four."

I was laughing so hard I had to stop talking. What a wonderful relief it was to have finally figured out the essential secret of life: four. Everything came in fours. Once you realized that, you realized it all. *Chip* had four letters. So did *Paul*. So did *John*. Only *Billy* had five, but wait—*Ray* had three. Three and five were eight, and half of eight was four. It was infallible!

"Why don't you ask me to dance?" I said to Aladar.

"You want to dance? Okay, lady."

He held out his arms, and I walked over the water like

Jesus, and into Aladar's waiting arms. We started to dance on the water, very very softly, very very slowly. Marie Antoinette gazed at us and nodded.

"Let them eat merde."

"Go away," I said. "We don't need you anymore."

"Who you talking to, lady?"

"The Queen of France, before she had her head cut off. DuBarry had hers cut off, too. She screamed all the way to the guillotine. She kept saying, 'I'm not guilty, I'm not guilty.' Marie Antoinette didn't scream. She just kept saying, 'Let them eat merde.' That was all she said, as people threw shit at her when she was in the open carriage, going to her death. But I can't remember what happened to her children. Maybe they were guillotined, too. Maybe she killed them first. I think that's what she did. She killed them before they could be guillotined. I have to brush up on my French history. Louis XVI was guillotined, too. Louis XV died before the revolution."

I couldn't stop thinking of the fate of Marie Antoinette's children. What would be the fate of my unborn child? I knew I was pregnant. I didn't have to wait to hear the results of the rabbit test. I didn't have to take a rabbit test. I didn't need Dr. Oiseaux to tell me I was pregnant. I knew. I knew everything. I knew that Parker Mason wasn't the father of my child. I knew that Leonard Stein's poison-green carpeting was beautiful, a sea of green water on which I was dancing

BECAUSE I KNEW
THERE WAS NO FATHER
I HAD DONE IT ALL MYSELF
I KNEW HOW TO MAKE BABIES ALL BY MYSELF

"Why you laughing so much, lady?"

"I'm going to have a baby. *Baby* is another four. Do you see how it all fits together? And there is no father. Do you know why there is no father? It's simple, it's so simple I don't know how I could have overlooked it before this. The reason there is no father is because *father* isn't four. It's six."

"*Mother* is six, too."

He couldn't trick me, I was too smart for him, too clued into the secrets of the cosmos. I KNEW. "Ah," I said, "but *Mary* is four."

And we danced until the Orientals reappeared.

About the Author

This is Joyce Elbert's third novel. She is now working on a fourth book, *The Three of Us,* which will be set in London, Venice, and Trieste, the cities which she has recently visited in search of the intimate verisimilitude which is her particular hallmark. The results of her trials are forthcoming.